KNOXLEY HALL

EDDIE HEATON

Matador
9 Priory Business Park,
Wistow Road, Kibworth Beauchamp,
Leicestershire. LE8 0RX
Tel: 0116 279 2299
Email: books@troubador.co.uk
Web: www.troubador.co.uk/matador
Twitter: @matadorbooks

ISBN 978 1788033 756

British Library Cataloguing in Publication Data.
A catalogue record for this book is available from the British Library.

Printed and bound in the UK by 4edge limited
Typeset in 11pt Minion Pro by Troubador Publishing Ltd, Leicester, UK

Matador is an imprint of Troubador Publishing Ltd

For Faz

ONE

It was the early hours of Sunday morning and progress was slow through the drunk-infested streets of Soho. Todd had to bump along in first gear for fear of hitting one of the multitude of inebriated clubbers who swayed and staggered around on their loud and unsteady journeys from West End pleasure houses to night bus stands and mini-cab offices. At one point he was forced to stop altogether as a gang of drink-crazed twenty-somethings hurled themselves into the street right in front of his wheels. He felt an intense desire to press down on the accelerator pedal and wipe a few of them out but resisted the impulse and instead just waited for them to move on and out of his way. He wasn't in any great hurry as the man he was on his way to see was already dead.

He would have turned left off of D'Arblay Street and into Wardour Mews, which was where he'd been instructed to go, had it not been for the red and white plastic police tape that was stretched across the top of the cul de sac. A large uniformed policeman stood in front of the tape with his arms folded in front of his barrel sized chest. He was just as big as Todd and twice as ugly. Both of which were considerable achievements.

Down at the blind end of the alley there was a squad car with its doors open, the light on its roof illuminating the squat grey buildings and then plunging them back into shadow again with its every sweep of electric blue.

Todd got out, showed his ID and was nodded through. He lifted the tape and made his way to where two of his colleagues were standing over the remains of a human being and having a good old laugh about something trivial and coarse.

'Don't work too hard, lads,' Todd said, 'Think of all those forms you'll have to fill in if you find out who killed him.'

'Hello, Sherlock,' said D.S. Norcross. 'Got your magnifying glass?'

This was a man with more pockmarks on his face than there were lampposts on Piccadilly. He was wearing a Saville Row suit that someone on his salary shouldn't really be able to afford, and which didn't go at all well with his facial disfigurement.

'If there's any paperwork to be done it's you that's doing it.' Norcross went on. 'We've been told to hand the whole case over to you. They want a preliminary report at the station, sharpish. They must know how much you love your paperwork. We're just here to put on a show for the public and the plods.'

Todd took his first long look at the stiff on the tarmac. He knew who the dead man was but kept the information to himself.

'Some dirty tramp,' Norcross told Todd, 'just a dead smelly nobody.'

Norcross turned to D.C. Barrowclough, who had a clearer complexion and a more reasonably priced suit, and invited him, with a comradely wink, to laugh along. Barrowclough forced a laugh, and then a full-on grin that made him look like something dead that was being worked by strings.

Todd made a cold, hard face and kept his thoughts to himself whilst he stared at the dead man. The corpse did the same thing back.

It could have been mistaken for an empty bundle of rags if there hadn't been a human head sticking out. The back of that head had been bashed in with something blunt and heavy, leaving an indentation the size of a soup dish.

'No ID.' Norcross said, 'nothing whatsoever to go on. Forensics did a bit of street cleaning but I don't think they found fuck all.'

'That's a double negative,' Todd told him, 'just like you two.'

Norcross sneered and looked at Barrowclough and Barrowclough sneered too. It was that kind of relationship.

Then they moved away to the open end of the alley, trying to look policeman-like and failing. When they got to the tape they stopped and waited for the uniformed man to lift it for them but he didn't bother and so Barrowclough had to do it.

They were scurrying away from the case of a lifetime. Todd found it hard to believe that neither of them seemed to know who the dead man was; only a couple of years earlier he'd been all over the papers and on every TV news bulletin. His name was Terry DeHavilland and he was a newspaper reporter who'd been sent down for phone hacking, was the first one to have ever been prosecuted for that particular misdemeanour. The only reason he hadn't got away with it like everyone else was getting away with it at that time was because it was a Government Minister's phone that he'd hacked. Now that just wasn't on. That was really taking the piss. So the judge had decided to make an example of him and had given him a couple of years inside which must have been especially rough for an upper class, middle-aged type like DeHavilland but nowhere near as rough as being beaten to death in a Soho side street.

Todd carried on musing until the meat wagon arrived and poor old Terry was hauled unceremoniously aboard. Then he got back into his car and drove out into D'Arblay Street. The throng of drunken morons was even thicker than before. They lurched noisily around Todd's car; braying and guffawing like members of parliament at Prime Minister's Questions.

But then another group appeared. Younger and quieter. Hooded. About a dozen of them jogging down the middle of the street behind their leader like ISIS on manouevres but without the black flags and with trendy grey hoods instead of wrong way around balaclavas. The leader stopped, took a long hard look at the large, uniformed policeman and then casually and wantonly kicked at the wing mirror of a parked car until it came away from its bracket, somersaulted into the air like a miniature gymnast and then fell noisily onto another car's bonnet on the other side of the street.

The braying Hoorays fell silent. The large policeman pressed a button on the short-wave radio that was attached to his shoulder and then started to talk into it, his head cocked to one side but his eyes remaining fixed on this second group's leader. This individual shrugged and didn't run away; a deliberate and blatant show of defiant disrespect. Then, after a little time had passed he decided that enough defiant disrespecting had taken place for the time being and he moved his men on. They jogged off, hoodie fashion, into the Soho night.

Todd remained behind the wheel of his car and wondered if any of this had anything to do with him. He decided that it didn't and so he pulled away from the kerb and headed back to base.

TWO

The senior duty officer at West End Central that night was a thin-faced sergeant called Jenkins. He was sitting in an elevated glass cage watching his minions deal with the procession of drunks, drug users and punch-up merchants brought before them. One by one these miscreants supplied their names and addresses, emptied their pockets, took out their shoelaces and were taken off to the cells.

Todd had no office of his own and had to request use of a shared one every time he entered the building. So he approached Jenkins who looked away from the induction processes and gave Todd a cold and hostile smile that didn't quite extend to his eyes. Then he thrust a piece of paper at Todd that he must have had typed up all ready for him. Todd glanced at it. It had login details and a case number on it, nothing else. He pointed behind Todd to a row of doors with numbers on them and said: 'Lock yourself away in one of those boxes and get your briefing from the computer, and don't ask me any stupid questions. I've got enough on as it is.'

'Why am I on this case?' Todd asked him. 'Batman and Robin were first on the scene.'

'What did I just say about stupid questions?' Jenkins

mouthed through the glass. I've got Ascot or Henley or some such bollocks. Upper class twats getting fucked up all over the West End. Oh yes and there's a riot kicking off in Hackney. They want me to send them reinforcements. And now I've got you.'

'They're rioting in Soho as well,' Todd told him. 'It's probably better to concentrate your forces there. No one gives a fuck about Hackney.'

'Go and do your job, Detective Sergeant,' Jenkins said, 'and let me do mine.'

The small, windowless office had just one chair and a Formica covered table with an ancient pc and an old-fashioned telephone on it. Todd turned the computer on, wondering how many police hours were wasted waiting for decrepit old machines like this one to warm up. Eventually, however, there were signs of life and he entered the log-in details and the case number.

The forensic report had already been added but it told him nothing. Unknown male, indeterminate age, the cause of death was a blow or blows to the head with a blunt instrument, possibly a hammer. No personal belongings. No witnesses. The body had been spotted by a member of the public and reported anonymously from an untraceable mobile phone number.

Todd took his own phone out and dialed a number. No signal. There was an old-fashioned landline phone on the desk but there was about as much chance of him using that as there was of Terry DeHavilland coming back to life and telling Todd who'd killed him.

He put his jacket back on and went out through a side

door into the car park and the cool night air. He dialled the number again, not really expecting anyone to answer and was surprised when someone did.

'What's happened?' The Voice asked him.

'TD got done in.' Todd said.

'Are you sure it was him?' the Voice asked.

'Sure as I'll ever be.' Todd said. 'What's next, Skipper?'

'Go to his house and have a shufty. I'll text you the address.'

The line went dead. Todd went back inside and turned off the computer. Nothing to report.

Then he went back out to his car. His phone beeped. DeHavilland's address.

Islington. The scruffy end. Off the Essex Road.

THREE

He drove past the house three times. There were parked cars on both sides of the street but there was no one sitting in any of them so far as he could see and no vans or other large vehicles that might have contained a surveillance team. Even so, he parked three streets away and walked back.

It was an end of terrace and there was a side entrance, a high wooden gate. No houses opposite, just a little park. There was no one around so he took out the jemmy that he carried around with him for just this sort of situation and pushed it into the gap between the gate and the gatepost. He applied just the right amount of pressure to force the gate to creak open. He was inside the garden with the gate closed behind him in one brisk movement.

It was dark in there. The moon was skulking behind the clouds and a tree blocked out the light from the streetlamp. He stopped and listened. All was quiet. He got his little torch out and turned it on.

There was a dirty old barbecue rusting away on a crazy-paved patio. Todd needed something to keep the gate closed so he manhandled the lump of rusty iron up into position behind the gate. He didn't want anybody wandering in off the street.

He'd seen where the back door was so he turned the torch off and waited until his eyes got used to the dark. Then he walked up the path to the door and turned its handle. It was locked. He shook it a couple of times. It carried on being locked.

Then there was a sudden scurry of activity. A plastic bin went flying and a slender dark shape appeared from nowhere and then disappeared again just as quickly as it had arrived through a hole in the fence. It was just a fox, but it got his heart pulsating almost out of his chest.

There was no point in being quiet any more after all that racket so he kicked the back door. It didn't seem to mind being kicked so he carried on kicking it until it flew open and nearly off its hinges. That felt good.

Once inside he put his torch on again. The kitchen was small and didn't look like it had been used much. There were a few utensils lying around on one of the work surfaces and a Keith Floyd cookbook that might not have been opened since the roaring eighties. There was a musty smell about the place that reminded Todd of a derelict caravan that he'd once been forced to occupy due to straitened circumstances.

He walked through the kitchen and into the living room. There had been two rooms at one time but the dividing wall had had a big hole punched into it transforming two very small rooms into one not quite so small one. Todd was no interior decorator but he didn't suppose that that had improved the aesthetics of the place or added much to its market value. The inexpertly applied wallpaper had been covered unevenly with a coat or two of magnolia and the threadbare carpet was a dirty grey and didn't look like it had been troubled by a vacuum cleaner since the alterations had been carried out.

Everything about the place said 'rented accommodation.' The furniture was cheap and barely functional: a dining table and four chairs; a writing desk; a sofa bed that looked about as comfortable as a neglected park bench.

Todd had never got to know Terry Dehavilland but he'd formed enough of an impression of him to know that this was not the sort of place in which he would choose to live.

He turned his attention to the writing desk. Only one of the four drawers was locked so Todd didn't bother much with the unlocked ones. He forced open the locked drawer and found some books and papers and a laptop computer.

That was probably the mother lode, so he left it there while he checked out the rest of the place. He wanted to be sure he was on his own. For all he knew there might be some terrified lodger skulking in one of the upstairs rooms, trying to pluck up the courage to sneak down and hit him over the back of the head with a frying pan.

There were only two bedrooms, one small one and one even smaller one. The main bedroom was at the front of the house. The bed was made up with a nice burgundy coloured duvet neatly arranged on top of it. There was a wardrobe, a chest of drawers and a dressing table. Zero signs of female occupancy and not much sign of any human activity at all. Todd didn't need to be that much of a super sleuth to figure out that DeHavilland hadn't spent much time here, that this wasn't his main abode.

The spare bedroom had an exercise bike and a few weights in it. It didn't look like they'd had much use. The only other thing in there was a modern chest of drawers whose contents were of no interest. Todd stared out of the window and down into the gloom. He could just make out the derelict barbecue that was still guarding the back gate like some bizarre sentry.

He went back downstairs and took the papers and the laptop out of the drawer he'd forced open. The papers were all legal documents; a rental agreement, divorce papers, birth certificate. Important stuff. Which surely meant the laptop contained something important too. Todd turned it on. No password required. There was a folder on the desktop called 'journal'. He opened it. There were about a hundred word documents in there, arranged in three columns. No names, just numbers. Todd ran the cursor over them and a little window opened telling him the date that each one had last been modified. The oldest one was three years old and the most recent had last been worked on just a week before.

He went upstairs and into the spare bedroom and moved a chair so he could be nice and comfortable whilst keeping an eye on the back gate. If that rusty barbecue moved, even the smallest fraction of an inch, then Todd would know for certain that there was someone trying to get in.

He settled himself down for some late night reading.

FOUR

J o took charge of all the funeral arrangements in her usual super-efficient manner. All the high-borns were notified but only one of them bothered to turn up. I couldn't have cared less but it was rather amusing to watch the reaction of Jo's husband, Jeremy, the social climbing banker wanker who almost came in his pants when he was introduced to the one titled oaf who did bother to attend.

Of course, I hate the bloody lot of them. I remember mummy's stories of how they deliberately humiliated her. They disapproved of her because she was a Catholic! I mean for Christ's sake! Darling daddy would have had the title if he'd just been born a few minutes earlier, rather than later, than his twin brother, George. I'd like to say that I couldn't care less. But to be honest, when you're as broke as moi the idea of getting paid a pretty decent amount of cash for doing absolutely bugger all is actually rather appealing and the carte des vins at the House of Lords is absolutely second to none.

Anyhow, after the church service was over we all trooped back to Daddy's house where Jo had organised *some refreshments. The sight of vino and victuals cheered them all up no end and it wasn't long before a veritable shindig was in full swing.*

Daddy's sister Lou had a few too many glasses of Pinot Grigio and got a bit loud and opinionated, which I found hilarious. I'd never seen her like that before and she was terribly funny. Her lady friend, Fiona, was with her. I think they're probably lesbians.

*'Jo and Terence are both writers,' Aunt Lou announced to all and sundry in a voice that was several decibels louder than it needed to be, 'isn't it marvellous? Terence writes for one of those terribly serious political fortnightlies and Jo does society pieces for the "*Mutt and Nag.*" It is the "*Mutt and Nag*" isn't it, darling?'*

*'It's the "*Horse and Hound*", Aunt Lou and you jolly well know it is,' Jo said, trying to pretend that she wasn't offended.*

I just came right out with it and told Aunt Lou that I'd been sacked. I suppose I must have been a bit pissed as well. I had been tippling all day.

Aunt Lou seemed to think that that was terribly funny and asked what I was going to do with myself.

I told her I might have to go and work in corporate comms for some hedge fund or investment bank churning out lying press releases (bound to end badly) but that it was more likely that I would make a living by uncovering the indiscretions of disobedient backbenchers and then selling the information to the party whips.

She seemed to rather approve of this half formed, somewhat dastardly aspiration and agreed that I should give up any pretensions of being a serious political commentator and move entirely into the realm of the scandal sheet and of "digging the dirt".

'...and I don't meant the sort of society drivel that your sister and her chums like churning out. Tell the world what the dirty buggers are really up to! That's what the masses want to read. And believe me, darling, there's plenty of merde to rake up!'

She promised to get me into the 'right drawing rooms' as she put it. The idea immediately appealed. So much more interesting than all that dreary Westminster stuff...

It turned out that Auntie Lou and I have rather a lot in common. She too started out all political and "holier than thou" back in the fifties before feminism got trendy and when communism really wasn't trendy at all except amongst the Hampstead elite of which she was a somewhat sceptical member. She quickly became disillusioned with lefty politics and decided that the best way to subvert the system (and make herself a pile of cash at the same time) was to either publish or threaten to publish salacious rumours about some of the rather badly behaved establishment types who happened to be operating within her immediate social orbit.

'Teddy Tomlinson was the first. Before your time but you've probably heard of him – Sir Edward Tomlinson. He was foreign secretary for a spell later on. Anyway, much earlier on in his career, when he was still a junior minister, he'd been married off to some gormless debutante at twenty-one despite being as queer as a coot. He used to go to all the gay clubs which were illegal at that time. Homosexuality *itself was illegal then. So I grabbed the opportunity, darling. I had a word with the editor of the Sunday Wotsit who was a personal friend of Mummy's and tried to sell the story. But he said we'd need evidence. So I set poor Teddy up with a couple of Earl's Court rent boys and had a few lovely snaps taken. Of course it never got published. He just got the cheque book out and I was off and running. He was the first of... oh... dozens and dozens darling, I never bothered to count them. Now, I know what you're thinking, Terry darling, but it really isn't blackmail. You see, we write the story and then go to them, present them with the evidence and ask them to comment. If they offer money and we decide to take it, then that's a perfectly acceptable business transaction. Of course, what we mustn't do is to demand money in exchange for non-publication – now that really would be terribly naughty.'*

I looked around to make sure we weren't being overheard, which would have been a bloody miracle as she was using a booming baritone that was in danger of disturbing poor old daddy in his newly dug grave, but no-one seemed to be taking much notice and I was rather intrigued.

'My goodness, Lou, you really are a bit of a dark horse aren't you? But, you know, being gay isn't seen as that much of a problem these days, even in the Tory party... morals are a lot looser now – I'm not sure if that's a good thing or a bad 'un...'

'There are still plenty of things they want to keep quiet,' she told me with a wicked glint in her eyes and I couldn't help seeing her side of it.

'I'll bet if we look at the latest generation of the same families I had so much success with all those years ago we'll find a rich new seam of wickedness.' The wine was taking over and she was slurring her words now. 'These buggers pass their dirty habits down from one generation to the next just like they do with their stately homes and their strings of pearls.'

It all got a bit messy after that and I think I disgraced myself by saying something unforgivable to Jo's dreadful husband while the last time I saw Lou she was dancing cheek to cheek with her friend Fiona, doing a Bogie and Bacall impression, despite there being no music on. I don't think they play music at funerals.

We met up again a few days later and compared address books and intriguingly enough we did know lots of people from different generations of the same families. So that became our Modus Operandi. She would identify the families who she knew to be particularly dissolute and I would skulk around the latest additions looking for "merde to rake up". It was just a question of going to the right clubs and parties and keeping one's ear to the ground. My kind of graft.

My first one was Tubby Entwistle with whom I'd been to school. He was shacked up with a bum chum in a little flat near Sloany Square which was all fair and good except for the fact that he was a front bench M.P. and was claiming expenses for the mortgage on the pad that they were sharing and then charging his live-in lover an arm and a leg to reside there too. The rent was paid into a joint bank account they'd set up on Grand Cayman. Naughty boys!

That one got me out of debt and paid six months' rent on my flat in Chelsea. The cherry was well and truly lost and there was no looking back.

There were about half a dozen clients in that first year and I soon started to find sharing the profits with silly old Aunt Lou was becoming a little tiresome so I told her to bugger off. I'd had all the useful information out of her that I could use and she'd become superfluous to requirements. It may have started with those dissolute aristocratic politicians who'd inherited their degeneracy along with their titles but it certainly didn't end there. Quite soon I was roaming freely in that strange nether world of those who are "famous for being famous". In fact I soon learned that I had to be careful because some of the weirder ones actually wanted their vile habits to be circulated to the general population in order to sufficiently increase their profiles so they could get themselves a slot on some third rate reality TV show.

But there were plenty of genuine 'clients' out there, too, and that first year I had payoffs from a couple of sexually incontinent politicians, a cross-dressing, crack-smoking morning TV presenter who wanted to keep his wholesome image intact and hang on to his superbly well paid job, and a footballer with a coke and gambling habit that was making him a prime target for the match fixers.

Nor was it always the case that I was paid to keep quiet about whatever grubby little indiscretion I managed to uncover. Sometimes the client just told me to sod off and do my damnedest and so I damned well did. I then had no option but to take my information to the street of shame, *metaphorically speaking of course, there hasn't been a newspaper on that particular EC4 thoroughfare since Auntie Lou's day. At any rate, I became rather adept at haggling with the tabloid editors. It was quite a trick one had to pull off – to divulge the level of chicanery and the status of the individual without letting on exactly who the client was or the exact nature of the wrongdoing, or those double-dealing pro vultures would as sure as hell just go off and get the stories themselves. So it was about getting paid a decent amount up front whilst divulging as little as possible. I soon realised that there was one tabloid in particular that paid higher rates than all the rest and I decided that whilst continuing to get paid for not publishing whenever possible, once it was clear that the client wasn't prepared to cough up, that it then made sense to only sell stories to that particular rag, although of course I did do everything I could to give them the impression that they were in a bidding war with their competitors.*

The red headed dominatrix who was editor of that mass circulation daily had her own little network of information gatherers and would always try to screw me over given half the chance, but I soon had a pretty good record for getting some serious wonga out of her.

Then, one fine winter's day just as I was about to pack my suitcase and take a well-earned sabbatical in Amsterdam, a wonderful journalistic opportunity presented itself to me like a big fat line of coke just waiting to be snorkled up a nasal passage.

I was putting the squeeze on a nasty little faggot who'd been caught bang to rights on Clapham Common with his pants around his ankles and a rent boy's dick in his mouth – the divulgence of which would never have been in the public interest if he hadn't been a C of E bishop and a sitting member of the House of Lords. At any rate he blubbed a bit when I showed him the piccies but claimed he didn't have the necessary lucre to grease my palm. I didn't believe a word of it and told him that if he wasn't prepared to cough then I would have no other option than to tell his torrid tale to a tabloid.

He was sobbing like a baby by now and I suppose he really must have been broke, but then a light bulb seemed to come on in his head and he blurted out an offer to give me some really meaty hearsay by way of payment. He offered me a story that he said would pay me many times over what I would get for selling his nasty little tale of woe.

'What would you say if I told you that certain extremely high-ranking establishment figures are involved in something that involves children. Something that involves institutions that exist to protect vulnerable, parentless children; children's homes, approved schools, borstals. What if I were to tell you that young boys are being systematically whored out for abuse by the very people who are supposed to protect them and that some of the ones doing the actual abusing are very well known indeed?'

I shrugged, not wanting to seem too keen, but it did sound as if it might have legs. I told him he had to give me names and pretty soon they started to come to me by email. The names involved were positively galactic.

I started to lick it into shape and it came together like iron filings on a magnet. I managed to convince myself that

20

I was destined to reveal all to the world and to become rich and famous in the process. But even so I had to admit that this was probably too big for me to deal with on my own. This was a large scale operation being run by a network of rich and influential paedophiles, not just some individual saddo who happened to be one of the political elite. I needed resources and I needed the back up of a major National. So I put in a call to the redhead.

But before I could even start to tell her just what a hell of a scoop I had to offer she told me that from now on, under no circumstances, was I to contact her directly or to go near the paper's offices. From now on, she informed me, I had to negotiate with one of her operatives, who, on this first occasion, I was to meet in a rather disreputable West End night club called the Purple Pussycat. She told me only the woman's first name, Dolores: They would book a table for me and all I had to do was wait.

'Dolores,' I said, when I saw her, 'what a surprise.' 'Not a nasty one, I hope?'

'Of course not,' I lied. I was looking at my ex-wife.

I remembered with a sinking feeling just how pally she'd always been with good old Auntie Lou.

She had a Kir Royale in front of her and was vaping on an e-ciggy with those ruby red lips of hers. Her raven black hair swept the contours of her face and created shadows that I wanted to kiss and lick. Our previous involvement had ended catastrophically – for me at least. She'd taken all my money and broken my heart and still managed to leave me with the feeling that it was all my own fault. I'd opened up to her then and she knows things about me that you *wouldn't want your best friend to know and, believe me, Dolores isn't my best friend or anyone else's. She wasted no time in reminding me of all the little secrets that she knew about me and then when we got down to discussing the business at hand she told me that what I had wasn't enough and that I had to get more. More, more, more! That's Dolores all over. Nothing's ever enough.*

FIVE

Todd heard a noise from outside so he flicked his flashlight off, got to his feet and looked down onto the garden. The rusty barbecue was no longer behind the gate. It had been pushed over and to one side and was lying in pieces in what used to be a flowerbed. The gate was open and was rocking backwards and forwards on its rusty hinges and making a noise like a dying rodent.

Somebody was coming up the stairs and it sounded like they didn't care who knew it. Todd got himself behind the open bedroom door and waited.

As soon as his uninvited visitor had entered the room he closed the door firmly with the side of his fist. It slammed and stayed shut and the door frame shook a little.

A young woman swirled around and faced him. She had wavy, auburn hair and big brown eyes. She was wearing a fluorescent jacket and a rucksack and was carrying a bright yellow cycling helmet.

There was a moment of silence whilst they checked each other out. Todd rather liked the look of her.

'Who are you?' he asked her, without trying to be nice, and when she didn't respond he said, 'I'm a police officer.' And he reached for his warrant card.

'I know who you are, D.S. Todd,' she told him, confidently.

'Oh. You'd better tell me how you know that.' He said. 'Or I'll confiscate your bike.'

She took a phone out of her pocket and started pressing buttons.

He said, 'You can stop doing that until you've explained yourself.'

She ignored him so he took a step towards her and tried to grab the phone. She kicked him violently on the shin. It was like being pecked by a butterfly. He managed to ignore the pain and stood his ground, directly in front of the bedroom door in case she tried to make a run for it.

'All alone here, are you, D.S. Todd?'

Running away wasn't on her "to do" list. She crossed her arms and looked him up and down.

'Like I said,' he told her again, this time with a little more steel in his voice, 'I'm a police officer, here on police business.'

'That surprises me. I thought you might have some young, unfortunate woman with you. Blackmailing women into having sex with you is a speciality of yours, isn't it?'

'I don't have the slightest clue what you're talking about,' he said.

'I suppose there have been so many different instances of that nature that you're not even sure which one I'm talking about.' She had the clean and precise accent of the privately educated daughter of someone rich, and vicious.

'You've got the wrong man.' He said. 'I don't go for the unfortunate ones.'

'Oh I think you do.'

'I don't know who you are or what you're talking about.'

'I don't suppose you remember Emma Naylor, an unfortunate, vulnerable young woman you blackmailed into performing an indecent act? You pretended to be looking for drugs and when she gave you the… crack cocaine wasn't it? You produced your Metropolitan Police ID and told her that if she didn't perform fellatio on you that you'd charge her with conspiracy to supply a class A drug.'

Todd thought about that for a little while and then said, 'I remember nicking her and I remember cautioning her. She then informed on the next person up the drug distribution chain who I subsequently arrested. I let her go because I like to let the little fishes go. That's the way I catch the bigger fishes. There was no sex involved. Somebody's made that up. Who are you? Press?'

She pursed her lips, tut tutted like a head girl handing out a detention and said, 'Very well. I suppose you have a right to know. Yes. I am a journalist. My name is Lucy Mainwaring. Now, I've given you Miss Naylor's version of events and I've heard your response but it doesn't tally at all with statements we've been given by the victim herself and other police officers. I should inform you that I intend to make a full statement to the police complaints board immediately after we publish the story.'

Todd said nothing but that didn't mean he had nothing on his mind. Someone back at the ranch had poisoned his water hole.

Lucy Mainwaring pressed on with her allegations: 'You thought you'd got away with it, didn't you? Your colleagues told you they weren't going to press charges. Well, guess what? They've changed their minds. They're co-operating with my paper's investigation and I suggest you do the same. That might do you some good when the matter comes to court.'

Todd's nervous twitch got started. 'Who sent you here?' He asked her. 'How did you know I was here?'

She gave him the prissy, pursed-up look again and said, 'I got a tip off.'

'You got a tip off? Or your boss got a tip off?'

'I don't see what difference it makes.'

'So your boss got a tip off. Or at least that's what he told you.'

'How do you know it's not a she?'

'Ok then, that's what she told you.'

'Well… actually it is a he, but that brand of casual sexism isn't acceptable anymore and the sooner people like you learn that then the better it will be for everybody.'

Todd said: 'Your boss sent you over here. *He* sent you over here. All on your own. He told you I'd be here and that I'd more than likely have a little crack whore for company and that you just might be able to catch me red-handed with my John Thomas stuck in her gob.'

'There's really no need to be quite so disgusting.'

'Does this look like a crack house to you?'

She was too busy thumb tapping her phone to reply and he didn't suppose she was checking out the football results. Just then the moon came out from behind a cloud and shone its light through the window and across her face. She couldn't have been much more than twenty.

'Do you know whose house this is?' Todd asked her. Lucy shrugged, like she cared more about whose horse had won the Epsom Derby.'I thought it might be yours. Isn't it? Whose is it?'

'It's Terry DeHavilland's.'

Todd watched closely as her sharp young mind processed this fresh piece of information with all the speed and efficiency of Silicone Valley's latest operating system. She swiftly found a duplicate data point.

'He's a tabloid reporter,' she said. 'He was imprisoned for illegal phone hacking.'

'Bingo!' said Todd. 'Exactly right. And this is where he lived.'

'Lived?'

'He's dead,' Todd told her. 'He's been murdered. But don't tell anyone. It's a secret.'

That stopped her thumbs from tapping. She even paid him some attention. 'I think you're just trying to deflect me away from – '

'Which rag do you work for?' He asked her.

'*The Defender,*' She told him, 'And it's not a rag.' Then she started with the phone again.

'You're being used,' he told her. 'You and your employer. Whoever gave you the tip off must have been somehow involved in DeHavilland's murder. Nobody knows that DeHavilland is dead. Except for me and whoever killed him.'

'I don't believe you,' she said. 'You're playing games.

Terry DeHavilland isn't dead. I just checked. You're lying. You had a girl here but she must have left before I arrived.'

There was as much chance of him winning her over as there was of the boys back at West End Central having a whip round for the Home Secretary, so he grabbed the laptop, opened the bedroom door and walked out of the room.

Lucy Mainwaring flew out after him like an angry bird and was already chirping into his earhole before he even reached the top of the stairs.

'Leaving, are you, D.S. Todd? Is it something that I said?'

He went down the stairs and she fluttered down after him.

'What do you say to these allegations, D.S. Todd? Have you been abusing your authority in order to prey upon unfortunate young women?'

She pushed her smartphone under his nose and he saw enough of it to register that she had a recording app turned on.

'D.S. Todd, please answer my question. What do you say to Emma Naylor's accusations that you coerced her into having oral sex with you in exchange for promising not to charge her with supplying drugs?'

He stopped and faced her as they reached the flimsy kitchen door that he'd kicked in earlier.

'I've already told you I didn't do it,' he said, setting off again towards the garden gate and the broken barbecue. 'Come with me and you'll get the story of a lifetime.'

She said: 'I'm here to follow up a case of alleged sexual harassment by you of a vulnerable young woman and you're asking me to go off God knows where with you in the middle of the night. You must think I'm insane.'

But she followed him anyway.

He said: 'Your editor knows you're here and with me. I'd have to be the insane one to do you any harm right now, wouldn't I?'

She said: 'Come on, Todd, this is just a ploy to stop me turning you in. Why don't you just admit that the game's up? That will work out better for you in the long run.'

'This is the story of a lifetime.' He told her. 'Come with me and I'll prove what I'm saying is true. What have you got to lose? You know all about DeHavilland. Don't you?' He stopped and faced her.

She stopped as well and said, 'It's the Knoxley Hall story isn't it?'

'Go on,' Todd prompted her.

'It was a boys' home in Barnes. Child abuse went on there back in the eighties. Everyone knows about it but no one can prove anything. Lord Warrington's name seems to keep cropping up. The word on the street is that he was either involved in what seems to have been a pedophile ring involving a number of prominent politicians or that he covered it up.'

Todd drummed his fingers on the laptop and said, 'Terry was sent down for listening to Lord Warrington's phone messages and now Terry's dead and his diary is on here. The proof is on here.'

She gave the laptop a long and covetous look and seemed to be coming around to his argument but then her phone beeped. She read what was on it by the light of the moon and said: 'You're lying. Terry DeHavilland isn't dead. Our news room would know if he was and they just messaged me to say that he isn't.'

'No one knows he's dead yet. They're keeping it quiet.'

'So how come you know?' They were in the street now. Still she followed him.

'Look, I suggest you come back to my office and we'll take it from there,' she said.

'Not on your life,' he said. 'Whoever sent you to that house knows DeHavilland is dead and whoever gave you the made-up story about me is most likely part of the same conspiracy that enables rich perverts to commit evil acts on orphaned children.'

'Oh don't be so ridiculous.' she said.

But he could see that she was far too ambitious to risk missing out on the scoop of the century. Her desperate desire to be an acclaimed investigative journalist was practically palpable.

'We'll go somewhere and read it together,' he suggested, 'and then back it up. I haven't had the chance to read it all myself yet. But what I have read is pretty fucking explosive.'

'All right,' she said, 'but this stays on.' She held the phone up in front of him.

They'd reached his car by now and he got in behind the steering wheel, put the laptop under his seat and pushed the passenger door open, inviting her in.

There was a pause before she finally got in alongside him and dropped her cycling helmet on the floor in front of her.

'Where are we going?'

'We'll go to a hotel and read what's on here, back it up and then talk to your editor.'

'I'm not sure about this… I'm…'

'Are they listening to all this?' He asked her, pointing at the phone.

'Not unless I press send.'

'Don't send it just yet then. Let's make sure we know who we're dealing with first.'

'I'll save it as an audio file and send it directly to my editor. I think we can trust him, don't you?'

'I don't know. I don't know who to trust.' He started the engine and pulled away from the kerb. She got busy with her phone again, texting or messaging.

'Now what?'

'I'm scared,' she said.

She didn't look scared.

'What are you doing?'

'Never mind.'

'Hang on, who are you texting?'

'Shit!' she said, 'I've dropped my phone.'

'I'll pull over.'

'It's okay… I've got it… no… I've dropped it again… yes… pull over here, will you?'

They'd reached the bright lights of Upper Street by now but it was three in the morning and there was no one about. Todd pulled over.

As soon as he applied the hand brake she opened the car door and was half way through it before he could stop her. She'd taken the laptop from under his seat and was about to disappear with it. He managed to lunge over and grab her arm. She punched him with the inside of a closed hand and then dragged her nails down his cheek. Despite that he was able to hold on to her and get a hold of the laptop with his other hand. She pulled herself free of him and let go of the computer and then ran back the way they'd come. He watched her in his rear-view mirror.

Her cycling helmet lay forgotten on the floor in front of the passenger seat that she'd so hastily vacated. He tried not to worry too much that she might fall off her bike and bang her pretty head.

SIX

'The Voice asked: 'What did you find?'

Todd said, 'A laptop computer with names, dates everything.'

'Good,' the Voice said, 'you've got plenty to go on then.'

'What do you mean?'

'Time to be a policeman. Chase up those leads.'

'Why don't we just hand it all over to someone at the very top? Tell themDeHavilland's dead and give them the laptop.'

'This goes all the way to the very top. No one can be trusted.'

'There was a reporter there.'

'Christ! What was his name?'

'It was a her. Someone told her I was there. 'They gave her some phony story that I'd shagged a female crack head in exchange for not nicking her.'

'They've placed you at his house. Before anyone was supposed to know he was dead. The only person who could have known he was dead was the person who killed him. What did you tell the reporter?'

'That DeHavilland was dead. I tried to get her on

board but she ran away. She tried to nick the laptop and she ran away.'

'So not only have they got you at the house. They've got you blabbing that DeHavilland's been done in before any one is supposed to know. And they've got you at the murder scene.'

'How's that?'

'You turned up at the crime scene. No orders for you to attend. The guilty party drawn inexplicably back to the exact place where he committed his evil deed.'

'You told me to go there.'

'I don't exist.'

'Norcross and Barrowclough were expecting me and Jenkins told me to file a report.'

'Which you didn't do. No one is going to stand up and say you had orders.'

'Still… that's not enough evidence to convict me; not even enough to bring charges.'

'There won't be a trial.'

'How do you mean?'

'My guess is that they're going to kill you. Now they've got you nicely in the frame, they'll do you in and make it look like suicide.

'You bastard.' Todd said. 'You sent me to that house. You knew what was going on.'

'You'd better get to them before they get to you.' The Voice said, and then hung up.

SEVEN

"**D**olores in tonight?' Todd asked Stan, the manager of the Purple Pussycat, and was quite surprised when Stan nodded and pointed her out. She was down at the far end of the bar sitting on a stool and vaping on an e-fag. Her hair was as black as the inside of a derelict coal mine and she hadn't spared the blood red lipstick. Just the way Terry had described her.

Todd stood up and was about to pay her a visit when Stan put a hand on his arm.

'I never said you was allowed to chat her up. What you want to talk to her about anyhow? Sit down for a bit and talk to me first.'

Stan had a long, ferrety face with tiny, pale blue eyes and a thin-lipped mouth that was no longer blessed with its full complement of teeth.

Todd didn't like being handled. He considered it an intrusion on his personal space and a mark of disrespect to the badge in his pocket that identified him as a detective sergeant in one of the world's great police forces.

On the other hand, the big black bouncer who'd been on the door when he first came in was now standing close enough to give him a nice big cuddle. Except he didn't look the cuddling type. He looked more like the type who might tear off someone's arm with his bare hands and gnaw on it like it was a chicken wing.

Todd just shrugged and sat back down on his bar stool. In any case, he needed a little thinking time. He told the barman, who'd come up to their end of the bar, most likely in the hope of a bit of trouble, to bring him a pint of lager and a packet of mini cheddars.

The Double P hadn't changed much in the last twenty years or so; the pole dancing / lap dancing craze had come and gone but the management at the Purple Pussycat hadn't bothered with any of that. Dancing, of any kind, was strictly forbidden. The place had a formula that worked: a system of monetary re-distribution that involved middling amounts of cash being channeled from middle aged men to much younger women and then onwards to another, different group of middle aged men. Sometimes there was sex involved but more often than not the punters just handed over their dosh without getting anything in return and hardly ever complained.

The bar area was illuminated whilst the rest of the place was in semi darkness. At the back of the room were alcoves with lighting that was so dim it shouldn't really get called lighting at all. Todd could just about make out the shady outlines of men wearing suits talking to women wearing next to nothing apart from "come here and fuck me" attitudes.

Stan was short for Stanislav not Stanley; he was from one of the former Yugoslav countries. Todd couldn't remember which one and he didn't like to ask. For the time being he just kept shtum and ate his cheesy biscuits.

Stan made a point of turning his back and chatting to the woman on a stool the other side of him. All Todd saw of her was a flash of leg and some cleavage. He didn't care to see more so he concentrated his attentions on psyching out the barman by staring right at him in a cold and unfriendly manner.

Eventually, Stan, having shown his minions who was boss by keeping Todd waiting, turned back around to face him and said, 'What's all this about?'

'Police business.'

'If you don't tell me what you want to talk to her about then you ain't fucking talking to her, mate.'

Todd sighed, scoffed some more cheesies and washed them down with a swig of warm, flat lager. 'Remember Terry DeHavilland?' he asked Stan.

'Went down for phone hacking. Posh cunt. Yeah, I knew him. Why?'

'Brown bread,' Todd told him. 'Murdered. This is a murder inquiry and the body's still warm. They've given the whole mess to me to get what I can before the press are told and those bastards start crawling all over it. We're asking a favour Stan, best if you play along, eh? Nobody's suggesting this has anything to do with you or the club but he was a regular here and Dolores was his ex-wife. She ditched him but then they got pally again – in here.'

Stan looked like he cared more about the Middle East peace process than he did about who'd killed Terry

DeHavilland and as far as Todd was aware Stan had no interest at all in foreign affairs.

'When was the last time you saw him?' Todd sharpened his tone.

Stan shrugged. 'Ages back. I never liked the twat so I never bothered talking to him.'

'Who did he knock about with, apart from her?'

'That's all you get from me,' Stan snapped and the big man behind him stiffened in readiness for the order to attack.

'All right,' Todd said, 'if that's the way you want it. I'll go and get a search warrant and a van full of plods.'

He made as if to leave but Stan put his grubby hand back on Todd's arm and said, 'I was only 'aving you on, mate. Course you can talk to her. Go and sit in a booth and I'll send her over.'

'Tell her I'm a punter,' Todd said. 'And don't tell her Terry's dead. I want to see if that comes as a surprise or not.'

Stan nodded and Todd went over and seated himself in one of the dimly lit alcoves.

She came over right away and sat down opposite him.

'Friend of Stan's, eh?' she said. 'I expect you'll be wanting special treatment.'

She leaned towards him, which had the twin effects of giving him an unavoidable eyeful of her plunging neckline and an almost overpowering whiff of her pungent perfume. 'What's your name, Dreamboat?' She was laying it on thick. Like she'd laid on the mascara.

'Todd.' He told her. 'Detective Sergeant Todd.'

That spoiled the mood a little.

Just then the barman came over with a bottle of cheap fizz in a rusty ice bucket in one hand and two dirty champagne flutes in the other one. He opened the bottle, splashed about a fluid millimeter into each of the two glasses and then dropped the bottle into the ice bucket with the minimum amount of style or finesse. Then he retreated back behind his bar. Neither of them bothered to drink.

'I understand you were married to Terry DeHavilland?' Todd asked her.

Her whole face tightened up and all of a sudden she wasn't quite so alluring any more. She made to get up but Big Boy came over and told her to sit back down. Then he turned his huge back on them and stood directly in front of their booth. Either Stan was co-operating more than Todd could have expected or both of them were being held there. Stan himself had disappeared. Maybe he was on the phone to his contact in the Met. That could turn out badly. In any case, Dolores sat back down.

'It wasn't really a marriage,' she said. 'I was only rinsing him.'

'That's what marriage is,' said Todd. 'Anyway, that's not what I'm interested in. Tell me about the story he was working on for *The Planet*. You were a go-between weren't you? Between him and the paper?'

'How do you know about that?'

'I'm asking the questions. And as soon as you answer them we can all go home to bed.'

'If I told you the truth, you wouldn't believe it.'

'Try me. But you'd better make this good. Terry's dead. He was murdered last night. Not far from here, as it happens.' He watched her closely. She was either genuinely shocked or a very good actress. – the finest leading lady in the whole West End.

'Any ideas who might have killed him?' He asked her in a nice even tone, not wanting to upset her any more than he already had.

'A bunch of fucking lizards!' She snapped at him, and then tried to pour herself a drink. Her hand was shaking so much she was getting more bubbles on the table than she was in her glass. Todd took the bottle away from her and finished the job.

'I never thought they'd be nice friendly folk,' he said, 'but never mind. 'Lizards eh? I'm going to need names.'

She shook her head and grinned at him. 'I mean it,' she said. 'They're shape-shifting lizards from outer space.'

'Don't fuck with me,' he snapped at her. 'Not in the mood, love. Now give me some names. Or one, at least.'

'No names. Not yet. Not in here.'

'So tell me about the story he was working on just before he got sent down. Why did it never get made public?'

She rubbed her thumb and forefinger together in the International gesture for money and plenty of it.

'Look,' he said, 'I'm just trying to find out who killed him and I'm guessing that whoever it was had something to do with that story. You know the one, the one that involves those lovely people that abuse kids in care. People like that belong behind bars, don't they?'

She nodded almost imperceptibly then drained her

glass and moved her body across the table and motioned for him to do the same. He did so until her mouth was right close up against his ear.

'Lizards,' She whispered.

'If you say that one more time…'

'You as hard as you look?

'Harder.' he said.

'Get us out of here then and I'll tell you everything you need to know. Make it look like you're forcing me to go.'

'All right. Slap me,' he said, into her ear. 'And then I'll slap you back.'

'Make it realistic.' She had the tone of voice that made him think that she kind of liked being slapped. Then out loud she said, 'Why don't you just fuck off, you bent fucker! You're not getting nothing out of me!' And she slapped his face hard.

He slapped her back, hard, and then grabbed her arm and twisted it. Pulled her up and out of her seat.

'Right,' he said, 'That's quite enough of that. I'm arresting you for withholding evidence. You don't have to say anything but anything you do say may be used in evidence against you – '

Dolores screamed and beat him over the head with her free hand.

The bouncer turned around to face them. It was like watching an oil tanker turning – the type that has to turn around at sea because the docks aren't big enough. Once he'd completed that maneouvre he tried to grab Todd but Todd slipped past him and out of the alcove. Then the big man threw a punch, which is what tends to happen in those situations so Todd was expecting it. He let the punch sail past his head, moved to one side and gave Big Boy a nice firm push. That was all it took. His weight and the momentum of the wayward punch caused the big man to fall flat on his face. Todd kicked him in the small of his back a couple of times to discourage him from trying to stand up. That worked a treat. The big man made no effort to stand; he just lay there on the nightclub floor and made a noise like a dying buffalo.

The next item on the evening's entertainment was when the barman came screaming over at Todd swinging a large shiny baseball bat. Todd had been trained in unarmed combat by the British Army but taking baseball bats away from fear-crazed night club bartenders hadn't been in the manual, which meant that Todd had to improvise. But that was all right, he'd always been pretty good at that when it came to acts of violence.

The Barkeep was swinging wildly, like a number eleven batsman who's in a bit of a hurry to get back to the pavilion, so it was easy enough for Todd to get inside the swing arc and give his assailant a nice big bear hug and a Glasgow kiss, which is a forcefully administered head butt on the bridge of the nose. The barman screamed, held up his hands and, when Todd released him, ran away screaming and holding his face. The baseball bat spun up in the air and then dropped and bounced off the wooden floor at just the right height for Todd to catch it. And catch it he did, just as Big Boy was trying to get up on his feet. Todd belted Big Boy with the bat, twice, once across his back and once across his shoulders.

The whores in their alcoves stayed in their alcoves with their terrified punters. The ones on the barstools stayed on their barstools. The music had stopped but no one was complaining.

Todd grabbed Dolores by her arm and pulled her over to the door. Stan was there now but he stood to one side to let them pass. It was the best thing he could have done. Todd's blood was up.

'You've not even supposed to be here!' Stan shouted after him as he and Dolores reached the top of the stairs. 'I checked with your station. I hope you know what you're doing.'

'So do I.' Muttered Todd, to himself.

They got a cab back to the cheap hotel he'd checked into earlier on. There was no one in reception but his key card let them into the building and then in to the elevator and then into his room.

Before you could say *Strangers in the Night* they were both naked and in bed. There was something about committing acts of extreme violence that always got Todd's sex drive going, and it turned out that Dolores had the same hang up.

He quite forgot to pump her for information.

When he woke up in the morning she was gone. There was a handwritten note on the bedside table with a mobile number on it and some kisses.

He had a shower and made himself some coffee. Then he took the laptop out of the hotel room safe and carried on reading from where he'd left off the night before.

EIGHT

'They're not even sure that this one's worth bothering with.' Dolores told me as she took a drag on her phony cigarette and blew the vapor at me. It didn't quite reach.

We were sitting at a window table in that rather blingy bar/restaurant on the top floor of the Park Lane Hilton, although we might as well have been in Winston Churchill's wartime bunker for all we could see of the great metropolis. The sky was as black as Dolores's heart, assuming she's even got one, and the sleet and the hailstones flew straight at us like shotgun pellets.

'They know all about this filthy business,' Dolores continued. I could see she was relishing the opportunity of passing me some demoralisingly rotten news. 'It's been bubbling under the surface for months, years. I'll admit that a bonking Bishop is always a nice little hook but what else have you got? Have you got any actual proof, Terry? Any statements? Any witnesses? Was your Bish actually present at any of these nasty little get-togethers?'

'Oh come on.' I said, hoping that her lack of enthusiasm

was just a negotiating tactic. 'Wait until you see the whole list. What I've given you so far is just the tip of the slagheap. As you say, my extremely reliable source happens to be a C of E Bishop and member of the House of Lords and will swear on a pile of holy books what was done, by whom, and when. And you know what I'm on about.'

'So he was there?'

'Well… he says he wasn't,' I told her, 'but when you think about it he must have been. Or how would he know so much about it?'

'So we can't even place him at the child abuse soirees? He's denying he was there?'

'Yes,' I said. 'But he would, wouldn't he? Look, he's ready to crack. All we need to do is just apply a bit of pressure in the right places. You're good at that, Dolores.'

'Alright,' she said. 'Let me see the pics.' I hesitated and she said, 'Come on Terry. You'll get paid. You know you can trust me.'

She's about as trustworthy as next door's cat but I really didn't have any other option than to reveal all if we were going to make any progress, so I got the sordid evidence up on my smart phone and showed her.

'Bit boring aren't they?' She said. 'Let's spice them up a bit.'

She grabbed my phone, emailed the pics to herself and then pulled a tablet out of her bag and started messing around with them. It was news to me that she was a dab hand at photo shop or whatever it's called but she evidently was because she soon had the shady figure in the bushes all dressed up in his Sunday best, I mean in High Church

Vestments – big, silly, boat shaped hat and all but still on his knees with the rent boy's dick in his mouth.

'Now that's much more dramatic.' she said, once she'd managed to stop giggling. 'Why don't you send it to him and see if he wants it spread across the webosphere.'

I did so, and he phoned me within seconds.

'That's not me,' he said, 'and you bloody well know it's not.'

'Take a closer look and I think you'll find it is,' I told him. 'That's going viral, your reverence.'

'You can't do that,' he said, and started to cry.

I looked in my heart for any spare pity that might be lurking around but there just wasn't any there. So I went all butch and got down to business.

'We want names and sworn witness statements,' I told him. 'Once I get all that then this can just disappear as quickly as holy smoke on a Sunday morning.'

He said, 'I told you, I'm not prepared to give you any more information. Do what you will. Tell whom you wish.' He sounded terribly brave and noble.

'Oh, so you're going to tell everybody what you and your wicked chums did to those poor little kiddiewinkies?' I said.

'What?' he managed after quite a long pause.

'Oh come on! It's obvious that you were involved.'

'I absolutely was not!'

'So how come you know so much about it?'

'One of the victims came to me... for help and... consolation. I did my best to help him. I told the police for goodness sake and they did nothing. I absolutely was not involved.'

'But we can make it so you were,' I told him. 'We can put you in there with the rest of them. Just like we put you on Clapham Common in your work clothes.'

A strange noise come out of his throat and down the line to me. It sounded like a cross between a lavatory flushing and a volcano erupting.

'What kind of a fucking monster are you?' He screamed at me.

'Now now, Frobers,' I said. (I must admit I was rather enjoying myself.) 'That's not the kind of language we expect to hear from a man of the cloth.'

He'd started blubbing again, like an insecure three-year-old being forced to watch his favourite teddy bear being hung, drawn and quartered.

'Get me what I need,' I told him, 'and we'll no longer need you as bait.'

The sobbing subsided a little. 'How do I know you'll keep your word?'

'You're just going to have to trust me, old chap. But let's face it you're rather a small fish compared to some of the other sick bastards whose names we're hearing.'

'Yes,' he said, 'And there's much more to this than I first told you. You only know the half of it.'

His voice was full of hope again. I think he rather liked the idea of being a small fish. And I was intrigued and rather excited by the notion that this whole scurrilous episode could be even bigger than it already seemed.

'Alright,' he said, all businesslike now. 'I'll put you in touch with someone who was there, who witnessed what went on and who will testify. Some of the men who were *involved have done rather well for themselves and are now very well-known indeed. You will be amazed.'*

I kept my mouth shut and waited for him to amaze me.

'If I put you in touch with someone who will actually testify… do you swear to leave me out of it?' He was trying his best not to beg but not quite succeeding.

'Yes,' I said, 'of course I do. I absolutely swear to do everything I can to keep your name out of this whole sordid mess.'

'And the Clapham Common thing?'

'It will be as though it never happened, Frobers, old chap. And those nasty litte piccies will disappear forever.'

'Okay,' said the Bishop, after a brief silence. He almost sounded like a member of the establishment again. 'I'll make the call. Can I assume that there is money on the table? For him I mean, not for me. I want nothing.'

Dolores had been listening, her ear up next to mine, and she nodded her assent. I passed on the good news.

'Very well,' he said, 'I'll arrange a meeting.'

NINE

Ａnd so it came to pass that later on that day, in a
well-known gay pub at the Earls Court end of the
Old Brompton Road, Maurice (Mo) Miller shuffled into my
life like the dirty shadow of an evil age. He sat across the
beer-stained table from Dolores and I, took a quick, furtive
glance at each of us and then stared sullenly down at his
pint of lager.

He had to be in his forties but he didn't dress his age;
he was in baggy jeans, tennis shoes and a hoodie. There
were wrinkles around his eyes but it didn't seem likely they
were there through excessive smiling. He had a round, snub
nose and a wisp of hair on his chin that passed for a goatee.
His mouth was like a baby's mouth that was just about to
suck on a nipple. His eyes were small and hard to read,
particularly as he didn't point them in my direction all that
much.

I don't think Dolores had been in a gay bar before and
she seemed rather disappointed that the place wasn't full
of pretty little leather boys with their dicks sticking out of
their lederhosen rather than just a lot of mustachioed men
standing around drinking pints of beer, and ignoring her.
She was wearing a red leather skirt, a tight, red sweater and

the usual seven layers or so of dramatic makeup. I have absolutely no idea who she was trying to impress.

'What you got, Mo?' She asked him. She never was one for niceties.

Mo ignored Dolores and spoke to me. Strategic error.

'More than you could possibly hope for,' he said. His voice was like a choirboy's on the day his balls descended. 'What have you got for me?'

'How much do you want?' I asked him. Dolores just smoldered.

'Fifty K.' he said, and for the first time his eyes came up to meet mine

'Dream on,' Dolores said.

Now he looked at her. 'I'm not going to haggle,' he said. 'I'm taking a massive risk. And this is a massive story. And I've had other offers.'

Dolores said: 'Don't give me that bullshit Mo. You've told us what you want, now tell us what we get. I'm not even sure there is a story here at all. Your first job is to persuade me that there is. Then you'll have to be able to come up with the evidence. Personally, I don't care if you do or you don't. I can walk away from this without a backwards glance.'

Mo said: 'Fuck off then. Like I say, I've got other interested parties.'

I said: 'Let's just all calm down a bit. Mo, what exactly have you got?'

'No.' He said, 'Fuck you, I'm going.' And he started to get up.

I was about to try to persuade him to stay but Dolores put her hand on my arm.

'Let him go,' she said. 'He's got nothing.'

I shrugged and kept shtum. Mo sat back down in his chair.

'Nothing?' he said. 'You must be fucking joking. I've been putting this together for years. I've got signed statements from about a dozen victims and witnesses all alleging the same thing against the same people. Most of them don't know each other. Couldn't possibly know each other.'

'Go on.' Dolores said.

He said: 'Listen. I've been threatened, told I would get hurt or even killed if I didn't keep my mouth shut. You've got to promise not to tell anyone that I've… given you this.'

'You haven't given us anything yet.' Dolores said. 'Get me interested. Give us one name. Then if the name you give is stellar enough and you can come up with those statements, we might be able to do a deal.'

'Don't worry Mo.' I told him. 'No one will find out it was you.'

He seemed reassured by my soothing tones. He nodded imperceptibly and then looked down at his lap and placed his fingers up to his temples. Like he was getting a signal, receiving a message from somewhere scary. Hell or Valhalla or somewhere like that.

'Once you've got the name you'll screw me over.' He accused.

'Oh for Christ's sake!' Dolores snapped. As if we'd just hand over fifty grand with absolutely nothing in return.'

'Alright' Mo said slowly and quietly. 'I'll give you one

name. Then I want some money – something at least – before I give you the paperwork.'

'Alright,' Dolores puckered her lips at him for some reason, which seemed to freak him out. He rocked back in his chair and it took him a couple of seconds to recompose himself.

There is one... individual... who we would all swear was there. He was as famous then as he is now.'

Then, rather than just telling us who this stellar sicko was, he paused for what seemed like an age, like the judge of a reality TV show who's about to divulge who it is who won't be coming back next week. Then he hit us with it.

'Lord Warrington.' He said. He didn't even bother to lower his voice.

Dolores eyes shone and I'm sure mine did too as we looked at each other with barely concealed excitement. It was one of those rare and beautiful moments that happens maybe only once in the long and sordid career of every muck-raking hack. The Peer in question was a Political Beast of the largest proportions.

'And you can get sworn statements?' Dolores asked him, almost breathless now.

Mo's little mouth pursed in concentration.

'Yes,' he said. 'But you're not getting sweet fuck all... until I get paid.'

Dolores wasn't fazed. 'All right, but I'll need a couple of days to sort it out.'

'Quick as you like, love.'

They exchanged numbers and then Mo put a bit of icing on the bun. 'There's much more to this than you can even imagine. This is the story of the fucking century, dear.'

'Okay,' she said. 'Well… if we can put Lord Warrington in there…'

'That's just the beginning,' he told her, 'They're still at it now. Do you think that people like that would ever stop? They never got caught so they just carried on.'

His dirty eyes came up slowly and faced mine.

'They think they're above the law,' he said. 'Maybe they are.'

TEN

I t was good to get out of there and into a world that contained more women than just Dolores. I needed another drink so I talked her into one of those big old Victorian boozers in the Earls Court Road that used to be full of Aussies on around the world trips but that are now full of Slovaks and Albanians swapping hints on benefit fraud.

Half way through her second glass of sparkling wine she disappeared outside for a bit, presumably to make a phone call.

I had a premonition she was going to put a damper on things and so it turned out.

'They want more,' she said. 'If this is still going on we can catch the whole filthy gang of them. We'll get Mo's and his mates' statements but we're going for a set up. We're going to do his phone.'

'Whose phone?' I asked. 'Mo's phone?'

'No, you simple bastard,' she sneered. 'Lord Warrington's phone. Do try to keep up, Terry. You're going to do his phone and you're going to worm your way into his entourage. You can do it!'

'I'm sure I can,' I told her, 'but I'm fucking well not going to.'

She said, 'Yes you are, darling, because if you don't we'll have you banged up for blackmail.'

'How so?' I asked her, 'when I haven't blackmailed anybody.'

'Good old Tubby Entwistle begs to differ,' She told me.

'I didn't blackmail him,' I said. 'He paid me not to publish something. That's an entirely different matter.'

'Beg to differ, sweetie. At any rate he's prepared to make a statement to the police. He's really manned up since his wife divorced him. You see, that was the consequence that he feared the most and now that it's actually happened... well he has nothing left to fear. Apart from fear itself. By the way, he wants his money back.'

'Well,' I said, 'if you're going to blackmail me for blackmailing Tubby then I'm jolly well going to blackmail you and that supercilious redheaded bitch for blackmailing me!'

'Oh don't be so bloody stupid,' she said. 'She's got every politician in the land squirming around in the bottom of her Gucci handbags. She goes to weekend house parties with the fucking PM for Christ's sake.'

I sat back and took a swig of the cheap bubbly we'd been served and tried not to show her how devastated I was by the way things were turning out. A few minutes earlier I'd thought I was on my way to the biggest cash payment I'd ever managed to get my greedy little hands on but now it looked like I was going to get sweet bugger all except a great big pile of grief.

Dolores had the paper arrange an interview with Lord Warrington. That was easy enough to pull off; he had his own comms team and The Planet contacted them on the pretence that we were doing a piece on the lifestyles of the rich and famous. I still checked out as a journo and that crappy but immensely popular little rag was friendly, obsequious even, to the great man's political party.

We met him at his club, 'The Brook Street Club', which is just a few doors down from Claridges. It was just as you'd expect really, all crystal chandeliers and mahogany panelling, and he looked just like he did on the telly, except he was sitting in a leather armchair with a dry sherry in front of him.

Apart from myself and Dolores there was another young woman present, some public relations Doris who was there to make sure we didn't ask him any awkward questions. She was called Harriet. But we weren't there to interrogate him, just to get into his confidence, get his phone number and then start digging.

We'd looked him up of course and he was patron of one of the big opera companies, so I asked him about that and some other cultural matters and he droned on a bit about how terribly important culture was to the spiritual wellbeing of the national community. He was so boring that I found it difficult to follow what he was saying but I nodded and grunted at the appropriate moments. I didn't write down everything he said because I was taping the whole charade on my smartphone but I did make the occasional note to make him think I was paying attention and that what he was saying was terribly important. So there was a fair bit of eye contact going on and I soon got the impression that he fancied me. It was as if the two women weren't there.

'I am,' he said, 'very much a one nation conservative and the over-riding reason I got into politics was to try to make sure that everybody else gets the same chance in life that I've had...'

He was just about to qualify those remarks, presumably to stop himself from sounding like too much of a leftie when Harriet intervened.

'Yes but this isn't about policy, is it? More of a lifestyle type interview?'

'Yes. Quite.' I told her with as much disdain as I could muster and I turned away from her and back towards him. I could see that the manner in which I'd dissed her had brought a twinkle to his eyes.

'Now, moving on.' I said, 'I understand that you're heavily involved in caring for disadvantaged youngsters. Working with children's homes, that sort of thing...'

'Yes,' he said, 'I am a trustee of a large institution of that type and I chair one of the leading children's charities. And I find both of those roles enormously rewarding.'

He turned to Harriet and said, 'Would it be appropriate to name the institutions in question?'

'No.' she said. 'Actually, no. I don't think it would be.'

There was a bit of a silence then. For a moment I couldn't think of another question but then I came up with one, I said: 'Moving on to your domestic arrangements... you're not married are you? Is there a significant other in your life just now?'

It was an open secret in the Westminster village that he was as gay as a royal butler and he was acting so camp with me I thought I might as well play the reporter and see what

I could winkle out of him. Harriet, of course, stepped in at that juncture and said, 'please don't go there, that's really not appropriate.'

He shrugged and as much as told me with his lust-filled eyes that he would have liked to confess all but that his hands were tied. I got the impression that the Party wasn't ready to 'out' him just yet but that he himself was more than ready to declare his undying gayness to the world. I managed to get a cheeky question in about same sex marriages.

'Of course I'm in favour,' he declared. 'If two human beings are in love they should, of course, be allowed to marry...' and so on – ad nauseum.

'Well thank you ever so much, Lord Warrington. I think that should do it. Would you mind letting me have your number? In case I need any clarification or extra information once I've actually written the piece.'

'I'll deal with that,' Harriet said. 'You have my card.'

It was a tricky moment, but the minute her back was turned his Lordship slipped me his card with a wink.

So, we had his phone number. That very same day I sat down at my kitchen table with a couple of cheap mobile phones, a digital tape recorder and a notebook and pencil. I placed his lordship's number on the speed dial of both phones and then pressed call *on one of them. I briefly heard his patrician tones, hung up and pressed* call *on the other phone, knowing it would go straight to voice mail. Then all I had to do was to press zero four times (which is the manufacturer's code that hardly anybody ever bothers to change) and I was able to remotely retrieve the dirty old bastard's voice mail messages.*

But there was nothing there. Not a sausage. There were messages right enough but the usual dross. 'I'm in a cab on my way over to see you.' 'Meet me at the club at eight pm.'

There were messages from his executive assistant that were of a business nature 'don't forget your luncheon meeting with the chair of this or that or the CEO of that or the other.'

There was some racy stuff on there, he was clearly gay and liked the company of much younger men but there was nothing that could be construed as illegal or immoral, not on his part anyway. The young men who called him tended to be on the make, enquiring about some overdue gift, usually of money, but sometimes trips abroad or shopping excursions.

Dolores was terribly disappointed and didn't hesitate to tell me so.

'You're going to have to do better than this, Terry. We've put a lot of money and resources into this and we really must get some results.'

'What the hell do you expect me to do? I can't make people call him and leave incriminating messages.'

She thought about it and then said. 'Okay, call him and ask if you can do a follow-up interview, but this time just the two of you.'

'The problem with that strategy,' I told her. 'Is that the last interview we did wasn't even sodding well published.'

'So tell him there wasn't enough in it and that you need more stuff but be sure to tell him that you can't do anything if Harriet's going to be present.'

So I called him.

'I wondered when you'd call,' he said, 'I haven't seen the story.'

I said, 'I need to do a couple of fact checks.'

'Off you go then,' he said.

'I'd rather do it face to face if you don't mind. And could we do it one to one? I promise it's a friendly piece. I just want to highlight all your wonderful achievements.'

'Very well,' he said, 'come to the House of Lords on Wednesday. Shall we say twelve noon?'

I almost alerted him to the fact that this might cause a clash with a select committee hearing that he was due to attend but I managed to keep my mouth shut.

I announced myself to some MI5 man disguised as a British bobby at the gates of the Palace of Westminster and a few minutes later a lackey was sent down to meet me and accompany me up to the bar.

He welcomed me with the kind of smile that Caligula might have used on his unsuspecting little sister and we were soon ensconced at a cosy little table for two that looked out over the river.

'So what is it that I said last time that you didn't quite catch?' He asked me.

'Look,' I said, 'you've seen things change a lot haven't you?'

'In what way?'

'You know, attitudes.'

'Towards?'

'Sexuality. I thought you might be ready to declare...'

'I have absolutely no compulsion to do so,' he said. But he just had.

'Off the record then. In fact, it's actually a favour I'd like to ask.'

'Pray continue.'

'I've heard there are some rather racy parties, you know, men only ones, that are terribly fun to attend and that will get you a yard or two up the greasy pole.'

'And to which greasy pole are you referring?'

Oh how we laughed.

'All right,' he said, 'but if you print anything at all about any of this. I'll have your genitalia served to me on a silver tray. There might be something coming up. But I'll have to have you vetted first.'

I shrugged as if I couldn't care tuppence if I was vetted or not but my guts were churning over like an ice cream maker on a hot summers day. I'd got nothing more out of him and now I'd made him suspicious.

So I had to go home empty handed. Back to the kitchen table and the hacking operation and there was still bugger all of any use in his voice mail.

Dolores was her usual sympathetic self. She said: 'If you don't come up with something sharpish not only will you not get paid but we'll have you banged up for blackmailing Tubby, and we'll fit you up for the... Great Train Robbery... the Madeleine McCann abduction and whatever else we want to bloody well fit you up for. You'll be finished. Now, go and make something happen.'

All this time, Mo had been waiting for his payday. I asked Dolores when the money was likely to come through and she got all inscrutable and said that it might not be a bad idea to make him wait a while but that we should keep him nice and keen in the meantime.

I went to meet him again and tried to get some more out of him but he wasn't prepared to go on the record until he got paid and was given a new identity and a personal bodyguard.

'This is fucking dodgy,' he said, which was a bit rich coming from him. 'You'd think they'd pay anything for those signed statements.' His face got all scrunched up and a line of sweat appeared on his upper lip. 'They're going to try and get them off me by force.'

He was terrified at the prospect of Lord Warrington and his cronies getting away with their wickedness and then wreaking a terrible vengeance.

'Give me something,' I said. 'Anything at all. So they have *to pay up.'*

Those dead eyes of his made a rare appearance when

next he spoke. 'This is much bigger than I've let on,' he said. 'Much, much bigger. There's more to this than a few naughty politicians bumming a few kids' home rent boys.'

There was nothing to say to that, so I just kept shtum.

'They murdered some of those kids. Bloody tortured them to death! Just for jollies mate, just for fucking jollies! And it's still going on.'

I didn't really know what to make of that, but when I told Dolores you'd have thought I was the bearer of glad tidings. Her eyes positively sparkled.

'So it's true then,' she declared.

It looked like this new revelation was confirming something that she or the Planet's other reporters had already suspected.

But what really got to me was that she never at any time seemed to spare even the tiniest thought for those poor, innocent kids. All she could think about was how fucking huge the story was getting.

It was then that I started to realise I was getting in with a pretty bad crowd.

ELEVEN

The *Brook Street Club* wasn't easy to find. It kept itself to itself. It had no online presence and its physical location seemed to be a closely kept secret. Admittedly it *was* in Brook Street but Todd had to stride twice along that string of imposing Mayfair terraces, all the way from Bond Street to Grosvenor Square, before he finally spotted the classily understated little brass plaque that read: *The Brook Street Club.* Todd pressed the classily understated little brass button that was next to it.

The door opened and he found himself in a grand hallway with a high ceiling. Ahead of him there was a lounge area with leather armchairs and mahogany paneling and on his left was the entrance to what looked like a reading room or library.

The little man who had opened the door for him was wearing a blazer and an old school tie; an ensemble that made him look like a wrinkly-faced public schoolboy.

'I'm here to see Lord Warrington.' Todd told him.

'Are we expected, sir?' asked the ancient retainer who would have looked down his nose at Todd if Todd hadn't been two feet taller than he was.

Todd showed his Metropolitan Police ID card and said, 'This is a police matter. Please inform his Lordship that I wish to see him.'

The little man scuttled off and Todd stood alone in the grand hallway and awaited developments. It was cool in there. A clock ticked. He could see the sunlit pavement and the street beyond it through the front door that hadn't been closed properly. Cars and taxis trundled by, stopping and then starting again at the lights where Brook Street and Bond Street intersected.

An ancient gentleman, wearing a dark blue three-piece suit with an old-fashioned watch and chain in his waistcoat pocket and a confused expression on his face, came out of the lounge and towards Todd. He was helping himself along with an expensive looking walking stick. He stopped for a moment and looked all around him as if he was unable to remember who and where he was. Then he appeared to have a moment of lucidity and turned towards the entrance to the library. He had a stooping gait that placed his upper body almost at right angles with his waist and suggested he was well into his ninth decade.

A waitress wearing an old fashioned black and white uniform complete with bonnet and white pinny appeared, opened the door for him and helped him through it. The old boy stumbled through without so much as a word of thanks.

Once the old gentleman had gone, the waitress turned and looked at Todd. Then turned away quickly. He'd seen her before. It was Lucy Mainwaring. Realising that he'd already seen, and recognised her, she stopped and turned and their eyes met.

Todd was about to approach her when the little porter waddled back into view with a peevish expression on his face and said: 'Lord Warrington has requested me to inform you that if you wish to see him you should write to him at the House of Lords. Will that be all?'

Todd took another look at the girl. She flicked her bonneted head towards the back of the building. She either had a nervous twitch as bad as Todd's or she was telling him to meet her at the back door.

Todd said, 'Did you make his Lordship aware that I'm here on police business?'

'Yes, sir,' the porter said. 'Will that be all?'

Todd showed the little man his back and exited the premises without wasting any more words. He heard the door slam shut behind him.

He walked a little way towards Bond Street and then turned immediately right into Brooks Mews, which was quite the busy little West End side street that morning. There was a coffee shop on one corner and, on the same side of the alley, a row of unassuming little Mayfair mews houses. Todd wondered briefly how much one of them would cost but soon came to the conclusion that they were comfortably outside his price bracket. On the other side of the street were the tradesmen's entrances at the back of what had once been a row of impressive town houses but were now expensive restaurants, hotels and the gentleman's club where he was so unwelcome.

Members of staff from the various six-star establishments stood around smoking and complaining about their working conditions. Todd didn't see Lucy amongst them so he walked back to the coffee shop and bought himself a cappuccino. Then he sat outside and waited.

She sauntered over about ten minutes later. Male heads swiveled. Todd fancied her too but he didn't have time for any dalliances. He just wanted to know why she was there.

She seated herself at the table right opposite him and folded one of her legs over the other one. Seen close up they were quite impressive.

'I'm under cover,' she said.

Todd just grunted and did his best to keep his eyes on her face.

'That wasn't particularly clever,' she told him with the prim authority of a primary school teacher, 'Did you really expect him to agree to see you?'

'Why wouldn't he see me? Surely the fact that he wouldn't see me means he knows DeHavilland is dead. I reckon it could have been him who ordered it done. He's got half the Met in his pocket and he knows I'm working for the other half.'

She'd been looking away, watching the club's back door but now she turned to face him. 'If DeHavilland is dead why didn't you put that in your report?'

'Read that, have you?'

'No, but I know what's in it.'

'Who told you that?'

She didn't bother to reply.

Todd said: 'So you know all about the Knoxley Hall affair and that his lordship is involved.'

'Of course I do. I'm a news journalist. We're looking into it. Lord Warrington's name does keep cropping up but there's no evidence against him.'

'I've got the evidence. You tried to steal it from me last night.'

'Oh, you mean on that laptop, the one you so jealously guarded?'

'Yes. The one you tried to steal from me.'

'It doesn't belong to you. I had as much right to take it from you as you had to take it from that house. You didn't have a search warrant and you haven't handed it in. Anyway, what's on it?'

He said, 'It's absolute fucking dynamite. You won't see a bigger story than this one if you live 'til you're a hundred.'

She didn't respond – just looked him up and down, like he was Gary Glitter.

'Why do you think I was at Terry's place?' Todd asked her.

'I might have been asked to look into that story too, Todd, but I'm still on sexual harassment. Are you prepared to make a statement yet? We have statements from the girl and from two of your colleagues.'

'You're completely wrong, love. I never sexually harassed anyone in my life. They're screwing me over. You'd have figured that out by now if you had any journalistic instincts at all.'

'You found out the girl had made a complaint and that your colleagues were ditching you and so you used the murder of some vagrant to divert attention away from the shit you were in and then tried a smoke and mirrors number by breaking into DeHavilland's house and putting out the story about him having been murdered. You're just trying to tempt me with the prospect of a big story. You must think I'm very naïve.' Then she leaned over towards him and said, 'Why don't you come back to *the Defender's* offices with me and make a statement. I can't promise anything, but that just might do you some good.'

'You're making a massive mistake. You've got the whole thing arse to bollocks. Lord Wotsisface is front-page sleaze. Joe Public loves a good old paedo story, so you really could break a massive scoop. This other thing is fake news, a set-up. It will fall apart before a single word of it is even printed. I think you know that's true. At some level.'

'It's just one of a series. A feature. About police harassment of women.'

'You know this is bullshit. Someone at your paper is working for him. They're using you to frame me for a murder that someone committed to cover up what they did to those kids.'

She said, 'We've all heard the rumours about this kids' home thing but there's no proof and we can't go around accusing establishment figures like Lord Warrington of serious crimes without – '

'You're no journalist. How many stories have you worked on before this one?'

She blushed. 'Alright. This is my first big story. But I'm totally qualified. I have a first in English and a Masters in journalism. It's only because I'm a woman that they've had me on all that... minor celebrity crap. I've earned the right to cover something... valuable... and important. And you're not going to spoil it for me.'

And with that she uncrossed her legs a lot less decorously than she'd crossed them a few minutes earlier, stood up and walked back to the Brook Street Club's rear entrance.

Todd kept his eyes on her as she crossed the street and made a mental note of which back door she went through. Then he lit a cigarette and smoked it slowly. Another smoker came along and asked him for a light and he supplied one. They exchanged smokers' nods.

Once he was done smoking he got up, approached the back door of the club and then strolled through it as if he owned the place. He got one or two inquiring looks but no one cared enough to ask him if he had any right to be there. He walked straight through the kitchen, where the shouting of chefs and the banging of pots and pans suggested that lunch was being prepared, and out into the same lounge that he'd seen from the front hall.

And there was Lord Warrington, sitting on his own in a leather armchair with a glass of dry sherry in front of him reading the Daily Telegraph. He was every inch the grandee, immaculately attired in a three-piece pin stripe suit, white shirt and blue silk tie. He had a full head of bleach-white hair with eyebrows to match.

He seemed to sense Todd's arrival and his cold blue eyes came up and swiveled towards him, hard and sharp and ready for a fight.

Todd said, 'May I join you?' and sat himself down.

'You're not wearing a tie,' Lord Warrington said, 'Shall I ask one of the servants to get you one? They keep a tie for people like you. It's a hideous bright pink one. Intended to embarrass people into dressing themselves properly the next time they decide to visit us. In the unlikely event, that is, of them ever being invited back.'

'Too damned hot for me.' Todd said, in an affected accent. 'Too damned hot for you? Is it?'

Lord Warrington took a sip of his sherry.

'Well, it's going to get a damned site hotter.' Told told him. 'ready for the heat, are we?'

'I'm expecting guests for luncheon.' Lord Warrington said. 'One of them is the Permanent Secretary at the Home Office but I don't suppose you'd even know what a Permanent Secretary is, would you?'

'Terence DeHavilland was beaten to death last night.'

Lord Warrington took another sip of his sherry and gave Todd the kind of contemptuous look that a chief constable would give to a traffic warden who's just put a parking ticket on his Bentley. 'Terence who?' he said.

'He used to be a newspaper reporter, until he was sent to prison for listening to your mobile phone messages.'

'Oh that one,' Lord Warrington said, 'Beaten to death, eh? Poor bastard.'

'The tone of his voice suggested that he had about as much sympathy for Terence DeHavilland as the Great British Public had for Myra Hindley.

'Have you spoken to him since he was released from prison?' Todd inquired.

'Of course not.' The Grandee sneered, 'Why on earth would I?'

'I'm sure he would have tried to reach you. He was investigating allegations of child abuse at a boys' home called Knoxley Hall.' Todd pronounced the name of the institution slowly and deliberately and maintained eye contact.

Lord Warrington didn't blink. He just looked away towards the front hall as if there was something there that had attracted his attention.

'My guests have arrived,' he said. His tone was suddenly light and cheerful. His eyes lost their coldness and danced a little. I can see them in the front hall. So, if you'll excuse me –'

'DeHavilland left a journal. You feature.'

Lord Warrington stood up. Todd stood as well, positioning himself between the peer and his luncheon guests. 'Knoxley Hall,' he said, 'was a boys home in Barnes. The boys there were routinely abused. Some of them were abused to death. The abusers were members of your party about the time you were Chief Whip.'

'Get out of here, before I have you thrown out.'

'No one throws me anywhere,' Todd said and he straightened himself up to his full, rather impressive stature. 'Just think of it. DeHavilland's journal. Names, names, names. Your name keeps coming up. More often than any of the other names.'

'I think you should leave now.' This came from a female voice that was right behind him. It was Lucy. Todd hadn't noticed her presence. For all he knew she could have been there the whole time.

'You have absolutely no idea what you're dealing with.' Lord Warrington told Todd.

Just then the miniature Hall Porter arrived with Lord Warrington's guests. Three old men in suits.

Todd's work there was done, so he turned on his heels and took himself off through the nineteenth century décor and out into the street.

TWELVE

He was half way up South Molton Street before he realised that she was following along behind him. He stopped and faced her. She was still wearing the maid's outfit and looked a bit out of place amongst the shoppers and tourists.

'Where are you going now?' she asked him.

He gave her a short, dismissive laugh.

'Come on, Todd. Don't go all strong and silent on me. If your story's true you won't mind answering a few questions.'

He thought about it. Why not? He had two leads left; Mo Miller and the Bishop. The sooner he found them and bullied them into telling him the truth the better. She would slow him down but she was a lead too. Her presence at both the Islington house and the Brook Street Club meant she was involved. She was being used and he needed to find out who was using her.

'Go and get changed,' he said, 'or we'll attract the wrong types. I'll wait here for you.'

'What would you like me to change into?' She gave a little twirl, 'Sexy schoolgirl or nubile nurse?' and she strolled back down South Molton Street like a Downton Abbey extra who wasn't going to be an extra for very much longer.

Todd sat himself down outside Widow Applebaum's Strudel Emporium, lit a cigarette and waited for her to come back.

He took out his phone and saw that he had a missed call from Dolores. He pressed the call back button and she answered right away.

'About time.' He said. 'What have you got for me?'

'Don't be so fucking rude,' she said. 'I don't suppose last night means anything to you but you could at least be civil.'

'Get to the point.'

'I've put my head on the block just to try to help you, you bastard. I've arranged a meeting at the Coleherne, or whatever it's called these days – with Mo Miller. Be there at one. Arse against the wall, tiger. And watch out for lizards.'

Dolores hung up and Lucy reappeared. She was wearing a pink and yellow summer frock and Doctor Marten's boots. Not many girls could have pulled that one off but Lucy managed it with ease.

She sat down opposite him, leaned forwards and said: 'Is there anything you need to get off your chest?'

'The story about me and that girl is completely untrue. Just for a minute accept that and then think of the implications.'

'My editor – he's won all manner of awards – gave me the lead. We all know that this abuse of female suspects by police officers goes on all the time but that it's rare,

75

for obvious reasons, for any of the victims to lodge a complaint or go on the record with the press. This girl has been brave enough to tell us what happened and we have a source in the Met who is also prepared to testify against you. This whole Knoxley Hall business is complicating everything and yes, of course my instincts are telling me to follow that up as well. But there's no doubt in my mind that you did what Emma Naylor said you did and that it's not an isolated incident. This disgusting practice has to be uncovered and stopped and you just happen to be the first one to get caught. It doesn't matter to me how much you deny it. We know you did it… my editor –'

'What's his name, this editor of yours?'

'Adam Rifkind.'

'Never heard of him. But I've just added him to my list of suspects.'

'Oh don't be so fucking ridiculous.'

'You're being used. Maybe Rifkind is too but it seems more likely to me that he's in on it. He sent you to Terry DeHavilland's house knowing I'd be there and then to that fucking museum.' He nodded his head towards the *Brook Street Club*. 'He knew I'd be there. They want someone to testify that I was in both those places soon after Terry was killed – and you're that someone.'

He saw a flicker of doubt in her eyes. It was just a flicker but it was there.

She took out a reporter's notebook and said, 'I've got some questions.'

He looked at his watch and shook his head. 'Sorry. I don't have time.'

'Oh, how very convenient!' The flicker of doubt was now a flame of anger.

'Look, I'm not evading your questioning. I really do have to go. I have to go to Earl's Court to talk to someone who was abused at Knoxley Hall.'

'Alright. I'll come with you.'

'Good. But please don't tell your friends where we're going.'

'Very well, but one false move and…' She held up the smartphone and gave it a little sideways jiggle.

He gave her his coldest smile. Then he felt a twitch coming on. He tried to restrain it but it got away from him.

They walked up to Oxford Street and jumped into a cab. West past Selfridges. South down Park Lane. The park was packed solid with carefree sun worshippers; barely a blade of grass was visible.

Lucy's phone whistled a little tune. She took it out of her bag and looked at it for a few seconds. Then she rounded on him and said: 'Who are you, Todd?'

'What do you mean, who am I.'

'You're not a policeman. Not in the Met anyway.'

He pulled out his ID and gave it to her. She looked at it and then gave it back and went back to her phone.

The cab took them around Hyde Park Corner, along Knightsbridge and High Street Ken and then turned left into the Earls Court Road.

Finally, she stopped texting and said: 'The only Jack Todd they can find who's around your age and fits your description was dishonourably dismissed from the army two and a half years ago. According to our records he's serving time in a military prison for mistreating Iraqi prisoners.'

'Does it look like I'm in a military prison?'

'Curiouser and curiouser. 'We'll have to get to the bottom of this.'

'What do you do in your spare time? Hunt down Nazi war criminals?'

'I don't have any spare time. What do you do in yours?'

'Sleep,' he said. 'Sometimes.'

THIRTEEN

Terry's Journal

A
fter my first failed attempts to find anything incriminating in Lord Warrington's voice messages the *Planet* ran the following story on an inside page alongside a large photograph of 'Belinda from Birkenhead' whose breasts were so large and round that one doubted if they could be real:

'The Planet *has received a number of allegations of the organized and systematic sexual abuse of children, some as young as eight years old. These vile practices allegedly took place at Knoxley Hall, a boy's home in southwest London. One ex-resident of that institution, now in his forties has given us details of how these innocent, vulnerable young boys were taken, late at night, sometimes to a nearby guest house and occasionally to a well-known luxury apartment complex in Westminster where they were abused and raped. One or more of them may even have been killed. One of our sources is quite certain that at least one of the evil perverts who was responsible is now a senior politician, possibly, even a member of the government. The Planet is determined to get to the bottom of what happened at Knoxley Hall and has launched a large-scale investigation, which will continue until the truth of this matter has been uncovered.*

'Were you, or was anyone you know a resident of Knoxey Hall in the late eighties or early nineties? If so, please contact The Planet *on 0789 4079656.'*

It was an attempt to smoke the buggers out and it worked. Lord Warrington's mobile phone messaging service now got busier than a freefone number offering half price cup final tickets.

The first voice I heard was so recognisable, that I thought I'd tuned in to the Today *programme by mistake. He was a prominent Minister of State.

He said, 'Jeremy, I think you'll guess what this is about so call me back. Immediately please.'

Of course that wasn't at all incriminating but I could tell by his tone of voice that he was as guilty as the jack of hearts and I now had his identity and his phone number. Now we could get into his phone too and see what turned up there.

Soon the other papers picked the story up and started to publish articles that were rich in innuendo and hinted strongly of establishment involvement in organised child abuse. But, needless to say, without naming any names. This little blast of publicity lasted about three days and then the news agenda moved on, as it must, to more pressing issues; the obesity time bomb or the rights of gay footballers or some such guff. But in the short period when we were headline news, I managed to intercept a whole series of frantic messages from terrified sounding men. I recorded and transcribed every single detail and made a copy of everything for my own benefit.

I handed it over to Dolores and she told me it still wasn't enough.

'I thought you said you were expecting an invitation to one of their naughty parties?'

'The invitation must have got lost in the post,' I told her. 'Not much I can do about that.

'Make things happen,' she said. 'Call him... flirt with him... get him all a flutter at the prospect of seeing you and then take him back to your place and fuck him up the bum. Or let him fuck you up your bum – whichever way around it is you like to do things.'

'That might be how you operate,' I said, 'but I'm not much kop at that sort of thing and darling – I'm straight. And if I was gay I don't think I'd fancy him much. He's a revolting old sod and when I think of all the dirty games he must have played...'

'Oh come on, Terry,' she said, 'you're about as straight as the north circular. We tried, remember? And it didn't quite come off. Did it?'

'It worked alright at first,' I told her. 'Then I think I just got bored with you.'

That went down like a politician's intern. Her eyes got steely hard and her mouth went all peevish. 'Don't even think you can quit on me now, you fucking loser. That whole Tubby Entwistle affair is still hanging over your head like the sword of... wotsisface and the last thread is starting to fray. Get yourself invited along to one of these dirty little dos. Then let us know the happy day and the venue and we'll get you all wired up with a titchy little camera in your buttonhole. Then we'll have the buggers red-handed. Won't we, darling?'

What choice did I have? I called him, got his voice mail and left a message. He called me back later on that evening.

'Ah Yes! Young Terence,' he said. 'I haven't forgotten you.'

'Well. I must say. I was rather hoping to hear from you before now.' I said, trying to sound like a spoiled little gay boy and disgusting myself in the process.

He said, 'I've got some friends coming over tomorrow evening. Why don't you join us?'

'Oh I'd love to, I gushed. 'What's the address?'

'I'll have you picked up,' he said, 'What's your address?'

I gave it to him and we hung up.

I called Dolores and she told me I was a very good boy. 'I was beginning to think you didn't have it in you.' She said.

'If we don't play this right it won't be the only thing I've got in me.' I said.

FOURTEEN

Mo Miller was sitting at a corner table and staring down sullenly at a half-finished pint of lager. He looked up just once, as they arrived at his table. His pupils looked like badly crafted full stops that had been drawn on his irises with a ballpoint pen.

Todd showed Mo his badge and said, 'We want to talk to you about Terry DeHavilland. Have you spoken to him since he was released from prison?'

'Oh. He's out is he?' said Mo. His voice held nothing. 'I haven't spoken to him for over a year. He offered to pay me for something. But he didn't come up with the cash so I didn't come up with the something.'

'But you told him about Lord Warrington?'

'Someone must have or he wouldn't have been hacking the dirty old bastard's phone, would he?'

Nobody spoke for a bit but then Mo did.

'Lord Warrington's a child molester,' he said to the bubbles on the top of his pint, 'He was part of what the papers call 'the Westmister paedophile ring.' Once Terry DeHavillland started prying into it he had to be kept quiet. My bet is they offered him a deal and he took it. I'd have done the same thing.'

'Terry's dead, Mo. They found him in the West End with his head bashed in.'

Mo took an excessive gulp of his beer, spilling most of it down his chin and his mohair sweater. Then he made a half-hearted attempt to wipe himself clean with a shaking hand.

'Will you help us find out who killed him?' Lucy asked.

Todd looked at her and said, 'Working together now, are we?'

'For the time being,' She looked back at Mo and said, 'I can see you want to help. What is it that's preventing you from telling us what you know.'

'I know who you are,' Mo said to Todd, 'that other bint filled me in on you. But who the fuck is this one? She looks like she should be at a One Direction concert.'

'I'm a reporter,' Lucy told him, her hand made a little flourish like a royal wave. 'If you help us then we'll help you.'

'I fucking well want paying this time.' Mo said. 'I got nothing before. Apart from threats.'

'Who threatened you?' Lucy asked him, and when he just snorted by way of reply she said, 'This is a big breaking story now. Nobody is going to suppress it this time around. You'll be well paid.'

Mo got up, muttered something incomprehensible and stumbled over to the gent's toilet. The door swung closed behind him.

Todd said, 'So you believe me.'

Lucy said, 'Not entirely, but for the time being I'm going along with it.'

'Why do think I'm running around after these fucking weirdos? I am telling the truth and you're going to be the first reporter to break this massive story. I'm sure that will bring you all the happiness in the world.'

'Let's hear what else he has to say.'

They waited in silence for a few minutes and then a few minutes more. Then Todd got up and went into the gents to see what had happened to him. The toilet had two entrances; one that served the room that they were in, and another one that led out into another room. Todd pushed the stall doors open one by one with a fair amount of apprehension as to what he might find. But they were all empty. Mo Miller had left the premises without so much as a by your leave.

FIFTEEN

Terry's Journal

It was a male only affair. Older males and younger males with nothing much in between. There were one or two what you might have called boys but they weren't as young as all that. Late teens, maybe. Early twenties, possibly. I couldn't remember what the age of consent was for shirt lifters. Was it eighteen or twenty-one? In any case, they certainly couldn't be described as children and they all seemed to be there of their own free will; in fact, they seemed to be enjoying themselves. Lots of kissing and groping and the whole place fairly stank of cannabis resin and amyl nitrate.

Lord Warrington was standing with a much younger man who was wearing a frock and a handlebar moustache. Maybe he was in the RAF.

'Ah, Terence!' Lord Warrington greeted me. Only my mother and father had ever called me Terence and hearing it from him rather despoiled their memory.

'This is Bernard.' he said, pointing to the oddity that was called Bernard. Bernard seemed to find me quite interesting.

'I say, Jeremy' he said, 'where have you been hiding this one.'

A glass of champagne arrived from somewhere and Bernard put his hand on the side of my head and started fiddling with my ear.

'Stop it!' I said and pushed his hand away. I took a long swig off the bubbly. I have to say it wasn't the best.

'Off you go now, Bernard. Lord Warrington said. ' I'd rather like to have young Terence, here, all to myself.'

Once Bernard had gone, Lord Warrington turned his lust filled eyes on me and kept them there. There was something utterly revolting about being regarded in such a manner by such an old and wrinkled specimen.

'Is this what you were expecting?' he asked me.

'Not exactly.' I said.

'Don't worry. We're expecting some rather more appetising guests. They'll be here shortly.'

His revolting expression deepened in its revoltingness. His look said: You know exactly what I mean, don't you?'

My look back at him was intended to say, yes, of course I know, but might have said something altogether different.

He said: 'What happens here, stays here. I hope that's very clear?'

'All absolutely off the record.' I assured him.

That was when I realised I was in the deepest do dos. There was no way he would have invited me to this little happening knowing nothing about me except that I was a journalist, especially if the 'rather more appetising guests' turned out to be quite dramatically younger than the legal bumming age.

He looked over my shoulder at the doorway through which I'd entered, grabbed me by the arm and said, 'Come. Our little friends are here.'

I tried to turn around to catch a glimpse of 'our little friends' and, more importantly, to let my little camera record their entrance, but his Lordship pulled me away.

That was when things started to go all swimmy, but I do remember being pulled into an adjoining room and then through that room and through another door into what looked like the security man's office. There was a nude calendar on the wall with Miss November on display. He must have liked her because this was February. They seemed to know where the camera was and they removed it and then confiscated my phone whilst I was busy passing out.

I dreamed of a childhood scene, a playroom with a rocking horse and a dolls' house and a train set. The train trundled around and the boys – boys my own age (and I was less than six) – took turns at driving. There was a helmet that was passed from boy to boy – whichever boy's turn it was to drive the train got to wear the helmet. I kept thinking it would be my turn next, but they kept ignoring me and I could feel a tantrum coming on.

But then it was bedtime and that was then the nightmare started, the dream within the dream. Men wearing Vivien Westwood creations and large eccentric moustaches were doing unspeakable things to me whilst the Home Affairs Select Committee stood around and watched. I screamed and I screamed and then I screamed some more.

I came around in the back row of a multiplex cinema

in Leicester Square, the one that shows cult classics from different eras. No idea how I'd got there. The film that was showing was Invasion of the Body Snatchers *– not the original, the re-make with Donald Sutherland. Or was it Kieffer Sutherland? In any case I got asked to leave because I threw up all over the place. Luckily there was no one sitting directly in front of me. The security men just picked me up and threw me out, didn't even try to find out what was wrong with me. That's the West End for you.*

SIXTEEN

The long hot August day was finally ending and a sheet of blinding sunlight was descending beyond the westerly end of the Old Brompton Road. Like there was a fire ship going down near Putney Bridge. Todd shaded his eyes, hoping that Mo hadn't got too far, but could make nothing out. He looked back the other way towards South Ken but there was no sign of his star witness in that direction either. Just as he turned to go back into the pub Lucy came out and met him at the open door.

'Have I done something to offend you boys?' She asked him.

'He's done one, Todd said. 'There was another door out of the gent's. He's given us the slip. I must have spooked him when I told him Terry's had his head smashed in.'

'So now what?' she asked, arms akimbo, 'what are you going to do now, DS Todd? Or whoever you are.'

'I've got plenty of leads to follow up. They're on that laptop. The one you tried to steal from me last night. I'm just going to keep on digging. You can help if you like. Think of the fame and the money. Or do you still think I'd make up a murder just to stop you from giving me grief about some trumped up sex allegations?'

'Maybe the dead man really was a vagrant. Maybe your imagination tricked you into thinking it was Terry DeHavilland. The mind can play funny little games you know. Mo told us nothing. Did he? Or have I missed something?'

Todd shook his head and set off with quick, long strides up the Earls Court Road, hoping that she'd follow him and at the same time hoping that she wouldn't. She did. Just like she had the night before when they'd come out of Terry's house and just like she had earlier that day when he'd left Lord Warrington's club. At least this time she wasn't pressing buttons manically on her phone.

The sidewalk traffic thickened as they got closer to the tube station. Todd maneuvered his way through the cosmopolitan crowd that swarmed around the station's entrance.

Then, into this Earls Court normality, came something unexpected and abnormal. First there was a loud crashing noise and then a series of quieter ones. The traffic stopped gradually. Horns sounded impatiently. Drivers leaned out of their car windows. Some of them turned off their engines and got out of their cars. It all went very quiet. No one could see the reason for the silence or the cessation of traffic on this road that never sleeps.

Then the reason came in to view from the direction of Chelsea, although they didn't look much like Chelsea types to Todd. They were wild and hooded. They were kicking cars and shop doorways. They weren't looting, just smashing things up.

Then a police siren sounded and they were gone. They

just melted away like icicles. The traffic started moving again and the music of the street resumed its steady rhythm.

None of this was any of Todd's business, so he walked briskly down the great cast iron stairway to the eastbound platform of Earls Court Station. Lucy stayed in his slipstream every inch of the way.

He sat down on a wooden bench. She stood with her arms folded firmly, between him and the sunset, blocking out the light. He could see her in silhouette only. Like a Bond girl.

'Just what on earth is going on?' she asked him.

'I don't know,' he said. 'Maybe it's the apocalypse. Would you mind not standing there, I can't see you for the sun.'

She shrugged and moved over about an inch.

He was going to have to trust her. He had to go back to the Waterloo Road and his hotel now and he assumed that she would tag along with him, all the way. There was nothing he could do about that. Any attempt to shake her off would only serve to convince her of his guilt. In any case he didn't really mind her coming with him; he could turn that to his advantage. But sooner or later she would start with the smartphone routine again and he couldn't have her texting his location to her friends at *The Defender*. Somebody there was working for the other side. For *them*, whoever *they* were.

An eastbound train trundled noisily to a stop but he didn't try to board it. He said: 'Give me a chance to prove what I'm saying is true.'

'And how?'

'Come back with me and read Terry's journal. He was on to them and they framed him and had him sent down. The coppers and the press were all involved as well as some senior politicians. When he came out of prison they had him killed and now they need someone to blame for his murder. That would be me.'

'Where do you live?'

'You don't think I'd go home, do you? I've booked into a hotel.'

'Very funny. As if I'd go in to a hotel room with you.'

His nervous tick started up again. It came and it went. 'Look, I'm not a sex fiend,' he said, keeping his voice low and light in the way he assumed that a sex fiend wouldn't. There was something absurd about how that came out and she laughed out loud, breaking the tension. He laughed as well, sensing some kind of breakthrough.

'Alright,' she said, 'I'll come along. But I'll have to let my editor know where I am.'

'No!' His voice rose again. People turned and looked and he lowered his voice and said: 'You can't do that.'

'Why not?'

'Because they're involved. They must be.'

'Oh, don't be so ridiculous.'

'Why did they send you to DeHavilland's house without telling you whose place it was?'

She walked back round, to where he couldn't see her face.

'And why did they send you to the *Brook Street Club*?' They told you I'd be there. Did they tell you that Lord Warrington would be?'

'There's absolutely no proof whatsoever that Lord Warrington has done anything wrong…' Her voice came out of the sun at him.

'He's as guilty as sin,' Todd said to her shapely silhouette. 'Every copper and every crime reporter in the land knows that. I'll let you read Terry DeHavilland's journal. That will convince you. But you've got to keep it to yourself for a bit. Then we'll break the story in our own time and through the right channels. We've got to keep the evidence hidden – for now. Later on, we'll tell one person – someone we really trust – and instruct them to blow the whole thing wide open if anything happens to either of us, or if anything even looks like happening to either of us –'

He stopped abruptly. Maybe he'd scared her, maybe he hadn't. At any rate, when the next eastbound train pulled up, they both embarked.

SEVENTEEN

Terry's Journal

Dolores was terribly disappointed. Not with me, just with the way things had gone, generally. She was actually quite sympathetic.

'Poor thing,' she said, 'Terry, how dreadful for you.'

I couldn't have agreed more.

'Look Dee,' I said, 'we can't do this anymore. Get me some money and let me go. Please? It doesn't have to be a fortune, just enough to get me to the other side of the world and set myself up when I get there. My cover is blown and I've seen what they're capable of. This is a highly organised outfit. I have to stop investigating them and get right away. You too, darling. Or you might get hurt too. Please? Darling?'

All right,' she said. 'Give me a couple of hours.' She didn't seem all that worried, which surprised me. Surely the fact that those weirdos had rumbled me also meant that they knew that she was my partner-in-crime. Perhaps she thought her close affiliation to the Planet would protect her.

In any case, she gathered together the collection of tapes, transcriptions, the list of names and phone numbers, *stuffed them all into her Hermes handbag and disappeared into the gloom.*

I felt an enormous sense of relief. I was out. I was free. I would jet off to California, marry a rich American widow, get a job writing bad TV shows and drink myself to death on Nappa Valley wine and Tennessee bourbon.

That wasn't quite how things panned out.

I waited for an hour or so and then became too restless to wait indoors any longer so I left her a message, telling her where I'd be and, braving the foul weather, I took myself around the corner to my local watering hole.

There was no one in there that I knew. That had become a fairly common occurrence. The old, rich but shabby Chelsea types who'd lived there for donkeys' years were gradually being replaced by a bunch of cosmopolitan bienvenues who I didn't really care for; off-duty Russian whores with ludicrously overdressed pimps and a smattering of Chinese brokers, badly educated hedge fund managers and various other nouveau riche nonentities who were somehow able to afford an SW3 residence.

I drank red wine steadily for a couple of hours until the barmaid refused to serve me anymore and suggested coffee. I vaguely remember verbally abusing her at the top of my voice, at which point a bouncer appeared and bounced me out through the door. That's what this country's come to – Eastern European bouncers, self-importance enhanced by those wireless microphones they wear on their faces – in an English pub.

Anyhow, this one had no need to radio for help, I was so drunk I couldn't have fought off a giant poodle and he just pushed me, unceremoniously, out into the driving rain.

And there they were, waiting for me in a big, black Peugeot – not the latest model.

The pock-faced man, who'd been sitting in the passenger seat, jumped quickly out when he saw me and flashed his ID. For all I saw of it he might have been from the gas board.

He told me to get in the back. I told him to fuck off and shouted for help at the top of my voice but my cries were lost in the wind and the rain. I tried to run but he grabbed me from behind, one hand on my arm and the other around my neck. I almost managed to wriggle out of his grasp but then the other one got out from behind the steering wheel and the two of them pushed me down onto the wet and freezing tarmac and got some handcuffs on me. Nice and tight. They bundled me into the back seat. One of them got in beside me, and we pulled away from the kerb and set off down Oakley Street towards the river.

They took me to that little business centre down by the Thames, the one that's right by Battersea Bridge, where you go to get your Lamborghini serviced or to get a consultation on how to furnish your ten million quid Chelsea town house. It was deserted at that time. A garage door slid up and over a drive-in entrance and we went into a loading bay. The garage door slammed down shut behind us.

One of them pulled me out of the car and pushed me down onto a concrete floor. The other one, the one who'd been sitting next to me, kicked me a couple of times in the guts and I vomited up about twenty quid's worth of Cotes du Rhone. I managed to get up onto my knees but then he kicked me again and I fell back down and rolled around in my own vomit a couple of times like a premier league football er trying to get his team a penalty. The ref wasn't having it.

I was hauled back up and then shoved back down again more times than I can remember. Then I must have banged my stupid head because I passed right out.

When I came to I was sitting on a hard-backed chair. I hadn't been kicked for a decent period of time so I was beginning to feel a little better.

'You can't do this,' I told them. 'This is England.'

'We can do what we want – to nonces.'

'No you can't and in any case I'm not one.'

'Yes, you are, look…'

And he showed me a picture of myself with two naked teenage boys. We were all playing with each other's private parts. Except I'd never done that. I've never had any interest whatsoever in that sort of gig. It looked to me like Dolores's dirty work.

'That's not me,' I said. 'That's my head pasted onto someone else's body. Look, you can even tell. Any expert could. Next.'

'Don't give me that. It's you!'

'No it's not.'

He punched me again, just the once this time, right around the earhole.

'What do you want?' I managed to groan at him.

'A full confession – to the Knoxley hall child abuse affair. You were the ringleader and organizer. Weren't you?'

'Fuck off.' I told him. 'I'm working on a story that will expose that very affair. You, you pair of bastards, you're

working with the abusers. You're covering up for them. You're protecting them.'

That got me a smack in the mouth from bad cop and a clip around the ear from slightly less bad cop.

'You know what happens to nonces like you in Wandsworth, don't *you?'*

'Don't tell me,' I said, 'they get an extra dollop of jam on their whole meal porridge, like?'

Either he didn't like me taking the piss out of his Essex accent or maybe he just liked belting me. Anyhow, he belted me. This time on the other side of me head. Every star in my microcosmic head universe flared up and glowed as brightly as Venus on a black and cloudless night.

Then they put a hood over my head and I think they buggered off for a bit. At least no one hit me or called me a paedophile for a few minutes, which probably meant I was alone.

I was wet through with vomit and rain water and my own blood, and I must admit I had a little sob to myself. I've never prided myself on being able to withstand much physical mistreatment, and this was the worst I'd had since I was a fag at Eton.

Eventually, after maybe half an hour, I heard them come back in. One of them whipped the hood off and I was temporarily blinded by an electric torch that was shone into my eyes from close quarters. I closed my eyes tight, and when I opened them again the harsh torchlight had gone and a normal light was on; a single naked light bulb, just like in the movies.

Essex man was holding a tape recorder. He turned it on

and we heard voices. I recognized them immediately. They were Lord Warrington's voice mail buddies.

'These were taken remotely from the voice messagin' service of this phone number.' He said and he read it out to me from a piece of paper he'd pulled out of his jacket pocket. 'That's not your phone number, is it?'

I just about managed to shake my head. It felt like it might fall off my shoulders at any moment.

'No,' he said, 'but you know whose it is, don't you?'

'Yes,' I said, 'of course I do. I was investigating the very child abuse activities that you seem intent on pinning on me. You must know that, lads.'

'You ownin' up then?'

'To what?'

'Mobile phone message intervention.'

Suddenly there was hope. 'Is that illegal?'

'Course it fuckin' is!'

'Well, what happens if I do own up?'

'All the other stuff goes away.'

'No extra jam on my porridge?'

He shook his head.

'Will I go down?'

'You gonna keep your marf shut?'

'About?'

'You know what.'

I nodded.

'You might get six months,' he told me.

Bloody marvelous! One minute you're contemplating a life of leisure on Malibu beach and the next you're looking at six months' downtime at Her Majesty's pleasure.

EIGHTEEN

Todd took the laptop from the hotel room safe, switched it on and opened the relevant word document. Then he placed it on the table. Lucy was waiting with folded arms and a cynical mouth. He would have liked to have read it again himself but he thought it best to keep a decent distance between them.

She started fiddling about with the machine's settings.

'Don't get any ideas about emailing it to yourself,' Todd said. 'He's disabled the Wi-Fi. It needs a password to re-enable it.'

A faint look of annoyance crossed her brow but then she made herself comfortable and started to read.

He lay on the bed and watched her, which was light and easy work, but it wasn't long before he started to nod off. He tried his best to stay awake but it was hot in the room and he'd not been getting much sleep.

Then he was in another hotel room. There'd been a girl in that room that day too. There'd been an overhead fan whirring around and she'd been brushing her hair at the dressing table and he'd nodded off then as well. Then she'd let them in. He'd woken up just in time and killed the first one at the door. He'd broken the man's neck the way the British army had taught him. The other one had already entered the room but was just about to leave in a hurry. Todd gripped him by the throat and was going to deal with him the way he'd dealt with the first one when he heard a woman's scream and realised that the intruders were a dream but that Lucy was real and that it was her neck he had a hold of.

He dropped her like an electric cable and she hurled herself across the room to the door. She struggled with the lock in a fit of fear and panic but couldn't get the latch on the door to yield.

'I was dreaming!' he yelled, 'and I thought you…'

The enormity of what he'd just done struck him like a roadside bomb. He put his arms around his head and cursed himself. When he looked up he saw that Lucy had stopped trying to unlock the door. She was rubbing her neck where his hand had been, breathing deeply and calming herself.

'What were you doing?' he demanded. 'Why were you up close to me like that?'

'You were snoring like a pig, I was just trying to turn you on to your side. What was going on – in that head of yours?'

'Flashback.' He said, trying to control a twitching fit. 'I was in Iraq, seconded to an infantry unit. We got caught in an advanced position, got taken prisoner by some Al Qaeda militiamen. Me and two others. Two private soldiers. Kids. Jarvis and Stokes. Geordie lads. Good as gold they were. Real good lads. I was a sergeant; they were privates. I wasn't *their* sergeant but that didn't mean that I wasn't responsible for them.

'Every day for a week the bastards played the same dirty trick on us – the mock execution routine. Put bags over our heads, made us kneel in the dirt, pressed guns against our heads. Then there'd be the click of an unloaded revolver and they'd drag us back up and back to the cage.

'Then, on about the seventh or eighth day, we were getting the usual treatment when a shot rang out. The shock nearly fucking killed me and when the bag came off my head I saw that Stokes had been shot and that half his brains were lying in the dirt. The next day it was Jarvis's turn.

'Then they just let me go. I suppose they wanted me to go back to base and tell everybody what had happened, just to put the shits up.

'I told the officer who'd de-briefed me that we'd been in a firefight and that the other two had both been killed in action and that I'd been concussed and wandering around in a daze for a week. I'm still not sure why I lied. I guess I was in shock and couldn't face up to what had really happened.

'They put me in a field hospital for observation and a couple of days later a pair of MPs came to my bedside and told me I was under arrest. Some Special Forces twat who was in the same ward had seen the three of us being taken. That made it look like I'd sacrificed their lives for my own.

'I got banged up and was expecting to be court martialed when some Major came in to see me. He said there was a big scandal breaking about British soldiers abusing Iraqi prisoners in Fort Basra. He said somebody had to take the blame and that I would fit the bill. He said if I signed a confession I'd get a couple of years in the Glass House and then a dishonorable discharge and that that would be the end of that.

I signed it and they let me go. That seemed a bit odd at the time but I soon found out why. They'd hired a couple of Iraqi mercenaries to kill me. They set me up with some Syrian bird in a hotel room and then sent the bastards around to do me. Same as now really. Give me the blame and then make sure there was no messy court martial. Just the same as now.

He looked into her eyes and said, 'That's who I thought you were.'

She nodded and touched her neck again.

'I managed to blag my way back into Fort Basra and reported for duty to my commanding officer. He was a decent sort and I trusted him. Anyway I had no other choice. He put me under guard. For my own good I reckon and then some civvy came to see me and asked me would I consider going back to Blighty under an assumed identity. He really didn't give me much choice.'

'So you're not really a policeman?'

He shook his head.

'So where are you from? What's your background?'

'Orphan.' he said. 'I was found in a cinema. Back row. They tried to foster me out but I wasn't a cute kid so no one wanted me. And I was violent. I've always been violent. I was brought up in kids' homes.'

'Oh, I see, so were you…?'

'No.' he said. 'They're not all kiddy brothels.'

There was a silence, which he broke. 'What about you? What's your background?'

'Not that dissimilar. My mother abandoned me as well.'

'So where did yours leave you? Royal Opera House?'

Lucy smiled sadly. 'She died in a car crash. Along with my sister, Isabel. We were on holiday in the south of France. She drove off a cliff in the hills above Cannes. I survived. Miraculously.'

'Still.' he said. 'At least you've got your dad.'

She shook her head. 'Not really. He's never really been there for me.' There was nothing more to be said about that. She changed the topic of discussion back to him.

'What is it about you that makes them always want to fit you up? The murder, the sex thing and now this.'

'How the fuck do I know? There must be something about my personality that makes me scapegoat material. One thing I do know is that this time there's no way out. This time I'm finished.'

'Don't talk like that,' she said. 'You're tired. Get some sleep.'

'Will you stay?'

'Only if I can tie you up. Otherwise you might try to strangle me again.'

They were on the bed now. That had just sort of… happened. He leaned across and kissed her and she didn't seem to mind. After a nice long snog she stood up and took off her dress. And then her underwear. Now she was naked except for her Doctor Marten's. That made him laugh, and she laughed along.

But then things got serious.

NINETEEN

Terry's Journal

Whilst I was on remand the wider phone hacking scandal started to break. Someone at The Planet turned on his own kind, blew the whistle on his comrades, and soon a plethora of outraged celebrities came to realise that members of the fourth estate had been listening in on their mobile phone messages. Poor darlings! It was enough to make me want to cry into my government supplied Quaker Oats.

But then something happened that changed everything; a young girl was abducted and eventually killed by some lunatic and those evil bastards at The Planet kept on doing her phone, listening in to frantic messages from the parents and then, stupidly, deleting them. That gave the poor girl's loved ones cause to believe that she was still alive. When the girl was found dead the police sussed out what had been going on and started to arrest the hacks and private investigators that The Planet had been using. That was the beginning of the great British phone hacking scandal. It took public indignation on to an entirely different level. I'd been the only person ever to be charged with phone hacking up until then, but by the time of my trial, phone hackers were being charged as frequently as Commercial Road prossies.

My trial was all hyped up to be a show trial It looked like it was going to be a right old media circus, but I spoiled their fun by pleading guilty. My lawyer, who was chosen for me by the police, (I was pretty certain that that was against the rules but I didn't see any point in complaining) didn't have much work to do; he just read out a statement to go along with my guilty verdict and his honour, the wigged wonder, gave me two years somewhere nasty. Take him down!

So, there I was, banged up in a cell in Wandsworth; four of us in a space that was designed, back in Victorian times, to accommodate two. Now there's progress for you. I was hoping for an easier billet, an open prison to which my status as a first-time offender and white-collar crook, might entitle me. I soon discovered that I was entitled to bugger all.

A couple of weeks into my stretch I realised I'd had no visitors and wasn't being allowed to communicate with anyone at all on the outside. This was all in direct contravention of my human rights, so I raised the matter with one of the few screws who seemed to be a reasonably decent human being. He said he'd have a word.

About a week later, I did have a visitor: Some dodgy solicitor from the same firm as the one who'd represented me in court. He was a pompous little Welshman about four feet nothing with a beer belly that would have looked a lot better on a much taller man.

He seemed to be listening patiently to my pleas to be transferred to an open nick and to my request for a visit from my sister. Then he changed the subject abruptly and asked me how I thought I'd get on if the other prisoners got the idea that I might be a 'nonce'.

The very idea of that sent an ice-cold shiver right up my rectum. My cell mates rarely talked about anything else. There was a 'nonce' on B wing apparently and the main topic of conversation was what they were going to do to him. And it didn't involve throwing him a nice surprise party with jelly and blancmange.

There had been a bit of speculation that I might be on – a nonce I mean – just a sly word dropped here and there, purely because I didn't join in with the general nonce hating repartee.

So I told my legal beagle friend that I'd much rather he didn't do that and he reminded me of the deal I'd made and that I'd better stick to my side of it, even though I'd been given twice the amount of prison time that they'd promised. That, he said, had been due to circumstances that were completely outside their control. So, far from improving my situation, all that happened was that, once again, I had it explained to me what a good idea it was for me to keep my big gob shut. They hadn't forgotten me then.

Then I started to get letters (not visits) from Jo, (no one else even bothered to write) and I was able to begin preparations for my eventual release. The lease on my terrific little pad in Chelsea had expired whilst I was on remand and Jo arranged to have my stuff, not that I had much, moved into storage.

So it was four in a cell and I was lucky to get my own bunk. My first group of roomies was an interesting and a varied bunch: an armed robber, a drug dealer and a shoplifter. I don't think any of them had attended Eton but you never know, standards there have slipped.

The armed robber was an old lag called Charlie Roberts. He'd spent most of his life behind bars and didn't seem too bothered about his lack of freedom. He was at the top of the pecking order, not only in our cell but, as I soon learned, of the whole wing – maybe even the whole nick. Even the screws treated him with respect. I wondered why, if he was 'The Baron' (a word I'd heard on prison movies but I never actually heard him referred to that inside) that he didn't have his own room with hot and cold running water and a breakfast bar but I soon found out why. The other two, Wayne, the shoplifter from up North somewhere, and Jesse, the crack 'shotter' a mixed-race kid from Peckham, were both quite young, and I suppose, if you'd been locked up for as long as Charlie Roberts had they were as comely as Kylie Minogue before she left the cast of Neighbours.

At any rate, the noises started the first night I was in there and it was a case of musical bunks every night from thereon in.

I wasn't invited to play at first, much to my relief, but then one morning the other two were moved out and it became rather evident as to why I'd been invited into that particular suite. By lights out I was already under zero illusions about what was expected of me. I was the chosen one! And there was nothing I could do about it.

There were compensations. Charlie protected me. Like

I said, the phone hacking scandal was breaking and my name was getting mentioned every day in the papers and on the news. I had become a bit of a celebrity and I think Charlie rather enjoyed having a celebrity as his bitch.

The story that the Planet had put out, that I was a lone, rogue reporter, the only one who had dabbled in the black arts of phone call interceptions, was starting to wear a bit thin. Other reporters were getting nicked and even editors and newspaper executives were falling beneath the long shadow of the law, spurred on by those hypocritical bastards who'd managed not to get caught. If they'd asked me I'd have told them what was happening, that every hack in London who was worth his salt was performing that particular dirty trick, that the entire cell phone network was being treated as Fleet Street's own private party line, but I wasn't in any position to tell anybody anything.

Anyhow, Charlie had the word put around that although I was a soft cunt, I was a good bloke for not grassing up my mates and that I should be left alone. Which made my last few weeks in Wandsworth a bit more bearable. Things got even better when they moved me to a cell with only one other occupant: a nicely spoken young embezzler who spent his time playing chess with himself and doing the telegraph crossword. Charlie had tired of me and found himself a new beau. Happy days. He told me if I ever needed him he was there for me. Ah! Bless! Last thing I heard was that he'd gone all religious, had seen the error of his ways and was in the process of converting the entire wing to Christianity. He must have been up for parole.

Then, one day, they came and collected me and drove me to an open nick somewhere down in Kent. The rest of my time was like an extended countryside break. Fresh air. Exercise. Time to think. And boy did I do some thinking.

TWENTY

Dolores lived in Pimlico, not far from the river, in a nice private square with a nice private garden in the middle of it. The kind you need a key to get into. It wasn't the largest flat in Pimlico but it wasn't the smallest one either. It looked like she was doing pretty well for herself, although there was always the possibility, thought Todd, as he pressed her doorbell, that she was blackmailing some poor sod to let her live there.

She greeted him in slippers and a dressing gown. It was the kind of dressing gown that keeps falling open at the front. Todd told her to go and get dressed. She seemed to like being told what to do. She sauntered out of the room and soon reappeared in a pair of slacks and a pink chiffon blouse. The blouse had the kind of buttons that come undone on their own.

Todd looked away from her nipples and focused on a forty-inch TV set that dominated one corner of the room. Twenty-four-hour news. Rioting mobs. Petrol bombs and tear gas.

Dolores's eyes followed his. 'Looks like the sales have started early.'

'I've got my own troubles. Who killed Terry? We can do this the easy way or the hard way.'

'Don't give me that crap, Todd. There's nothing else I can give you. I took a big risk getting you and Mo together. That was your big chance. What did you get out of him?'

'Nothing. He ran away.'

'Well you'd better run after him then, hadn't you? He's the best chance you've got.'

'There's something you're not telling me. There's something else. Somebody else.'

She shook her head. 'Sorry, Todd.' She picked up her electronic cigarette and gave it a loving lick. 'There's nothing more I can do for you. Maybe you should just… hand yourself in.'

Todd shook his head and spoke quietly, almost to himself. 'I was the one who cautioned him and charged him. They wanted my name involved. Even back then.'

'They're all in on it. It's a huge fucking web. It's a vice web, Todd. They make them join these weird cults where this ritual child abuse goes on. Oh it's not just Knoxley Hall. There was a boy's home in Northern Ireland. MI5 were involved in that. There have been others too that no one will ever hear about. It's fucking rife, Todd. The whole fucking establishment is riddled with the sick bastards. You've been caught up in it. So have I. But I'm getting out. Do what they want. I know what's going on, but I'm saying nothing. Maybe they'll get me anyhow just because I know. But maybe they'll spare me if I play along. You should play along too.'

'I can't. I have to find out who killed DeHavilland.'

'Why? Just drop the whole thing and fuck off abroad. I'll come with you. We could go to Ibiza, it's nice there.'

'I can't.'

'Why not?'

'It's complicated.'

'It doesn't need to be. Make sure your little news reporter friend knows all about it and then she can tell the world what's been going on. Then they won't be able to hurt a single hair of your great big ugly head.'

'How do you know about her?'

'Mo told me about her.'

'You two speak a lot then, do you? You and Weirdo Bollocks.'

She shrugged and took a phony drag of her phony cigarette.

'Give me something else,' Todd said. 'You know what's been going on. You've got to come clean. Give me some names.'

'I thought all the names were on that laptop,' she said, all vapour and cleavage.

'Some. But a laptop can't be cross-examined at the Old Bailey. I need to know who can be made to talk.'

She picked up a remote control and switched channels. 'Oh, look, it's the top of the hour. Have you seen the news today? You're bigger news than the riots. You've been on there all morning, Todd. On the hour, every hour.'

Todd looked at the screen and there, in ultra-high definition, was an old photo of Terry Dehavilland. It was captioned, 'found dead.' Then a more recent one of himself appeared captioned, 'chief suspect.'

The glamorous lady who read the news was talking to the world in a beautifully accented BBC tone of voice that was perfectly appropriate for the description of monstrous, criminal events.

'Terence DeHavilland,' she was saying, 'the tabloid news reporter who was imprisoned for illegally intercepting the private mobile phone messages of former cabinet minister Lord Warrington, was found dead early this morning in Soho. Police want to question Detective Sergeant Jack Todd, who is stationed at West End Central police station and was the last person seen with DeHavilland before his death. D.S.Todd, was heavily involved in the original phone hacking case and was the arresting officer who charged DeHavilland with the offences that eventually led to his imprisonment. According to Scotland Yard, D.S. Todd was facing suspension from the police force as a result of allegations that he was involved in the phone hacking operation and, also that he had sexually abused a vulnerable female drug user.'

The doorbell sounded. Dolores didn't seem surprised; it looked like she was expecting visitors.

He said: 'So that's what all the come on was about. I thought for a minute that you really fancied me.'

'You're all right.' she retorted. 'We had some fun but now it's over. I never said I was yours for life.'

She walked over to the door and opened it. It wasn't even locked.

'Hello Sherlock,' Norcross said as he and Barrowclough entered the room. 'That was quick. We were hoping we'd catch you with your trousers down.'

'Course you were,' Todd said, 'so you could wank each other off.'

'You going to come quietly, Todd?' Norcross said, 'or should we just finish you off here and say you resisted. Nobody would doubt it, would they? I mean you're such a desperate fucker with such a tragic history of violence and criminality…'

By now Todd's attention had been cornered by Barrowclough's right hand, which seemed to have grown a handgun.

Todd twitched: one long, intense one that seemed to affect the whole of his body and then three shorter ones that only affected his head.

'That's not standard issue,' he said.

'Don't do anything unexpected,' Barrowclough told him, 'or I'll shoot your cock off.'

Norcross produced some handcuffs and made his way behind Todd's back. Todd elbowed him in the throat and then swiveled and landed an old-fashioned swing punch to the side of his head. Norcross flew across the room, smashed against the wall and then slid down it like a cartoon cat.

Barrowclough stared at Todd like a rabbit stares at a headlight. Todd kicked the gun out of his hand and then broke his nose with a head butt that would have measured pretty highly on the Richter scale.

By now both his adversaries had lost their earlier bravado and were cowering on the sheepskin rug in front of the telly, bleeding all over it. That didn't seem to bother Dolores much. She seemed confident that her insurance would cover the damage. In any case she was concentrating on pointing Barrowclough's gun, which she must have picked up from where it had fallen, straight at Todd's belly button.

Todd walked over and took the gun away from her.

'Please don't hurt me,' she implored him. 'I had no option. They've got stuff on me. They're bastards, Todd. Go and hand yourself in to some real – I mean – straight coppers. Maybe it will all come out.'

Todd raised the hand that held the gun as if to strike her and she covered her face with her forearm. He lowered his hand slowly and then said, 'Boo!'

She started a little and let out a wail. Then put her hands to her face and started sobbing.

Todd waited a little while for his two adversaries to show some signs of consciousness. Barrowclough was the first to do so and so Todd dragged him up off the floor and held him up against the wall by his bloodied shirtfront. His nose was all over his face and he was groaning, like it hurt or something.

'Who killed Terry DeHavilland?' Todd asked him.

Barrowclough didn't seem to understand the question and in any case the interview was over because just then a siren could be heard from the street below.

'Time to go,' Dolores told him. So he went. He found a back way out. There's always a back way out.

The last thing he noticed was that Dolores' blouse was now all buttoned up.

TWENTY ONE

Terry's Journal

Once the euphoria of release had dissipated I began to realise that there were some pretty nasty realities to face up to on the outside.

For a start, I was totally brassic. Jo had rented me a scummy flat up the nasty end of Essex Road and put a few quid in my account and I suppose I should have been grateful for that but it was next to bugger all and it looked likely that I would have to sign on the Old King Cole in order to get my rent paid. But Jo came to my rescue again by getting me a bit of proof reading work for the Nag and Mutt. They even let me work from home. Jo let it be known that that was absolutely the last favour I would get from her and that she and her twat of a husband didn't want anything more to do with me; the phone hacking scandal was at its peak and the hacks who had hacked were persona non grata.

I half expected to have the press swarming all over me but Jo had been very discreet and no one had my new address. I'd changed my phone but they soon got my email address and it wasn't long before I started to get offers to blow the whistle on my fellow hackers. They weren't interested in Knoxley Hall, just who'd hacked celebrity phones. I didn't have a sodding clue! I hadn't once been in a newspaper office in my entire life. I just used to send in whatever *merde* it was that I'd raked up and a week later a lump of cash would appear in my bank account as if by magic. But those days were over. I now had about as much chance of digging the dirt on anyone worth writing about as I had of being asked to open the batting for the MCC.

I was as skint as a badger and had to get out there and hustle. Discreetly. Hoping to Christ that the bastards who'd stitched me up didn't get wind of what I was doing. Then I remembered Charlie's offer of help. He'd seemed to think that he owed me a favour, so I decided to call it in.

It was a pretty odd feeling walking back through the gates of Wandsworth nick so soon after being incarcerated there and into the visitors' room that I remembered from my own time inside. This time, thank Christ, I was on the other side of the glass partition. The right side. Charlie Richards was facing me through the glass.

'Charlie,' I said, 'we need to do God's work.'

'Yes,' He said, with a swivel-eyed stare. 'I am spreading the word in here. I am using my power and influence over others to make them see that the Lord's way is the only way.'

He sounded like a cross between Malcolm Muggeridge and Mad Frankie Fraser.

'That's grand, Charlie,' I said. 'I'm doing the same

on the outside. But we must root out the sinners. Those abominable creatures that abuse and murder the little children. Didn't Jesus have a particular affection for sprogs?'

Charlie looked up at the ceiling. Either he was contemplating the higher meaning of my words or his meds were wearing off and he was slipping into a manic episode.

'Yes,' he said, finally. 'Yes, he did.'

I was pleased we'd got that straight so I pressed home my advantage: 'I want to finish my work,' I said. 'I want to expose these terrible sins and have the perpetrators brought to justice. Then they'll get banged up in here and you'll be able to go to work on them properly.'

'God will punish them,' he said. 'He will consign them to the flames of hell for all eternity.'

'True.' I said, 'but don't you think He'd quite like to see them get a bit of the old dirty porridge routine in here first?'

'Yeah,' he said with a cold-eyed grin that reminded me of the old Charlie. 'Yeah, you're right.'

Was that a wink? I thought I saw the mask slip for a moment. I'd long suspected that this born again stuff was all just an act to get an early parole date. I wouldn't have put it past him.

'On the day I got out you offered to help me, Charlie,' I said. 'I'm trying to write this story but I'm getting stopped. I want to stop the child abuse, Charlie, and I want to bring these bastards to justice. But apart from all that... writing stories about celebrities' and politicians' private lives is the only way I know how to make a living.'

'Who's stopping you?' Charlie asked with a flash of protective anger.

'Bent coppers,' I told him, slipping into the prison vernacular that I'd learned to use during my spell inside, 'Two of 'em. They're called Norcross and Barrowclough and they work out of West End Central. Is there anything you can do? They beat the shit out of me once and then got me to cough for the phone hacking. It was that or get a ten stretch for kiddy fiddling, which I never done. You know that, don't you? Anyhow, once they catch wind of me nosing around after the nonce brigade again they'll give me a taste of the same old mustard. They'll just round me up and pin something on me and put me back inside. Or maybe even do me in. The stakes are high, Charlie, and this goes right to the very top.'

'Alright.' he said. 'I'll get a mate of mine to keep an eye on you. Bent coppers are a piece of piss, mate. We got plenty of our own. Chances are these two are on our payroll. I can easy take care of that. Anything else?'

'No.' I said. 'That's the main thing. Once they're off my back I can crack on and collect evidence and then write the story. I've got one of the broadsheets interested. I'll get paid and then be on my way.'

'Go to Spain.' he said. 'Magaluf. I got loads of mates down there. That's where I'm going when they let me out of here.'

Not much chance of that, I thought. But I didn't say so at the time.

I had already been approached by The Defender, that holier than thou, leftie 'heavy' rag that I had always despised but that now seemed to offer my only chance of survival. I decided to accept their offer and they took me on, commissioned me to write a book about Knoxley Hall that would be serialised in their pompous pages alongside some sanctimonious crap about zero hours contracts. It turned out the poor sods who dusted their apple macs and scrubbed their toilet bowls were all agency workers on zero hours contracts too, but that still hadn't come out at this time.

It was an interesting proposition, but what worried me was how they'd got to know that I knew what I knew. I was torn between fear of whoever it was who'd fitted me up and then had me beaten up and sent down, and the absolute necessity of earning a few quid and getting out of that shithole of a flat. No one knew where I lived. I could get the rotten job done, take the advance and be far, far away before publication. No less a personage than the Defender's editor himself gave me certain assurances that if the bad guys were to find out where I was living, and if I was threatened in any way, that they would have me protected and make sure the police, (the good policemen, presumably) would be told what was going on. Surely such a morally upright member of the fourth estate would never go back on his word and put my life at risk. What with that and Charlie's offer of protection I am now, as I write this, emboldened to proceed.

TWENTY TWO

It was a scorching hot day in the British capital and London was on fire – in more ways than one.

It was cooler though on the embankment by Vauxhall Bridge, where Todd could be found. The pavements were crowded but the multitude passed him without glancing his way. Millions of people must have seen him on TV but no one recognised him, even though he was a singularly recognisable man and the photo that they had shown of him on the news had been a recent one. In any case, he made no attempt to hide his face or avoid anybody's eye contact. He held his head up high. If they clocked him, they clocked him. They would be more likely to look at him, and maybe recognize him, if he cowered, with his head down. So he didn't.

He looked due south across the river and a plume of smoke caught his eye. And then another one. Then he remembered. The peasants were revolting. There were riots breaking out all over town. The Terry DeHavilland murder had been top of the news bulletins earlier on but he bet it wasn't now. He was on nobody's mind right now and even if someone did identify him and call the police, the Met, in the current state of affairs, wouldn't have the resources to come after him. Norcross and Barrowclough were crooked cops, they took their orders from the wrong 'uns. And that news bulletin had been released by the same dodgy outfit who were pulling their strings. The riots had come to his rescue.

Still, he felt deflated. They were setting him up. What had Lucy said? What was it about him that made the powers that be always want to put him in the frame for offences that he hadn't committed? Mind you, he thought, there was plenty of bad stuff that he had done, in Iraq, for which he hadn't been held to account. He'd never cared much about the rules.

Violence had been part of his life for as long as he could remember. When he had been in the orphanage the bastards had leathered him for even the slightest misdemeanor. That would have broken a lot of kids but it had hardened him up. He had never cried, never shown them how much it hurt and Christ it had hurt; it had hurt like hell. Then straight into the army at sixteen. He didn't even remember making a decision to sign up. Somebody had decided for him that he wouldn't be able to survive in the outside world and he had been moved swiftly from one institution to another. More violence as one or two of the older squaddies tried to put him in his place, but that hadn't worked out so well for them and, after he'd smashed a couple of noses and loosened a few teeth, they'd left him alone.

Then there had been the special services training, which he'd sailed through, and then the wars. Blair's wars. Good old Tony! Whatever would he have done without him?

He'd been perfect for the black ops, those false flag operations that the British Army is so good at. Violence had earned him respect, for a spell. He laughed then, thinking back about what he'd been through. He'd survived all that, hadn't he? Fuck 'em! He would survive this too.

He'd been getting a little het up as all those memories had streamed through his consciousness but now he managed to calm himself and stop twitching and weigh up his options. He soon came to the conclusion that he only had one, so he called her. She picked up right away.

'Where are you?' Lucy asked him. 'Have you seen the news?'

'Yes.' he replied. 'Just now. Rioting all over the shop. They're not blaming that on me as well are they?'

'That's not what I meant, but it does seem like you've been relegated to the bottom of the bulletins. Look, I'm with Emma Naylor and she's admitted that she lied. I'm sorry I doubted you.'

He had to think for a tick or two to remember who she was talking about. Then it came back to him: Emma Naylor, the girl who was supposed to have sucked him off in exchange for not nicking her.

'Apology accepted,' He told her, with genuine relief. 'So what made her change her story?'

'When I told her that this is about child abuse. She's got a kid of her own.'

'I need to get off the street,' he said, 'and I can't go back to that hotel.'

'Did you check out?'

'Yes.'

'Where's the laptop?'

'Stashed'

'How soon can you get it?'

'Right away.'

'Good. Wait a minute.'

Todd heard her talking to someone else. Then she came back on the line.

'You can stay at Emma's place for the time being.'

'What "time being?"'

'Until I can get the story out.'

He hesitated. The idea of sitting around helplessly whilst a young woman sorted his life out was less than appealing. 'Where does she live?'

'Battersea Park Road. On an estate called the Doddington. You'd better get here quick. I suppose if what you say is true and they're going to… try to… murder you… then now would be the time – now they've released the news of DeHavilland's killing.'

'Bloody right,' he said, 'they just had one jab at it. Two of them. With guns.'

'So, what happened?'

'I disarmed them.'

There was a brief silence, then she said, 'Right then. So get over here, sharpish. You'll have to stay in hiding until we're sure we can hand you over to the bone fide authorities.'

'That's no good either. I'll never get bail and they'll do me while I'm on remand.'

'You need a top-notch lawyer. *The Defender* will arrange that.'

'Are you sure whose side they're on? Somebody there knew about Terry before it was common knowledge. It looks to me like they're working for the other side.'

'They just got a tip off, that's all. They had no idea whose house that was or that Lord Warrington was at that Brook Street Club. They got a tip off you were there as well. If we can't trust the editor of *The Defender*, then we can't trust anyone. Look, there's huge press interest now. There's no way they can do anything to you.'

'They can do whatever they fucking well want,' he said.

'Get yourself over here without being recognised. Sit on top of a bus and read a paper or something.'

She gave him the address and he hung up, and then saw that he'd had a missed call from a number he didn't recognise.

He dialed it and the Voice said: 'I'm pulling you in, Todd. Get yourself to West End Central and wait outside the main entrance.'

'No chance,' Todd told him. 'I'm getting close now. Give me a few more hours. At the very least I can find out who killed Terry.'

'Have you got any proof? Against anybody?'

'Not yet. But I will have.'

The Voice hissed at him: 'Do you think you're going to be allowed to gather the evidence?'

'I can get a confession,' Todd said. That came out like a dirty secret.

The Voice laughed. 'And you think that's going to be admissible? After you've beaten someone shitless?'

Todd said nothing.

'Where's the laptop?'

Todd said nothing.

'Forget trying to find out who killed DeHavillland. If we're going to save your neck then we have to expose the paedo ring. That happens to be my job. And now it's yours too. There are signed statements of victims. Naming names. They're on the laptop. Haven't you found them yet?'

'I haven't had the chance to look,' Todd told him.

'They'll be scans,' the Voice said, 'most likely pdfs.'

There was nothing like that on the laptop, but Todd kept that to himself.

'Alright, if you won't come in, then I'm going to arrange for you to hand the laptop over to one of my boys,' said the Voice. 'Where are you?'

'No chance of that,' Todd said quickly. 'What if I just give you the names? Then you can go to work. The laptop stays with me.'

'Don't be a fucking idiot, Todd. Every copper in London is looking for you. Your face is all over the media.'

'You'll just hand me over,' Todd accused.

'Not if you do it my way.'

'No,' Todd said, 'You're going to have to do it my way.'

'You're bloody lucky to be getting this chance! You should be rotting in a military prison. This is bigger than you, Todd, and it's bigger than me as well.'

Just then the signal died.

TWENTY THREE

Terry's Journal

We had another meeting this morning. It didn't go quite so well as the first one. All I have is names – the ones that I garnered from the phone hacking project for which I was incarcerated. But of course that's not enough. There need to be signed statements from witnesses and victims, people who were actually there and saw what went on, and those victims and/or witnesses should preferably have no knowledge of each other and should be available for further questioning and be willing and able to appear in court or in front of a Parliamentary Committee.

But what I have got is dynamite – a list of about a dozen men, politicians, senior civil servants, high ranking churchmen – those sorts of chaps – who all contacted Lord Warrington in a bit of a tizz just after the 'appeal' for victims and witnesses had been printed in The Planet. I'd got their mobile phone numbers and from those numbers I'd been able to get their names and addresses. But there still isn't enough to publish anything. These are alleged perpetrators, not victims or witnesses, and it doesn't seem likely that they're going to *own up to anything or to inform on each other. I need some money to get the evidence against those lovely people. I'm running on empty, living in this dreadful, awful place that Jo has found for me. Bless her for helping me out but the place is most definitely not up to muster. Having said that, as awful as it is, it's better than the street, and that's where I'm going to end up if I don't come up with some rent, sharpish. At any rate, Adam Rifkind, the illustrious, award winning editor of* The Defender, *that illustrious, award winning, (dying), rag has magnanimously agreed to let me have* some *money – but nowhere near enough. For some reason it's never quite enough, is it?*

I had one chance, and it was a long shot: Mo had promised signed statements on the day Dolores and I met him in that Earls Court gay pub. She'd told me he had nothing, that he was just trying to blag as much money as he could out of the Planet. Then we got side tracked into hacking Lord Warrington's phone. If it had been up to me I'd have paid Mo and got those signed statements. But it hadn't been up to me, had it? I'd told Dolores that was the way to go but she'd insisted we take the phone hacking route. That bitch. She set me up. Of course The Planet *would have needed the same evidence. She led me down a route that let them off the hook. The only person who did get hooked was me. Maybe Mo hadn't been lying; maybe he did have some signed statements along with contact details of the signatories.*

The Defender *would pay for that.*

After a little bit of detective work I found out where Mo lived and paid him a visit.

'What the fuck do you want?' he asked me on the doorstep. It was a rhetorical question, so I ignored it and he stood grudgingly to one side and let me enter his abode. It was all chintz and lace inside, like a little old lady's country cottage.

'I want those scans.' I told him.

'Gone,' he said. 'Gone forever. I'm out.'

'There's money on the table.' I said. 'More than last time. I should think.'

'More than last time!' he squealed. 'I got next to bugger all last time!'

'You got a fucking sight better deal than I got,' I told him.

'Well, it wasn't nowhere near enough,' he said, and looked gloomily down at the carpet. (It's all about the money with Mo, isn't it?) 'Not for what I've been through. I've been threatened. I've been living in fear for my life. The only reason I'm still alive is because nothing's come out. I'm just starting to feel a little bit less afraid. I'm just starting to think I might be able to re-build my life. And now you expect me to go back to where I was? You must be joking.'

'They won't know it was you,' I told him. 'A lot of people know that they're out there and it could be any number of people who's sold them on. This is all coming out now and there's massive public interest. It's a seller's market, Mo, and you're the seller.'

I mentioned the amount I'd been authorised to offer him and he spluttered and gasped, brought his fists up to his face and almost screamed.

'When?' he said, finally. 'When do I get it?'

'Half up front and the rest when you deliver.'

He just couldn't say no.

He wanted the money transferred to his account, right there and then, and I thought that best too, before anyone else got to him or he just changed his mind. I wanted my slice as well, so I phoned Adam and he agreed.

'Stay with him,' Adam said. 'Don't let him out of your sight. If this goes wrong I'm for the high jump.'

So I sat there with him and we waited.

'What makes people like that?' I asked him, just for the sake of making conversation. 'What makes them do those things?'

'Black magic.' He said, in a stagey whisper. 'Dark satanic rites. These men are initiates of some sort of secret society and they need the blood of children for their ceremonies.'

I didn't believe a word of that but, let's face it – great copy!

We waited an hour and then I checked my account on my phone. It was there! At long last I'd had a decent payday.

Mo didn't have internet banking so we had to go out to the cashpoint and he checked his balance. He'd been paid too.

He took five hundred out in twenties and then set off at a brisk old trot away down the road. I went after him but he turned a corner and broke into a sprint. I cursed and continued my pursuit of him but he was well away. I kept going, more in hope than in any expectation of catching up with him, but my perseverance was rewarded: as I came *around the corner he was lying in the road. His face was bleeding. Two men stood over him. One was about six feet four and the other was about four foot six. Both of them wore overcoats but only one of them had knuckledusters on.*

'Alright Terry? Charlie says hello,' the big one said. 'Where do you want him?'

They took him back to his tacky abode and dropped him just inside the front door. But they didn't come in. Maybe they were too polite to enter without an invitation. And Mo was in no state to offer one.

Once he'd recovered, he went upstairs and came straight back down again with a tablet in a flowery knitted overcoat. He opened it up and sent me an email.

'Now, get out!' he hissed at me through a veil of tears. 'Just get out, will you and leave me alone.'

I checked out what he'd sent me and it was the real McCoy all right. PDFs. Signed sealed and delivered. So I made myself scarce; hightailed it back to Islington.

Once there I sent the scans to Adam and then stashed them on here, on this pc. They'll be hard to find but I'll leave instructions elsewhere. You can't be too careful.

Now I was ready to roll. There was more to it now: black magic, human sacrifice! Surely they couldn't turn this one down.

I worked feverishly on the story. I still am. The sooner I get it finished and send it over to The Defender *the sooner I'll get the rest of that lovely lolly. It finally feels like I've turned a corner in my life. Time to move on and away. Up, up and away to the glorious, sunlit uplands of Northern California.*

Although there has been one rather worrying development: I read the news today. Oh boy! Charlie Richards, my jailbird lover, was found dead. He's been beaten to death in his cell.

TWENTY FOUR

Todd left Battersea Park at its southernmost exit, strolled down the Prince of Wales Drive, with its upmarket Dakota style Mansion Blocks, and a couple of minutes later found himself on one of the nastiest, dirtiest, most drug-infested council estates in town; that's London for you.

There was a map of the estate on the corner of Queenstown Road that hadn't been completely vandalised so he was able to locate his destination: Harold Macmillan House.

The lift was broken, so he had to walk up four flights of stairs before he arrived on the landing he was after. Of all the desolate and depressing landings of Harold Macmillan House (and most likely of Clement Atlee House and William Gladstone House too) this was the most depressing and the most desolate. Filthy, forgotten washing fluttered from filthy, forgotten washing lines. Piles of what had once been poor people's private possessions bore witness to the latest evictions. It was where they shot the opening titles of Channel Four News.

There was a gang of kids at the far end of the landing. They were crowded around someone. They jumped up and down in unison flicking their fingers in that black 'gangsta' fashion whilst rapping an insistent hip hop chant.

The person they were crowded around was Lucy. She was shouting at them and they were chanting their unintelligible chant at her. It reminded Todd of a scenario that he'd once had to deal with in a medina in Ramalla that had just been bombed.

He stepped into the throng, pushing and pulling whichever young man came first to hand and forced a path through to Lucy, who seemed unharmed, if a little shaken and distressed.

He put an arm around her and tried to escort her out of the melee. The young men closed in around the two of them so Todd took hold of one of them by the shirtfront, held him out over the railing and offered him a free flying lesson. The noise dropped to a murmur and then stopped altogether. The whole crew of them backed right off.

'That's better,' Todd said, 'Now, get back in your rat holes.'

One of them took two steps forward, faced up to Todd and said: 'Get off this landing and take your bitch with you. You don't belong here and you got no business here.'

Todd dropped his hostage on the right side of the railing and reached inside his pocket for his ID.

'Police,' he said. 'We go where we want whenever we want to. Now get away from us before I call for reinforcements.'

'He's a copper!' someone yelled, 'what dat fuckin' pig doin' here?'

'You got a warrant, pig?'

'Who's he calling rats?'

'Shut up,' said the leader of the pack with a tone of authority that solicited an immediate, respectful silence. Then he turned to Todd.

'They was just asking what she was doing here. She wouldn't tell 'em nothing and that got 'em mad. I was just about to step in and make sure nothing bad happened. I'm the law here.'

'I'm here to see Emma,' Lucy said. 'I told them that.'

Numero Uno went over to numero 305 and banged on the door. After a second or two the door opened and a thin-faced young woman appeared.

'You know these?' the young man asked her, flicking his shaven, tattooed head towards Todd and Lucy.

'I know her,' Emma said, 'not him.'

'He's a copper,' the boss kid told her. 'Somethin' tell me he ain't official here but we gonna take his phone anyhow for the duration of his visit.'

'You're not going anywhere near my phone, sonny boy,' Todd told him.

The two men faced up to each other but only one of them had an army at his back.

Emma lowered her voice and spoke directly to the leader. 'He got no one to call. He that copper that the other cops is after. Don't you watch the news? He's outside the law now, Big. He's on the run.'

Big looked at Todd with a hint of surprise and then nodded slowly to Emma, who stood aside from the open door so that Lucy and Todd could enter her abode.

The flat smelled of stale tobacco and a blocked toilet but it was still a relief to be off that landing. There was a portable TV in one corner of the room and a small, mixed race boy of around seven or maybe eight years sitting cross-legged in front of it.

'I'd better go and straighten this out,' Emma said to Lucy. 'Watch Marcus for me.'

Lucy and Todd sat down on a battered settee, the little boy in front of them.

Lucy said, 'You could have handled that one better.'

Todd leaned back and closed his eyes for a second. After the standoff he felt a little drained. 'I just saved you from a fate worse than death.'

She shook her head. 'It was all noise and no action. And in any case, I can take care of myself. Although I'm not sure you can. Now your cover is blown. This block would have been a perfect safe house. Now some people know you're here. Why do you always have to play the fucking macho man?'

Todd opened his mouth but then closed it again without speaking. His twitch came on. A couple of quick ones and then a nice steady stream of facial jerks.

'This was supposed to be about getting you off the street,' She said, 'somewhere safe where no one would think of looking. Somewhere safe and anonymous. This place would have been perfect but now you've advertised yourself. You great big stupid sod.'

'Oh well,' Todd muttered, 'to be completely honest I don't really like this place much anyhow.'

'You've got to hand yourself in,' she told him. 'We

can't trust the police so we need to do it through *The Defender*. They'll get you a good lawyer and they'll arrange things with the police and the C.P.S.'

Todd shook his head. 'They've already got the evidence, according to DeHavilland. Why haven't they acted before now? They'll do me in. I'll get banged up on remand and they'll do me in the nick. It'll be front page news for a day and then everyone will forget about it. Your bosses have been frightened off, or they're in on it, or maybe they're just afraid of getting sued. That's what the libel laws are for – to stop the papers from telling the truth about people like Lord Warrington.'

'So what's the alternative? You're just going to stay on the run for the rest of your life?'

'Maybe I'll have to. That's nothing new for me.'

'Don't be ridiculous. There has to be another way.'

She looked thoughtful for a second. Todd sat with his head in his hands and started twitching again.

Lucy said, 'They think it's all on here.' She patted the laptop. 'Now, if they thought that what's on here would be revealed should anything happen to you…'

'Nothing much on there though, is there?' He said, 'No proof. Not many names and no fucking proof.'

'But they don't know that.'

'If you play it that way they'll come after *you*,' he said. 'They'll do me in the Scrubs or wherever I get banged up and then they'll come after *you*.'

'Not if we make it plain that should anything happen to either of us then all this will come out. See what I mean? That's got to be worth a try. At least let me try. I'll go above

Adam's head. He's only the editor, I'll go to the owners. And I'll pay Bishop Frobisher a visit. A source told me where he's holed up. A bishop's testimony might just still be worth something.'

Emma came back in. She looked Todd up and down accusingly and asked him a question: 'Did you just call my neighbours rats?'

Todd shrugged 'Heat of the moment. I'm sure they're lovely people.'

'Anyway…' Lucy said. 'Thanks, Emma, but I guess we'd better leave. Word will soon get out and –'

'No need,' Emma said. 'Only Big heard what I said and he won't tell anyone a word. I told him you were trying to get the child molesters and that brought him round.'

'Still, no point in staying here,' Todd said, 'I need to get out of town, out of the country…'

'Have you even got a passport?'

His twitching speeded up and then stopped abruptly.

She said: 'When I left you this morning I went to the office and spoke to Adam. He told me there was something big going down but that he couldn't tell me what it was. I asked him about you. The news of Terry DeHavilland's death had broken by that time and he tried to make me say where you were. I refused to tell him. I asked him why I'd been sent to Terry's house to question you about the sexual abuse story. He wouldn't tell me. I asked him if Emma had lied? He said that that had all been genuine, that you had abused her. I knew he was lying so I got in touch with Emma and once I'd told her that this was about kids being abused, molested, even killed, she admitted she's been paid to tell that story. She's got a kid of her own, you see.'

'But you still want me to trust this editor of yours?'

'No. To be honest I have lost trust in him. We'll have to go above his head. I don't know what he's doing but I do know that he's a fundamentally decent man. Whatever he's doing he's doing it for a reason. Maybe he's trying to play some kind of double game. Or he's being played. He claimed he wasn't aware that the house in Islington was where Terry lived or that Warrington would be at that club. He told me you'd be there but he didn't tell me why. I still don't know why he sent me there.'

'You're going to be asked, under oath, to say I was at both those places. At my trial. Or more likely at my autopsy.'

'Maybe so.' Lucy said, thoughtfully, 'In any case, he wouldn't answer me. He told me to wait in his office, said he needed to check something out, and then he left, leaving me in there. I waited a couple of minutes and then went out after him. I saw him talking to a security guard. So I left. Then I came to Emma's and I begged her to tell me the truth. Once I'd told her this was about child abuse she did. She told me they'd arrested her for possession and got her to lie about you in exchange for dropping the charges.

'Now she knows what this is about she feels bad about what she did and she says you can stay here until we can get your story out. She's taking a big risk. If you're not prepared to hand yourself in then wait here for a few hours and I'll arrange it so they daren't do anything to you, I'll let them know that if anything happens to you then the contents of that laptop will be revealed. So far as they know what's on there is enough to convict them.'

'Alright,' Todd said, 'I'll give you a few hours. If your way doesn't work, we'll do it my way. I'll go down fighting, take a few of the bastards with me.'

Emma spoke up. Todd had forgotten she was there. 'Don't you want to let the world know what's happening at places like Knoxley Hall?' she asked him, 'If that's still going on you're probably one of the few people who could help put a stop to it. Maybe you should concentrate on that, you selfish twat. Instead of just trying to save your own skin.'

He stood up and walked to the door in the hope of finding some cleaner air.

'I'm just not that good.' He told her.

TWENTY FIVE

Emma put Todd in the bedroom. The smell was slightly less nauseating in there but only just. He lay on the bed, lit a cigarette and blew the smoke at the ceiling, flicking his ash in an empty cider can that he found on the floor.

After a few minutes Emma appeared and said: 'You got any mint on you?'

'How much do you need?'

'Fifty?' He had a look in his wallet.'I've got thirty quid.'

'Hand it over then. Bedroom tax.'

'Hang on. What do you want it for?'

'Pay your fucking rent, mate. I've got a kid to feed.'

'Alright, alright,' he said, and handed it over. She went out.

After a few minutes he looked in on the kid.

'You all right, son?' he asked. The little one was immersed in the cartoon channel. He either didn't hear or pretended not to.

Todd sat down where the kid could see him and waited for some childish curiosity to kick in. None did. Todd found the remote and switched channels. He found a news channel. There he was, on a digital wanted poster. He flicked back to Danger Mouse but the kid was interested now.

'Wow!' he said. 'You're on the telly!'

Todd just shrugged and let off a twitch.

The kid looked startled and he made to get up.

'I'm not scared of you,' he said.

'You don't need to be.' Todd told him, 'I like kids. Once ate a whole one.'

The boy looked startled again but then Todd grinned at him and the kid saw the joke and grinned back.

'What's your name?' Todd asked him.

'Marcus,' he said. Then he looked around the room and asked, 'Where's my mum?'

'Gone out.'

'Where?'

'Don't know.'

'Most likely gone to score,' Marcus said, and went back to watching telly.

'So you know about that sort of thing, then?' Todd asked him.

'I might be a kid but I'm not stupid,' he said. 'Anyhow she's stopping soon. She promised.'

'Course. Course she is,' Todd said. He went back into the bedroom and lay back down on the bed. He was just dozing off when he heard her come back in. She turned the TV onto a news channel. Todd was half asleep but then sat bolt upright when he heard what the news presenter was saying in her immaculate BBC English.

'*Bishop Donald Frobisher, the bishop of Newark was*

found dead this morning in a startling development to the phone hacking scandal that has already claimed the life of Terence DeHavilland, the Daily Planet *reporter earlier this week.'*

Todd got up and went through to the lounge.

Emma had a plastic tube in her mouth. She was smoking heroin off a piece of silver foil. The little boy was watching her with a hostile look in his eyes.

Todd glanced at the TV. A photo of Frobisher, and then one of DeHavilland, and then one of himself. The announcer's voice droned on and on. Emma chased her dragon and blew the thick brown dragon smoke out into the room.

Todd went back into the bedroom, stashed the laptop in the bottom of a cheap, white wardrobe, went out into the hallway and quietly let himself out.

TWENTY SIX

Lucy got the breaking news about Bishop Frobisher's 'apparent suicide' at about the same time that Todd did. She was on the top deck of a bus when she happened to glance at her smartphone and there it was. Top story on *The Defender's* state of the art smart phone app. Oh well, she thought, at least I won't have to go to Newark.

Just then she got a call from a withheld number. She accepted it and an unfamiliar male voice came down the line.

'Good morning. Is this Lucy Mainwaring?'

'Yes, it is. Who's calling please?'

'This is Detective Inspector Norcross of the Metropolitan Police.'

'Good morning, Detective Inspector. How can I help you?'

'Is this a convenient time to talk?'

'Not really. I'm on a bus on my way to work.'

'I think you know what this is concerning, Lucy. We need to talk to you. Should we come to your office or would you rather meet somewhere else?'

'Not at my office, if it's all the same to you.'

'Meet me in Covent Garden,' His voice had an edge

to it now. 'North side of the Piazza. I'll be sitting outside.'

She called the office and asked one of her colleagues to check if DI Norcross existed and if he did whether he worked for the Met or not. The answer was yes to both questions so she got off the bus at Aldwych and walked up the hill.

They'd got there before her. Two of them. Two men in suits in a sea of tourists. About as inconspicuous as a pair of sausage rolls in a kosher bakery. When she got up close she noticed the bruises. One of them had a purple eye and the other a nasty looking thick lip.

Neither of them stood up. The one with the black eye and the bad complexion nodded at a chair they'd kindly reserved for her. D.I. Norcross got straight to the point.

'Where is he, Lucy? Where's Todd?'

'Why would you think I'd know that?'

Norcross inspected his notebook. 'Your editor sent you to talk to him on two separate occasions. The first time at an address in Islington and on the second occasion at a private members club in Brook Street, Mayfair. Is that correct?'

'Yes, that is correct but I haven't seen him since Brook Street and we barely spoke.He refused to answer any of my questions.'

She felt sure they couldn't prove otherwise. She couldn't blame Adam for telling them where she'd been sent. It was a murder case and he would have had to cooperate.

'So you haven't seen him since your meeting with him in Brook Street?'

'No.'

'After that meeting you went your separate ways?'

147

'Yes.'

'You didn't then accompany him to a gay pub in the Brompton Road?'

She opened her mouth to speak but then thought better of it. If they knew that much, then how much more did they know? 'I'm afraid that's all I'm prepared to tell you. I don't know where he is. Will that be all?'

Norcross licked his lips and grinned at her. Like a hyena that's just about to tuck into a half-grown gazelle. 'No. I'm afraid that will not be all. This is a murder investigation and you're refusing to cooperate. Your colleagues at *The Defender* are doing their bit. Now it's your turn. I'll ask you once again and please think very carefully before you reply. Lucy, do you know the whereabouts of D.S. Jack Todd?'

'No,' she said. 'No, I don't'

The two men looked at each other and shook their heads in mock indignation. When D.I. Norcross spoke again it was in a different tone of voice, one that reminded her of that friend of her father's, that nasty, slimy old man who'd once put his hand up her skirt.

'We'd like you to come with us, Lucy.'

'Oh. Am I under arrest?'

'Not at the moment but you soon can be. Withholding information relevant to a murder inquiry. That should get six months in Holloway don't you reckon, D.S. Barrowclough?'

'I'll say.' Barrowclough spoke for the first time. Like a ventriloquist's dummy. 'Can you imagine what they'd do to this little sweetie pie in Holloway nick?' He said to Norcross with a sideways leer at Lucy, 'All them bull dykes. They'd think it was Christmas, birthday, and Gay Pride weekend all rolled into one.'

Norcross shook his head with affected concern at just how bad that would be.

Lucy threw her head back, showed them the full expanse of her bosom and said, 'That sounds like fun. I like that sort of thing.'

That got her an identical pair of lecherous grins.

'All right,' Norcross said, 'You can go. But don't leave town. We'll be wanting another word before long, I should think.'

'I don't need you to tell me what I can or can't do, but I think I *will* be off now. Toodle pip.'

She stood up and walked back across the Piazza towards the indoor market aware of their eyes on her. She took a circuitous route to Holborn, making sure there was no one tailing her and then boarded the tube at Holborn Station.

She got off at Pimlico and texted Todd.

text me D's number and address.

Why?

Seen the news?'

Yes.

Maybe she's prepared to talk.

The number came back. Dolores's number.

She texted:

My name is Lucy. I want to talk to you about Jack Todd,

Who are you?

I'm a reporter.

Fuck off.

Look, I'm on his side – and yours. Meet me in the café at Tate Britain. I'll wait there for you.

Half an hour later she was facing Dolores in the tourist packed art gallery cafeteria over a couple of untouched cappuccinos. Lucy guessed that Dolores must be at least ten years older than she was and that she didn't much like the fact. She was dark haired and tanned and wore a pair of retro sunglasses for the whole time they spoke.

'Have you seen today's news?' Lucy asked her.

'News? The inflation figures, is it?' Dolores replied, waspishly.

'They're after Todd. They say he killed Terry DeHavilland. Now Bishop Frobisher's been found dead.'

'So Todd's on a killing spree is he? Bloody maniac!'

'Todd didn't kill Frobisher. I know he didn't. I don't think he killed DeHavilland either. Someone's out to get him. I think you know who they are and I want you to give them a message.'

'I don't have the slightest clue what the fuck it is you're talking about.'

The two women stared at each other with mutual hostility. Lucy was the first to speak. She made a conscious effort to soften her tone although that wasn't easy to pull off.

'Todd told me he went to the club where you work. You gave him Mo Miller's number and set up a meeting. I went with him. To that pub. The one in Brompton Road. The one you went to with Terry. Before you blackmailed him into hacking into Lord Warrington voice mail messages and then dropped him in the shit. If it wasn't for you he'd still be alive, wouldn't he?'

Her sunglasses hid the outward manifestation of any emotion that Dolores might be experiencing, but Lucy got the impression that there wasn't much there in any case.

'Terry was doomed from the start,' Dolores said finally. 'Most self-destructive person I've ever met.'

'We've got documentary evidence of your involvement in the Knoxley Hall cover up. We've got names and witness statements. Those same people killed Terry or had him killed. You're one of them.'

'Oh, don't be so bloody ridiculous!'

'Shut up and listen. This is what we want you to do. Tell your friends that if anything happens to him or to me then it's all going to come out.'

Dolores peeked over the top of her shades and said: 'You've got it all wrong. I don't want anything to happen to Todd.'

'Oh?'

'God no. He's the best lover I've ever had. I just couldn't bear the thought of that big, lean, virile man lying cold and dead in some back alley. That's what happened to Terry, isn't it? Oh and Frobisher got strung up in his own front room, I believe. Maybe that was Todd. Maybe his interrogation technique's a bit rusty and he just went too far.'

'Todd didn't kill Frobisher,' Lucy said.

'How do you know?'

'Because we spent the night together.' Lucy had the satisfaction of seeing Dolores squirm a little in her chair.

'Maybe he sneaked out and committed the foul deed while you were having a post-coital nap.' she said.

Lucy shook her head and smirked. 'Not a chance.'

Dolores leaned forward and said, 'and where do you think he came to after he left you? Wake up. You're nowhere near woman enough... for a man like Todd.'

Lucy held herself in, waited until she felt some composure return and then said, 'so will you come forward then?'

'No.' Dolores said, and shifted her body away.

'Why not?'

Dolores turned back towards her. Lucy could see her own reflection in the lens of Dolores's sunglasses. And behind her was a large, ugly man in a suit. He seemed to be paying attention. Dolores mouth twitched ever so slightly and she turned away again.

Lucy stood up. 'Just let them know what we've got on them! You can do that at least.'

Dolores waved a hand in a gesture of dismissal.

Lucy left the Tate and walked along the embankment. Her phone buzzed. She took it out of her pocket and looked at it. Adam.

He said, 'Lucy, if you know where Jack Todd is you absolutely must tell me. Protecting a source is one thing but harbouring a murder suspect is something else altogether.'

'No idea,' she said, 'the last time I saw him was in a gay pub in Earls Court.'

'Have you heard about Frobisher?'

'Yes.' she said. 'Who killed him? That can't have been Todd.'

'Suicide. Hung himself.'

She gave that the silent treatment, waited for him to start talking again and then interrupted him when he did.'Adam, why did you send me to Islington that night? You knew then that DeHavilland was dead, didn't you?'

'No. Of course I didn't. Come on, Lucy, it was you who got the tipoff that Todd was there and you pleaded with me to be allowed to go there. I had no idea whose house it was. Any more than you had. I wanted to help you file your first big story, the Emma Naylor story. I couldn't have stopped you even if I'd wanted to. Look, one never knows where these things can lead.'

You lying bastard, she thought. *You fed me that lead and let me think I'd found it all by myself. You must think I'm very stupid.*

'Anyhow,' Adam went on, 'now you've broken what could be the biggest story of the year... I mean, I know it was more luck than judgement... but you've done a cracking good job – but now we need a full team on it. I want you to let me have all your sources so we can go to town on a Frobisher / DeHavilland follow up piece for Saturday's first edition.'

'In your dreams, Adam – I'll do the follow up and I'll do it on my own.'

'It's not that simple,' he said. 'This is a big story now, even bigger than the riots. I've allocated half the news room – '

'Oh!' She cut in. 'I've just had a text from one of my sources. He wants to meet up. Better be off. Talk later.'

She hung up, found Mo Miller's number and dialled it as she walked into Sloane Square station. Voice mail.

'This is Lucy from *The Defender*, obviously we need to talk. The payment's been authorised. And in light of recent developments I think we'd better meet up right away. I'm in central London at the moment but I'll head out west to that pub. I don't want to mention it on here. Text me if you want to meet me somewhere else.'

She glanced at her phone prior to going down onto the platform. There was a text from Mo. It read: 'I'm here. 125 Riverside Road, Fulham SW6.'

She got out her other phone and dialled Todd's number.

There was no answer so she called Emma.'Where is he?'

'He went out.' Emma sounded a bit sleepy.

'What?'

Oh, you big, numb, stupid bastard!

She called Todd again and this time she left a message. 'Just what the fuck are you playing at? You must have the brains of a barnyard animal. I'm going to see Mo. I'll text you his address. He thinks I've got a cheque for him so he's sure to be in. Meet me there. Idiot!'

She swiped her debit card and went down onto the platform.

TWENTY SEVEN

Riverpark Road stretches all the way from Fulham Broadway to Putney Bridge, running parallel to the New Kings Road and the river. Its endless rows of identical redbrick houses, with their identical three-foot square front yards, were once workers' cottages. The majority of them have now been converted into flats and sold off to the kind of people who like to talk about property values over a vegetarian mezze.

On that hot and humid day, the roadside pavement of Riverpark Road was as deserted as any West London roadside pavement ever gets. Only Todd trudged along it, subconsciously avoiding the cracks between the paving stones. Then he realised what he was doing and stopped doing it. He didn't need to do that anymore.

Occasionally he stopped in front of one of the houses to check out its number. Some of them had numbers displayed and some did not. Some of the numbers were large enough to read and some of them weren't.

Eventually he reached number one-two-five. It was one of the few houses that hadn't been divided into an upstairs and a downstairs flat. Mo could afford the whole house and didn't need to be bothered by either an upstairs or a downstairs neighbour.

Todd walked through the garden gate and onto the crazy-paved front yard. He couldn't have avoided the cracks in the crazy paving even if he had felt compelled to do so but he didn't feel compelled to do so, so that was all right. He just walked across the yard in the same manner that anyone else would have done and banged loudly on the fancily decorated, white and silver door.

When no one answered he rang the doorbell. When there was still no response he both leaned on the doorbell and banged on the door simultaneously and persistently.

Still no one came, but Todd saw the rustling of a curtain at the downstairs window. In any case, he was entirely certain that Mo would be at home because right now he would be expecting Lucy to drop in on him with a big fat cheque in her handbag that had his name on it.

He stopped assaulting the front door and moved off westwards towards Putney Bridge Road trying not to think about avoiding the pavement cracks, and at the same time counting the houses. He counted eight between Mo's place and the end of the terrace.

He reached the gable end house. There was a gate between it and the first house of the next terrace. He climbed over it.

The rear gardens backed onto the gardens that belonged to the houses in the New Kings' Road. The New Kings' Road gardens were quite a bit bigger than the Riverpark Road gardens. Todd suspected there might be quite a bit of garden size envy going down. Just a passing thought.

He climbed the fence and jumped down on the other side. Garden One. Then he strode across that garden to the next fence. He was over that one quickly as well. Garden Two. Six more gardens to go. He hoped there were no barbecues scheduled. But it was a Wednesday and Todd felt pretty certain that the sort of people who lived in Riverside Road tended to work for a living and only had barbecues at the weekend.

He kept on climbing fences and crossing gardens. He visualized it as a British army assault course. He always used to complete *that* course with a shorter time than any of the other commandos in his unit. Always.

It was all going according to form and he was only two gardens away from Mo's garden when he hit an unexpected snag. No fence this time. Instead, he was confronted by an eight feet high brick wall. That wasn't so much of an obstacle to an elite, special forces warrior like Todd. Or at least it didn't seem that way until he ran up the side of the wall, commando style, and grabbed on the top of it prior to propelling himself over the other side. It was at that point that he discovered that the wall had broken glass cemented in to the top of it. There's neighbourly.

But Todd didn't let that slow him down. At his second attempt he was up and over so quickly that the glass barely touched him. Just one rip in his left hand and another one down the back of his shirt. Neither one delayed his progress.

He landed without a sound and crouched. There was a female figure in the kitchen. The back door was open and music from a radio blared out. The woman peered out into her garden. Maybe she'd heard something. But she saw nothing. Todd had 'become the shadow' the way they'd taught him in the army. The woman turned back into her kitchen.

He launched himself over the next wall. He was expecting more glass and he wasn't wrong. What would be the point in turning one of your garden walls into a deadly weapon and then leaving the other one harmless? In any case the glass was no deterrent to a man who'd spent three years avoiding IEDs in southern Iraq. This time he ripped his right hand open but the speed with which he moved kept the damage to a minimum.

If he'd counted correctly he was now in Mo Miller's back garden. This one was overgrown whereas all the others had been lovingly tended. This one was a mini-jungle – apart from a little patch of cannabis plants in one corner. Todd felt pretty certain that he was in Mo's garden so he kicked the back door in. (That was two in a week).

He saw Miller immediately, cowering by the sink.

'Are you going to kill me too?' Miller asked him, looking and sounding as if he would be more than happy to be put out of his misery.

'Yes,' said Todd. 'Unless you send me those scans. Terry seems to have lost them.'

He placed himself strategically between Mo Miller and Mo Miller's front door. He didn't want Mo bolting into the street and yelling blue murder. Not that anybody in Riverpark Road was likely to come to somebody's aid.

'So what's this all about, Mo? Some secret society? Ritual slaughter of innocent children. Been going on for decades?'

'Centuries more like it.' Mo told him. 'They do it because they think it makes them strong. But you already know that. You think I don't know you're working for them, you murderous bastard? You killed Terry DeHavilland. You killed Bishop Frobisher. And now you're going to kill me. But first you want me tell you the names of the others – the weak ones who might crack up and talk. So you can kill them too.'

'Who told you that?' Todd asked quietly. He didn't get a reply. He decided not to press the point. He was there to ask questions but that wasn't one of them.

He picked up a tea towel from the breakfast bar and wiped some of the blood off his hands but it just kept on coming.

'There are some decent people left.' Mo said. 'They're going to stop you, Todd. They're going to stop your little killing spree.'

'Shut up,' Todd said, 'I haven't killed anyone. They've just made it look like I did. I'm not one of them, Mo. But I reckon you are. You always were. You helped them didn't you? To save yourself? Isn't that right?'

'No!' Mo almost screamed it. 'What the fuck are you talking about? I was a victim. I was a child. They abused me. They raped me. They –'

'Who did? Lord Warrington?'

Mo shook his head. 'He didn't play. He just brought the others. At least I don't think he did. They all wore masks, you see.'

'I think it was you, Mo. You might have been young but you were older than most of the others weren't you?

159

You were fourteen. Some of the others were as young as eight. I think you and Warrington were blackmailing some of the other... players. Where are those young boys now, Mo? How many of them are dead? How many of them were tortured to death? Where are those scans, Mo? The ones you sent to Terry. We can't find them. You're going to have to send them again and this time we want more. We want names. All the names.'

'Money first,' Miller said. Bolder now. Greed was winning out over fear.

'Aren't you a clever boy?' Todd's question was rhetorical, 'selling the same thing twice, and to the same buyer too.'

The momentary boldness evaporated and Miller's facial expression reverted to its default setting: self-pity and suspicion.

'How do you know I –?'

'Don't worry, she's on her way. She'll be here any minute so we might as well make a start. Go get a computer and a pen and paper. You can send us the scans and give me all the names. All of them this time, Mo.'

Mo thought about it for a second or two and then nodded but didn't go anywhere. Todd had a root around in the kitchen drawers.

'What are you looking for?' Mo asked him.

'Gaffer tape,' Todd said. 'I'd going to mend your door.'

'What? With gaffer tape?'

'Just temporary,' Todd said. 'Just so it closes. We don't want anyone else barging in here. Do we?'

'There's some in the bottom drawer.'

Todd found it and said: 'Sit down, Mo.'

'Why?'

'Sit!'

Mo sat.

Todd taped him to the chair. Then he found the iron and an extension lead and he plugged the iron in. It soon started to heat up.

'There is no money, Mo. The only incentive you've got is the avoidance of pain. You need to start to tell your truth. I know enough already to know if you're lying or not. So don't. We already have some names but we need to know where they are now, what happened to them back then and if they're prepared to speak out now. Got it?'

He picked up the iron and moved it carefully towards Mo's face. Just to warm him up a little. Mo screamed so Todd put the iron down and slapped him.

'Start talking, noncy boy,' he said, between gritted teeth, 'or I'll de-wrinkle your boat race.'

The names came out quickly, like the blood from Todd's wounds. Mo's lips started moving and the words fairly tumbled off of them. Todd had to scribble like a maniac to get it all down. Eventually the words stopped tumbling. He picked up the iron again just to make sure Mo wasn't holding anything back. Mo's reaction left him fairly sure that there was nothing left to divulge.

Todd folded up the paper and put it in his pocket. He'd managed not to get too much blood on it. He used the tea towel again to clean his hands of blood and then he carefully placed it over Miller's head. Just for jollies.

Then the doorbell rang. Todd went in to the front room and peered out. It was Lucy. He opened the door a crack and said: 'Come back in ten minutes I'm in the middle of something.'

'What?' she said. 'What in Christ's name are you doing now, Todd?'

'Better that you don't know. Like I said, come back in ten.'

She started hammering on the door so he had no option but to let her in.

She brushed past him and went into the kitchen where Mo was taped to a chair with a blood-soaked tea towel draped over his head and a red-hot iron just two inches from the end of his nose.

Lucy put both hands over her face. 'Todd, what the fuck are you doing?'

'Just a bit of housework,' Todd told her.

Just then there was a loud crashing noise from the direction of Mo's front door. And then another even louder one. Someone was smashing their way in.

Todd left the scene. Through the kitchen. Out the back.

There's always a back way out.

TWENTY EIGHT

Lucy removed the bloodied tea towel that Todd had placed over Mo's head. His urchin features with those tiny, pinprick eyes stared up at her like those of a terrified rodent. He seemed physically unhurt but was shaking uncontrollably and sobbing like a small child. Every now and then he opened his mouth as if to cry for help but mouth and throat seemed unable to work together to make any kind of intelligible noise. Lucy wiped his face with the one corner of the tea towel that didn't have blood on it and then found a kitchen knife and cut through the gaffer tape that was attaching him to the chair. Then she unplugged the iron, wound the flex around it and found the space, in one of the kitchen cupboards, that looked like it might be its regular storage place.

Norcross and Barrowclough finally made their entrance. Norcross with his purple eye, Barrowclough, red faced and blowing like a carthorse. Lucy guessed it had been he who had been doing all the door shouldering whilst Norcross had stood and waited.

Mo stood up and pointed to the back door.

'He went that way!' he screamed. 'Out the back! He's

been torturing me with an iron! She's just turned it off and put it away.'

'Nasty business,' Norcross said, with a distinct lack of sympathy in his voice.

Barrowclough went through the back door and into the garden.

'I didn't crack!' Mo said, to Norcross, 'I swear I didn't. I swear to you I didn't tell him a thing.'

'Shut up.' Norcross said and he went and joined his colleague in the garden.

Lucy looked at Mo. He avoided her eyes and sat down at the kitchen table, buried his head in his arms and started sobbing.

He spoke to her through his sobs in his usual whiny voice: 'You need to keep out of this. There's no way you can win. If they've decided to get him then they'll get him. You'll just have to find yourself another piece of sausage meat.'

Norcross and Barrowclough came back in. It didn't look like either of them had fancied any garden fence hurdling.

'Can I help you, gentleman?' she asked them. Trying to be as irritating as possible.

'He smashed his way in!' Mo screamed. 'Then he let her in the front.'

'Breaking and entering,' said Norcross.

'And wilful damage to private property,' said Barrowclough. 'Eighteen months to three years.'

'Oh don't be so fucking ridiculous! I didn't break in anywhere or damage anything.'

'You're an accessory before the fact,' Barrowclough said.

Lucy looked at Norcross who was shaking his head in mock solemnity and at the same time struggling to keep his face straight.

'What the fuck does that mean?' Lucy asked him.

Just then Mo screamed out: 'They were going to kill me!' And he banged his fists on the kitchen table. 'If you hadn't have got here when you did… they… they would have killed me.'

'Oh do be quiet,' Norcross said, 'you smelly little faggot.' Then he turned to Lucy and said: 'Where's he off to then, Luce?'

'What about Mo?' Lucy said, 'shouldn't you call an ambulance? Oh, look. He's got blood on his face. Surely, D.I. Norcross, your first responsibility is the welfare of this poor, unfortunate little man. He's claiming he was assaulted, that his life was in danger.' She took her smartphone out of her bag. 'This has been recording us the whole time, D.I. Norcross. Your lack of compassion, your total disregard for this man's physical welfare, it's all recorded on here. In fact, it's already been downloaded remotely and is being transcribed right now, as we speak.'

'Do I look worried?' Norcross asked her.

She looked into his eyes where the absence of worry was clearly distinguishable.

'Why not?' she asked him. 'Why aren't you worried?'

He said nothing, just sort of drooled at her like some kind of scavenging dog that's been left with a carcass.

'I'm leaving,' she said and made for the front door.

Barrowclough stood in her way. She stopped, turned and gave Norcross an enquiring look.

'We'd like you to come with us,' Norcross said:

'No thanks.' She turned back towards Barrowclough. 'Can you let me through, please? Or am I under arrest?'

Norcross shook his head. 'Fuck, no. Perish the thought.'

'In that case, tell him to move.'

Barrowclough, rather unexpectedly, let out a brief and high-pitched giggle. 'We're to take you home to daddy,' he said, 'so's he can give you a good hard spanking.'

'What on earth are you taking about?' Barrowclough just giggled again and then stopped, abruptly. She looked at Norcross.

'Phone him,' Norcross said. 'Phone your father.' He was deadpan now.

It was a long time since they'd spoken and she had to look him up. She suddenly felt nervous and it took her a while but eventually she found his number and pressed the button.

He answered right away.

'Lucy!' he said, sounding relieved. 'Don't worry. This can all be straightened out.'

'There's nothing that needs straightening out. I haven't done anything wrong.'

'I know, darling, but please just let them bring you home? Please? Can you do that for me? There's more to this than… Look, just let them bring you. I'll explain when you get here.'

She hung up. The unexpected turn of events left her speechless and confused.

'Come on then, Juicy Lucy.' Barrowclough said.

'That's a good one,' Lucy said. 'I've never heard that one before.'

Norcross made a mock bow in the direction of the front door. She shrugged and moved towards the exit.

Mo said: 'What about me? I demand police protection. What if he comes back?'

'Dial 999.' Norcross told him. 'And if I were you I'd get that back door fixed.'

TWENTY NINE

Her father's Dolphin Square apartment was large and spacious. Some might have said unnecessarily so. The unnecessarily spacious lounge area was empty apart from a nest of uncomfortable chairs and unreachable tables. One of the uncomfortable chairs supported the hunched up figure of her father, a grey little man with a permanently troubled expression. This room, like the rest of the apartment, had been tastefully decorated by a local Belgravia firm and was consequently bereft of any semblance of warmth or personality. A monster sized TV was switched on but with the sound turned down.

Either he didn't hear her come in or he didn't bother to acknowledge her presence.

She went and stood in front of him.

'What's going on?' She asked.

'Lucy,' he said, without looking at her. 'You've got yourself involved in something that's a lot more complicated than you could possibly imagine.'

'Gosh, daddy. Have I really? Well, perhaps you could explain it to me. I'm all grown up now and I can understand some pretty complicated issues.'

'This man, Todd... How in God's name did you get mixed up with him? Do you know who he is?'

'Yes,' she said. 'I know exactly who he is. Do you?'

Her father stood up, walked across the room to the window and looked down onto the square where Norcross and Barrowclough were, presumably, still sitting in their cheap little car. He turned around and looked at her for the first time.

'I've just been briefed. It's a damned lucky thing for you that I have some connections. For a start you should know that he isn't a policeman.'

'I know that.' Lucy said. 'Tell me something I don't know.'

'He's a very dangerous individual,' her father continued. 'He's a highly trained Special Forces serviceman. Or rather, he used to be in the Special Forces. He was discharged for gross misconduct. On top of that he's mentally ill. That's rather a combustible combination, I'm sure you'll agree – trained to kill and sick in the head. He's capable of anything. He's killed at least two people in the last twenty-four hours.'

Lucy shook her head. 'I know for a fact he didn't kill Bishop Frobisher.'

'How could you possibly know that?'

'Frobisher was killed last night. I was with Todd last night.'

Her father's eyes flickered away from her and then back. 'You spent the night with him?'

'Yes.'

'Well, I've had a phone call from the Home Office.

Someone there, someone very high up, is convinced that he has committed both of those murders and they've asked me – ordered me rather, to get you to reveal his whereabouts.'

'Ordered you?'

'Yes. That's right. Welcome to my world.'

'What do you mean, ordered you? What is this?' *All she'd ever known about his professional life was that he worked for the civil service. She'd never questioned him much about what he did.*

'Lucy, they're going to find him anyhow and they'll shoot him down like a dog. Go with them and persuade him to hand himself in. If he's innocent, he'll be freed.'

Then he walked up to her and put his hands on her shoulders. That wasn't the sort of thing he did. 'Lucy,' he said. 'I need you to do this… for me.'

'Why? What's going on?'

'I'm in trouble,' he said. 'If you don't do this… I could be finished.'

'Trouble? Finished? Tell me what's going on.'

'I can't explain now. I will on another day. I promise.'

'Why not now?' she asked.

He just shook his grey locks

'In any case, I don't know where he is,' she said, rather too quickly. 'And I'm not going anywhere with those two. I've read a witness account of them torturing somebody. They're not regular British Bobbies, are they?'

'We're all working for the government,' he said. 'Just… different cogs in… different wheels. They'll protect you. I've received assurances… from the highest possible level.'

'What happens if I don't?'

'We'll both be arrested.'

'For what?'

He looked straight at her with something akin to terror in his eyes.

'I don't know where he is,' she said again.

'Lucy,' he said, 'I'm pleading with you.'

'Do you promise he'll get a fair trial?'

'I swear it, Lucy. I'd swear it on your dead mother's grave.'

That hit home. She nodded.

He picked up his phone and pressed a button.

THIRTY

Todd was jogging along the Wandsworth Bridge Road in the direction of the river. Both his hands were still leaking blood and every five yards or so he felt compelled to wipe the excess claret off of his hands and onto his shirt, or his jeans, or his face. His hair was matted and his face was streaked; an Apache on the warpath.

Cars whizzed past him in both directions. Drivers and their passengers stared. Surely it was only a matter of time before someone recognised him and made the phone call. He forced himself up a gear. Once he was across the river he would be able to get off the main drag and cut through the numerous council estates that lay between him and his intended destination. He had to get back there and pick up the laptop. He had names now. Some of those people would talk – even without a red-hot iron being held to the ends of their noses.

Once he'd recovered the laptop he would go and take some statements and then follow Lucy's advice and get his story, and the story of the Knoxley Hall victims, out into the open, for good or evil, through the honourable offices of the British media establishment, those seekers after truth.

On he went, his heart bouncing once for every forward movement of his scarred yet solid frame. Onward to the river and beyond.

But then the landscape changed. A gang of kids appeared. They were jogging too, towards him. The grey hoods they all wore made them look like junior reapers, of the grim variety. Todd could smell out violence from a mile away and this lot were a lot closer than that and they stunk of it. They were all tooled up with bricks and sticks and there was the occasional glint of sunshine reflected from a knife.

He stopped. Unsure what to do. To run through them or to cross the street. They had no quarrel with him so far as he knew, but then they looked like they might have a quarrel with the entire human race, particularly the Caucasian part, and if they got close to Todd they might, quite literally, smell blood and be unable to resist that primeval urge, the one that Todd knew all about; that invariably surfaces whenever young men get together and arm themselves to the hilt. He decided to cross the road; if they came across after him he would have a chance of picking them off, one at a time.

In the event he had no need to pursue that option. As the gang reached the first parade of shops its advance guard stopped and one youth, smaller in stature than the rest of them, although clearly held in higher esteem, gave the devil-sign signal with one of his hands, and with the other hurled a half-brick. His army followed suit and a hail of stones, rocks and bricks was unleashed at an antique shop window.

Within ten seconds or so there wasn't a scrap of glass remaining and a loud and insistent alarm was sounding out across West London. But that didn't worry them. The leader of the pack jumped up onto the ledge and through into the shop and the rest of them went in after him like Great War squaddies going over the top.

Todd jogged past, glanced sideways. His glance lasted long enough to see a small, balding Indian gentleman, who Todd assumed was the shop owner, pinned against the wall of his shop whilst the till was being emptied and the priceless antiquities either smashed on the floor or carried out into the street. It was like the liberation of the Baghdad Museum, except without the American soldiers standing around and watching.

Todd turned his back on them. He had other business at hand. He jogged on down towards the river and over Wandsworth Bridge. Onto the traffic roundabout on the south side of the water. Cars and bikes circled with horns blaring.

He took the subway beneath the roundabout. There was coolness and shade and the smell of piss, and the echoey sound of his own healthy panting. After a minute or so he emerged on the other side onto a footpath that led up the hill and away from the river. Trinity Road.

He trotted up the path until it forked into two and then took the left hand fork that took him away from the main drag and onto an estate. It was quiet, almost suburban, nicely kept council houses. Washing hanging out. Children here and there riding their scooters and kicking their footballs. He didn't hang around long enough to be recognised, just kept on moving on towards Emma's pad where he might find sanctuary from the friendless street.

Eventually the noise of traffic returned and he moved towards the main road. His sense of direction had told him this was Falcon Road but he soon realised that he'd taken a wrong turn and had come out on St. John's Hill. He knew this Manor well but he'd never seen it like this before. Groups of kids and young adults were wandering in and out of shops with a wide variety of consumer durables. Electrical goods from Carphone Warehouse, trainers and the like from the big sports shop on the large intersection at Clapham Junction. No one was doing a thing to stop them. There was no sign of the police. Fires had been set and were starting to rage out of control.

He walked past a bookie's at the bottom of Lavender Hill. A group of kids were trying to prise a flat screen TV off the wall. It was still showing the odds of the 3:45 at Haydock Park.

One foolish boy tried to grab Todd's mobile that he grasped in his hand, in case Lucy tried to call him. He wrested it back, put it safely in his pocket and then performed a perfectly executed right hook with barely any back lift that nearly took the young man's head right off.

A gang of his mates crowded around. Todd just stood there with his fists up and a manic grin on his face. Blood all over him. The kids thought better of the fight and went off to loot Debenhams instead.

One kid with a looted cappuccino maker under his

arm stopped and pressed the button at a pelican crossing and then waited for the green man to appear before proceeding. There wasn't even any traffic.

Falcon Road looked pretty clear but the big estate behind the station that was practically lawless at the best of times lay in that direction and he didn't fancy it. It was only a matter of time before he was outnumbered and trampled to death. So he walked up Lavender Hill in the middle of the road. Flames on either side of him. SW11 was on fire, the flames were spreading and more fires were being set.

He looked over at the terraced rows between Lavender Hill and the Common. Houses that had once been humble residences for the working poor but were now worth millions. Or had been until today. Todd could imagine a legion of yuppy householders cowering under their beds, agonising over the value of their properties.

The only man, as far as Todd could see, who was standing up to the mob was a large West Indian gentleman, who was standing in front of a hairdressers' shop, presumably *his* hairdressers' shop, and brandishing a golf club. They had him surrounded. Cornered. A pack of wolves closing in on the stag. But the stag wasn't done. The seven iron was swinging, threatening to cause damage to limbs and jaws. So the young outlaws were just keeping their distance for the time being and goading this middle aged fellow who was putting his life on the line to defend his property.

Todd stopped. This was none of his business and he had to get off the street as soon as he could. But it just wasn't in him to walk on by. Not when an innocent man was on the verge of being beaten to death by an unruly mob. So Todd steamed in with his fists and his feet. The fine young cannibals didn't fancy it much and after a few seconds they had all run away and just he and the shop owner were left.

The mob, as if it had one mind, surged up Lavender Hill and away from the Junction.

A strange quiet descended. A fire was blazing out of control. Debris filled the road. Plastic and cardboard packaging, half bricks and broken glass were strewn all about. In the middle of the road was the large flat screen TV set from the bookmakers' shop. Broken and useless.

Todd showed the man his ID. 'Have you called the police?' he asked.

The man laughed. 'Me and a few thousand others. Either they've just got too much on or they'd rather not get involved. Haven't you seen the news? It's all over London. It started in Hackney. Some kid got shot by the cops and that's what started it off. It's spread all over town. Brixton, Peckham. Croydon's burning, man.

'Croydon? What the fuck have they got to riot about in Croydon?'

'I don't know,' the man said, 'but they're burning it down.'

He looked at Todd more closely and for the first time noticed the blood and torn clothes.

'What the hell happened to you?'

'I've been fighting the good fight,' Todd told him. 'Like you have.'

Just then a fleet of police vans came screeching up the Falcon Road. They stopped and a squad or two of riot police hopped out and raised their shields. Todd and his new friend looked at each other and laughed. A fresh absurdity unfolded as a film crew emerged from one of the vans. There was a cameraman with his camera, a sound-man with his boom and a glamorous looking female presenter who took out a mirror and started to brush her hair.

Todd said, 'I got to go. Look after this lot. Make sure they don't get hurt.'

The man snorted and said, 'Twats like that caused all the problems in the first place. They is the problem. I'll just go and get my window boarded up in case the brothers return. I don't think they will though. There's nothing left to loot.'

Todd raised a hand in farewell and jogged on down. Impressed at the lengths a man would go to protect a few hairdryers and aerosol cans. In reality though, Todd mused, he'd been protecting much, much more than that – and Todd loved him for it.

He headed down the Falcon Road from where the riot police had just come. Immediately in their wake gangs of hooded kids had started to congregate again at the rear of the station and were trying to smash their way through the metal shuttering that defended the station forecourt and its franchises. Todd just jogged on by; he ignored them and they ignored him. He went under the railway bridge onto the lower part of Falcon Road which was deserted. The further from the Junction, the quieter the scene. Nothing to loot here.

Ten minutes later he was letting himself into Emma's place with the key she'd given him.

He could hardly get in the door. The hallway was packed from floor to ceiling with bulging cardboard boxes. Their labels announced what was inside them; TVs, computers, microwave ovens, a juicer and an automatic mixer. Everything the busy housewife needs.

He went through into his inner sanctum. This was the casual footwear department. Box upon box of brand new training shoes. All the trendy labels. At a hundred pounds a pair he reckoned there must be about ten grand's worth. He had a look around the rest of the flat. There wasn't an inch to spare. Shirts, fleeces, tracksuits, football shirts, onesies.

He found a designer shirt that fit him and got changed, throwing the torn and blood-soaked shirt that he'd been wearing into a corner of the room.

Just then he heard a key turn in the lock of the outside door. He heard male voices, grunts of exertion; more contraband was coming in through the door. He leaned against one of the piles of boxes and spoke in a poor attempt at a West Indian accent that came out more like a mixture of Welsh and Pakistani.

'This warehouse full,' he said. 'Use de one next door.'

The young black kid, name of Big, who he'd met earlier, came into view and said,'What the fuck? What you doing here?'

'I'm Emma's lodger,' Todd told him. I pay rent here. But it's ok, you can keep your stuff here for a bit.'

'What? Get the fuck out of here before you get hurt,

man, we need this space,' Big told him. Then he saw the empty shirt packaging on the floor and said, 'You stealing my goods, man?'

Todd couldn't help but laugh. But then he got serious again. 'I'm not going anywhere, he said, 'I've paid my rent. Don't push it, kid.'

'Bit of a hard cunt, yeah?' Big responded. There was a knife in his hand now. Todd wasn't sure how it had got there but it was there all right. Nice long one. Big took a step forwards and two more young villains appeared in the doorway behind him.

Todd was just getting into 'hard cunt' mode when he heard Emma's voice: 'Leave him, Big,' she said. 'He's paid his rent.'

'How much he pay?' Big asked her.

'Thirty quid.'

Big put a hand in his pocket and came up with three ten pound notes which he flicked contemptuously into Todd's face. 'There you go,' he said, 'now get the fuck out of here.'

'I need to be here. I'm waiting for somebody.'

'Waiting for somebody! He's talking about bringing people in here! Blood clot!' Then he put his face close up to Todd's, lowered his voice and said, 'You better just make yourself scarce my man or you're gonna cease to exist. There ain't no law no more around here. The Brothers rule these streets now and you know what? We rule the Brothers.'

Emma turned to Todd and said: 'Who you waiting for?'

'Your little pal, Lucy,' he said. 'Once she gets here we'll go.' He thought it was probably best not to tell them that she'd most likely be bringing a couple of bent cops along with her.

As he spoke, more hoodlums started pouring in through the outer door and the word that there had been a new development in this, the most exciting day of their young lives, was quickly passed back to them.

'Copper?' Todd heard one say. 'He's a fucking copper! Blood clot! Get me that fucking blade from the drawer, man. I gonna cut his white copper man throat.'

Todd had been in tighter spots than this; his training and his instincts told him that if he took the leader out then the others would more likely than not just turn and run. So he fixed Big in his sights and psyched himself up.

Maybe Big saw something in Todd's eyes that told him there would be no quarter asked nor given. Maybe he thought there would be no point in risking all the contraband and profit that he'd managed to accumulate in such a short period of time. At any rate, he yelled over his shoulder, 'Wait! I give the orders.'

Then he turned back towards Todd and said: 'Alright you can stay. I seen the news. You an outlaw, too, just like us, right?'

Todd nodded and then stooped to pick up the three ten pound notes. He held them out to Big who took them, stuffed them back in his pocket and left the room, pushing his compadres ahead of him.

Todd closed the door and then went to the wardrobe. He pulled the door open and lifted up the bedding that lay at the bottom of it. There was nothing underneath. No laptop. It had gone.

He put a fist through the wardrobe door. All that achieved was to start the bleeding off again.

THIRTY ONE

They drove silently along past the vast and mournful empty lot that used to house Chelsea Barracks and then down towards the river. Barrowclough was driving and Norcross was in the passenger seat next to him. Lucy sat behind Norcross. There was barely enough room for her legs so she stretched out along the back seat. She saw Barrowclough's eyes in the rear view mirror as they latched on to her bare legs.

'Eyes on the road,' she said. 'You dirty old creep.'

His grotesque features formed a grotesque leer but he did as he was told and she got busy on her phone.

She'd texted Todd before they'd left her father's apartment just to make sure he was where she assumed he was. He'd confirmed he was at Emma's and asked her to meet him there. But he had no idea who was coming along for the ride. Then she'd told them where he was and how to get there. It seemed they were acquainted with that particular estate. They'd asked her for the flat number and she'd told them that she couldn't remember but that she'd know it when she saw it.

Now she texted Adam and told him where she was going. Then she raised her voice and said, 'People know where I am and that I'm with you two. So don't get any funny ideas.'

Norcross leaned forwards and turned on the radio. The news was on. Some Johnny-on-the-spot reporter.

'Feral, hooded youths, some as young as eight, are strolling away from 21st-century megastores with hauls of looted iPod accessories and designer trainers. The absence of police officers to intervene in this orgy of looting has undoubtedly contributed to this breakdown of order that has turned large swathes of inner city London into something reminiscent of the lawless badlands of a failing state... scenes that are evocative of a desperate Parisian Banlieue... shops and businesses are being looted while scores of cars and buses are set alight, their torched carcasses littering what can only be described as an urban war zone... from Hackney to Croydon, gangs of teenagers are making roadblocks from burning cars... ransacking shops and restaurants... in Notting Hill, West London, diners eating in the two Michelin Star Ledbury Restaurant were attacked and mugged at their tables as rioters swept through the area... the Met's approach to this civil disorder would seem to comprise of standing by with a view to catching culprits afterwards through the use of CCTV footage.'

'Sounds like your boys are playing a real blinder,' Lucy said.

They reached the river, where a police car had been parked in the middle of the road preventing access to Chelsea Bridge. A uniformed policeman with an old fashioned pointy blue helmet stood in front of it. He held up one hand and used the other to try to wave them off westwards along the embankment.

Barrowclough drove up alongside him and Norcross showed his card and said, 'Let us through, please.'

'Is this to do with the riots, sir?'

'No. Separate matter.'

'I'd advise against going any further. There's been a total breakdown of law and order. Cars are being attacked and set on fire.'

'We have to go through,' Norcross said, 'We'll take our chances. This is a matter of national security.'

The policeman shrugged, flicked a switch on the walky-talky that was attached to his collar and gave the order. The vehicle that barred their way was removed and they drove on to the bridge and across into South London, where a huge congregation of teenagers was milling around, across the road in front of them and in and out of Battersea Park.

Theirs was the only car around and the mob surged towards it. Barrowclough didn't so much as think about stopping. The youths scattered like shotgun pellets but one of them didn't get out of the way in time and the car gave a sickening lurch as one of its front wheels went over what might have been a limb.

That slowed them up a tad and caused the by now enraged mob to crowd back around them. One tall, gangly youth, who looked to be about fifteen years old, climbed on to the bonnet of the car and started to hammer on the windscreen with his fists. Barrowclough jerked the car from side to side and the hitchhiker, unable to gain any sort of handhold went flying off sideways. Then a hail of stones and bricks lashed into them. The windscreen shattered and the riotous mob converged.

Lucy crawled down onto the floor of the car and put her hands over her head. Then she heard a shot. Someone had fired a gun, someone from inside the car. She lifted her head and looked out between the two front seats.

The crowd had scattered again at the sound of the gunshot, which didn't seem to have hit anybody. One or two of the kids weren't able to get away in time. Norcross was holding the gun and was pointing it at one terrified young man. The look on Norcross's face made Lucy fairly certain that he was about to pull the trigger. She pushed his arm sideways with her hand and the gun went off but its missile flew harmlessly up into the Battersea Park treetops. Barrowclough put his foot down and the windowless carriage sped southwards like something out of a Destruction Derby.

Todd needs to know they've got guns, Lucy thought, and she started to text him but Barrowclough saw what she was doing in the rear-view mirror and raised the alarm.

Norcross leaned over to the back seat and wrestled the phone from her. She tried to hold on to it but he was too strong and too vicious and he soon had her phone and was reading her texts.

'Thought so,' he said. 'She's been texting Lover Boy.'

'Ask him for the flat number.' Barrowclough suggested.

'What do you think I'm doing?' His superior officer yelled back.

They'd got to the Battersea Park Road by now. They turned right and then left into the supermarket car park that lay between the road and the sprawling estate.

Every shop window that Lucy could see, all the way down the Battersea Park Road, had been smashed. Those that had been shuttered had had their shutters prised open and then their windows and doors smashed in and their contents looted. Lucy shuddered at the thought of all those crazed young men carrying crowbars and tyre irons. Down at the other end of the road a double decker bus was on fire.

They got out of the car and walked on to the estate, which seemed pretty unscathed. No fire or broken glass here.

They walked to the entrance of the block. Then Norcross turned to Lucy and said, 'Take us to the flat.'

She tried to run but Barrowclough grabbed her and held on to her arm with a pincer like grip.

Norcross said, 'This is why you're here you stuck up little cow. Now give us the flat number or you will get hurt.'

Barrowclough increased the pressure, Lucy screamed and kicked his shin. Barrowclough yelled but didn't let go. Norcross hit her across the side of the head with a backhand swipe. She sobbed once and then fell silent. Her head went down.

By now a crowd had started to form around them.

A young woman ran at Barrowclough. 'You leave her alone, you. Great big man.' She said. 'You fucking bully boy, you just leave her alone.'

Barrowclough grabbed her and pulled out a gun. So they both had guns. His was an old fashioned revolver and he put it to the young girl's head and pulled back the hammer.

'Big white guy, bleeding like a stuck pig. Where is he?'

Either the girl didn't know or she just wasn't telling. She just shook her head and started sobbing.

'Blow the little bitch away,' Barrowclough said. 'Blow her away, go on. Breakdown of law and order. We can do what we want.'

'Alright, stop!' Lucy said. 'I'll take you there.'

'Lead on, little lady.' Norcross said, keeping hold of the girl and still pointing the gun at her head. Lucy led them four floors up and along the landing to Emma's door. With a single twitch of his gun hand Norcross indicated that Lucy should announce their arrival. She didn't have any other options so she banged on the door.

There was no response so she pressed the bell and knocked again and then bent down and yelled through the letterbox. 'It's me. Lucy. Let me in.'

Emma opened the door. Barrowclough pushed Lucy through and Norcross pushed the girl away from him onto the landing, went in after them and slammed the door shut behind him. They both had their guns out.

Todd stood facing them amongst the piled up boxes of contraband goods.

'Blimey Sherlock, you've been busy,' Norcross said, looking around him. 'Did you loot all this on your own then?'

Todd didn't reply. He just gave Norcross the evilest of eyes and the coldest of smiles. Then he twitched. Like one of those zombies that just won't die.

Big came out of the kitchen and threw himself at Barrowclough. Two more locals appeared and dived into the fray. Todd went for the Barrowclough gun hand. Pushed it up, just as Lucy had done in the car. Same result; a shot rang out but the bullet flew harmlessly upwards.

The sound of the shot stopped everyone in their tracks for a second; it was like being in a TV show that's been paused. Norcross broke the silence. 'Who wants to die?' He yelled. 'Who wants to fucking die?'

No one did.

Lucy knew he meant it: *Breakdown of law and order – we can do what we want.*

'They mean it, Todd,' she told him. 'Better back off.'

Todd backed off.

'Get down on the floor!' Norcross said. 'All of you.'

They did as they were told.

Emma's son, Marcus, came out of the bathroom and went and stood by his mother. Stuck his jaw out.

'Don't worry mum,' he said. 'I'll protect you.'

'Get in there, Todd.' Lucy heard Norcross say. She saw Todd and Barrowclough go into the bedroom.

'Now, fuck off the lot of you!' Norcross yelled. 'And don't come back or I'll start with the executions! It's time there was a bit of law and order around here.'

There was a mass exodus. But Lucy stayed. Norcross followed Todd and Barrowclough into the bedroom and

189

the door closed behind him. Lucy waited in the hallway and listened; there was a conversation going on but the voices were too low and muffled for her to hear anything.

Then all hell broke out.

First there was a thunderous hammering on the outer door and then riot police poured in wearing body armour and face masks and carrying batons and shields. There were a number of explosions as tear gas canisters and stun grenades were released. Lucy's eyes started streaming; the pain was unbearable.

A megaphone enhanced, robotic sounding voice cried, 'GET ON THE FLOOR! EVERYBODY GET DOWN ON THE FLOOR. RIGHT NOW!'

There was only Lucy in there and she was down already. Blind and petrified.

Then, what seemed like scores of heavily armed police officers, all dressed up in this year's latest riot fashions, booted their way in and trampled over and around her. More explosions. More gas. Then silence.

Then a wild-eyed Barrowclough came out of the bedroom and started turning the place over. Looking for something. But he didn't look hard. It was a hopeless task to try to find any one particular item in that Aladdin's Cave of stolen property and he soon gave up and kneeled down alongside Lucy who was by now sitting up and rubbing her bruises.

'Where is it?' He said. He pressed his gun against her cheek as he said it. 'You know what I'm talking about! Where is it?'

Lucy just shook her head to say she didn't know. He

seemed to believe her. In any case, he went back into the bedroom. Now, there was some more activity. An ambulance crew had arrived. A paramedic knelt down beside her and started to examine her.

Then a shot rang out. From the bedroom. Then she heard Todd scream. Then another shot. Lucy managed to drag herself up and hurl herself at the bedroom door.

'Let me through.' She yelled. 'I'm a newspaper reporter. How dare you obstruct me you…'

Then she began to feel a bit woozy. Maybe it was because of all the excitement. In any case, she lost consciousness for a spell.

After what seemed like an epoch, but was probably just a few minutes, she was picked up from the floor and carried out on to the landing. Emma and Marcus were there; Marcus had his arm around his mother's shoulders. Now he put his other arm around Lucy's. Brave little man.

But then Emma screamed and pointed as paramedics pushed past them carrying a stretcher.

Lucy turned around and looked.

Just in time to see Jack Todd's cold, dead body being carried away along the now deserted landing.

PART TWO

THIRTY TWO

6 months later

'We've decided to pass at this time,' said Henrietta, the TV Production Company Executive, who made a little sideways twitch of her head that enabled her to avoid eye contact with Lucy whilst dishing out the bad news. Lucy guessed she'd probably dished out quite a bit of bad news in her time; it seemed to be her specialty.

Outside it was snowing, but Lucy and Henrietta were snug and warm in an LGBT-friendly coffee bar in Old Compton Street. Lucy could tell the coffee bar was LGBT-friendly on account of there being such a large presence of Ls, Gs, Bs and Ts at the surrounding tables.

'You could have told me that on the phone,' Lucy said.

Henrietta was a plain and dumpy woman in her mid-thirties. She was wearing a green knitted dress and a small silver ring that protruded out from between her nostrils.

Lucy was wearing jeans and boots and a tight fitting, polo necked sweater. She was showing off all her curves. Henrietta had signed herself off as 'Henry' on the email that had confirmed their meeting and Lucy had made the mistaken assumption that 'Henry' was a man and had dressed accordingly. Maybe her blatant sex appeal strategy might still work, she thought, if Henry turned out to be an 'L'. But there was nothing in Henrietta's demeanour that suggested she was one.

Henrietta folded her arms and spoke tersely. 'Let's just be very clear about this. Adam told me you had signed witness statements. But that doesn't seem to be the case. There's no actual evidence, is there? We couldn't possibly make allegations of such a serious nature against such prominent individuals with what you're giving us.'

'Then don't accuse them directly,' Lucy said. 'At least not to start with. Just refer to them by their positions, by their status, just refer to them as… 'a high profile cabinet minister', 'a senior civil servant', 'senior members of the Anglican Church', 'high ranking police officers from at least three different police forces' and so on. That will flush out a whole army of new witnesses. There are hundreds of victims who are now adults. Up to now, they've been too scared to come forward. A documentary film on one of the mainstream channels will embolden them.'

Henry said: 'Look, without naming names there's really no point at all, is there? And there is absolutely no way we could accuse the people you've mentioned in here…' She lifted the dossier that Lucy had prepared and then placed it back on the table between them, '…without a lot more evidence. You need to get more evidence.' She emphasised the repeated word 'evidence' as if she were explaining something very simple to someone very stupid.

'Well… can you give me the resources to get the evidence?' Lucy asked, lowering her voice to a husky whisper for added effect. 'This is… really bloody enormous.'

'We'd hardly be breaking anything new, though, would we? It's a bit of an old chestnut. A lot of people either know or think they know what's been going on in this… shocking affair… but nobody's been able to get any credible witness statements and unfortunately I don't think you've succeeded where everyone else has failed. Your email gave the impression that you had unearthed something new, that you had some… mysterious new source prepared to reveal all.' She opened her palms in a gesture that spoke of emptiness and failure and said, 'There's nothing new here whatsoever.'

'I'm not going to just hand everything over. I'm not that green. I have got statements. Signed statements.'

'Then produce them,' Henrietta said. 'We'll give you a non-disclosure agreement.' She took a sip of her vegan macchiato and sniffed. 'But I must say I find it rather insulting that you think we're the kind of organisation that would steal your research.'

'Alright, I'm sorry I said that, but I'm this close.' Lucy illustrated to Henrietta with her thumb and forefinger just how close she was. 'Please, put some resources into this and you'll get something… unbelievable in return.'

'If you're asking me for money then I'm afraid that's not going to happen.'

'No. Not money. I need help with research and verification and all the legal stuff and… well maybe a little money just to keep me going and maybe incentivise some of the victims…'

Henrietta shook her head in feigned astonishment. 'You can't bribe witnesses!' 'Look, if you're able to produce signed witness statements then we might reconsider. Can you do that?'

Lucy leaned back in her chair and looked out through the large circular window at the flakes of snow that were fluttering down like petals onto the taxis and the tourists and the sex industry workers.

'Are you still with *The Defender*?' Henrietta asked her.

Lucy continued to ignore her and Henrietta pressed her point home, 'So can I take it that *they* won't put *their* resources behind this?'

Lucy turned her head away from the window and back towards Henrietta. 'I think one of their senior people is either one of the abusers or is protecting someone who is. I think it might even be Adam.'

Henrietta released a short, sharp laugh and looked at Lucy as if she'd tried to finger the Queen for the JFK assassination. 'Adam's been down the same road that you're on now. He had to 'cease and desist' for lack of evidence, just as you'll have to, eventually.'

Lucy said: 'You'll be sorry when this does come out and your bosses find out that you could have been the one to break it. What a story it is, Henrietta. Young children abused and then murdered and the people who are responsible are still out there, in positions of power. And it's still going on. Oh yes! Cuddly little kiddy winkys are still being used as sex toys by those fucking weirdos.

And not only that, Henrietta, love… there are all kinds of nasty, wicked blackmail webs being spun around the whole dirty business. This is a story that will just keep on giving. All we need to do is to turn over one slimy stone and all kinds of disgusting insects will come crawling out into the light of day.'

'Get the evidence.' Henrietta told her. 'I admire your enthusiasm but we have to be realistic.'

'You'll wish you'd listened,' Lucy said. 'I'm telling you, when your bosses find out you've turned this one down your career will be over. Goodbye.' She stood up briskly, grabbed her white fake fur coat from the back of the chair, pulled it on over her shoulders, pulled on her white cotton gloves, picked up her little white handbag and set off towards the door.

'Wait!' Henrietta said.

'Yes?' Lucy stopped and moved back towards the table.

Henrietta held out the folder and said, 'you've forgotten this.

Lucy snatched the folder, stormed out into the snowy street, and hailed a cab.

THIRTY THREE

Celebrity M.P., Barry Carter's big round backside was spread along an alcove bench in a well-known Westminster gastro pub. He took a manly gulp from his glass of tonic water, sinking half of it in one go. He didn't drink alcohol and hadn't done so since his student days when he'd realised that abstemiousness gave him a huge advantage over those who drank, which included just about everyone involved in student politics.

He had substituted binge drinking for binge eating and had gradually become larger and rounder until his body had assumed its present shape, which was extremely large and extremely round. To go with his large, round body he had a large, round face and wore large, round black spectacles.

Carter was a career politician – had been since university where he had studied Politics Philosophy and Economics and got himself elected to President of the Student Union and on to the NUS national executive. On graduating he had managed to get himself a position as an unpaid intern to another career politician, one of a previous generation, who had also never had a proper job in his entire life.

Carter soon became aware that his boss was gay. This was at a time before gay politicians were acceptable to the public at large and the older man was so desirous to keep his sexual orientation to himself that he'd entered into an arranged marriage with the daughter of one of the party grandees. As time went on it did become acceptable for politicians to behave as they pleased between their sheets but by that time the damage had been done and the cover up had become more of a potential embarrassment than the state of affairs it was attempting to cover. Carter hadn't exactly blackmailed his mentor but had never missed an opportunity to remind him that he knew the truth, that he felt his internship had gone on long enough and that it was about time that his years of loyal service were rewarded with a full-time, salaried position.

Thus he had become a political officer in the party's London HQ, a position he held for over ten years until, when the opportunity arose, he had himself parachuted into a safe parliamentary seat and was elected as the youngest Member of Parliament since Bernadette Devlin.

His meteoric rise continued; soon he had reached the dizzy heights of junior shadow minister for the environment with a specific brief to hold the government to account for its policy on sewers and drainage. This brief tenure earned him the unfortunate nickname of 'Smelly Baz.' But at least he'd managed to get his ample bum cheeks on the opposition front bench.

Then something happened that seemed like a disaster at the time but that turned out to be a godsend. The leader of his wing of the party, the faction to which he had allied himself at an early stage of his career and which contained all his political friends and allies, fell out with the party leadership over a matter of policy. There was a rebellion in which he was obliged to participate and, as a result, he lost his position on the front bench.

It was his first political setback and at first he was devastated, but he soon got over it and came to realise that the freedom of being a backbencher had its advantages.

He watched with great interest as the phone hacking scandal unfolded and listened intently to the indignant squeals of those celebrities who had had their privacy violated by tabloid newspaper reporters. Then, by process of subtle political manoeuverings he managed to set himself up as the celebrities' champion. Under the protection of parliamentary privilege he publicly chastised the tabloids, and one tabloid in particular, *The Planet*. This earned him the undying admiration of his party and of the all-powerful celebrities. Pressing home his advantage, he forced the setting up of a special committee to look into the matter.

He became famous overnight. Both his 'Smelly Baz' period and the rebellious episode were forgotten, and he soon began to attract praise from all sides of the political spectrum for being the only individual to have the selfless courage to bring the evil phone hackers to book. He milked his fame shamelessly. There were constant rounds of television and radio appearances where he was interviewed alongside 'national treasures' who had had their phones hacked, actors, pop stars, footballers, TV reality show hosts. How violated they felt! Something had to be done! And Barry was the man to do it.

Soon though, the phone hacking scandal, along with his own fame and glory, began to fade into history; the celebrities stopped phoning him, the media lost interest in him, members of the public stopped recognising him in the street and he was left with an unbearable yearning to return to the dizzy heights from which he had fallen.

Then, as if it had been ordained by the political gods that his star would continue to rise, another opportunity, like a carelessly handled fork load of steak and kidney pudding, fell directly and forcefully, slap bang into his enormous lap.

It had long been an open secret that there was a paedophile ring that was operating in Westminster that included a number of prominent MPs and senior civil servants, but that nothing was being done because of the proximity that members of this evil gang had to Parliament and even the Cabinet. This whole affair, Carter learned, had become known as the 'Knoxley Hall Affair' after one infamous institution in suburban south west London where a large percentage of the abuses were alleged to have taken place.

One morning Barry received a letter from a man who claimed to have been abused as a child by a prominent politician. The victim implied that one of the accused had been a close aide to a former Prime Minister. Carter discovered, after a minimal amount of digging, that there had been an inquiry into these allegations a decade earlier but that the inquiry had been closed. He immediately seized on this matter as his new *cause celebre* and publicly called on the Metropolitan Police to reopen the long-since closed criminal inquiry into the allegations.

Largely because of the influence that Carter wielded at this time, they did so, they established an investigation to look into the allegations, and after a few short weeks, the senior police officer who was heading the inquiry stated that a number of individuals had been identified. It was reported in *The Defender,* in a story that had obviously been generated by a leak from the inquiry itself, that police had interviewed a number of adults who claimed that they had been sexually assaulted as children by senior MPs and civil servants and that a 'large body' of evidence had been gathered. The Westminster Village and the rest of the Great British Public held its breath and waited for further developments. But then nothing. No arrests. No one held to account.

Carter suddenly discovered that the popularity that had disappeared when the phone-hacking affair started to fizzle out but which had returned when he had begun to look into the Knoxley Hall affair now began to disappear once again.

A vast array of individuals had supported him in his campaign against those evil phone hackers who had so unfeelingly 'violated' their celebrity victims but no one, it seemed, could care tuppence about a conspiracy of silence that was covering up horrendous crimes against children by members of the nation's elite.

By this time, as a result of his recent high profile crusade, he had been made Chair of one of Parliament's most influential cross-bench committees. He laboured briefly under the illusion that he now had some real power which he attempted to wield, but soon came to realise –

not the first politician to do so – that the levers of power would only work for a select few and that he wasn't one of them.

He hit one bureaucratic brick wall after another and could find no way around any of them. He had been given access to the names of some of the alleged perpetrators but it soon became clear that they were untouchable. Any attempt by the police or Barry's committee to subpoena, or even request to interview any of these individuals resulted in immediate 'super injunctions' being imposed. That made it unlawful to even whisper their names in the street.

Then, in a particularly unpleasant development, one of the prominent individuals on the list, one Lord Hunter of Hellifield was found dead in his London apartment. Suicide. Soon thereafter Carter began to realise that he was under attack; his fellow committee members had started briefing against him; sections of the press began, once again, to refer to him as 'Smelly Baz'.

Then, when he was just about to forget the whole sordid business and divert his energies to more promising political opportunities such as publicising modern evils like revenge porn and legal highs, he got a call from a contact in a TV production company with whom he had cooperated in the past. She informed him that a young *Defender* reporter called Lucy Mainwaring was claiming that she had unearthed a store of evidence against a number of the Westminster pedophile ring's paid-up members.

According to his source, this young reporter had become involved in the Terry DeHavilland affair that had hit the news six months or so earlier. Dehavilland, it seemed had been murdered by a rogue policeman called Jack Todd who had subsequently committed suicide. Carter had tried to get to the bottom of that business as well at the time but had soon realised that any attempt to open that particular can of maggots would only result in a large section of the political establishment turning against him.

But if this girl did have evidence – actual concrete evidence – then surely no one would be able to stand in the way of justice. Surely not. And what did he have to lose? He would give it one last shot. A meeting with the young reporter was arranged. He was waiting for her now.

He took another gulp of his tonic water and looked around him. Soon the place would be full of political fixers and lobbyists of every conceivable hue, but it was still early; only one or two tables were occupied and there was just one sole figure at the bar drinking an early lunch.

Then Lucy appeared in the doorway, found him with her sharp, young eyes and made her way over. He didn't stand or offer her a drink. She sat down across from him and turned on her charming smile. Then she turned it off again when he gave her one back.

'Perhaps you've heard of me,' he said. 'I'm the chair of a home affairs select committee.'

'Yes.' She replied, 'I do know who you are. How can I help you?'

'I've been asked to make some inquiries into allegations of child sexual abuse against certain members of the… shall we say… the establishment. I understand that you have some information that would help. I thought you might like to co-operate.'

'In what way?'

'I understand you have a list of names.'

'Yes. I do have a list of names but there's no proof… none at all… against anyone.'

'Even so. If there have been allegations against certain individuals we'd be perfectly within our rights to subpoena them to appear before the committee. Of which I am chair. Perhaps I already mentioned that.'

Lucy said nothing. Her body language said 'nothing doing.'

'Look,' Carter said, 'you have to give me that list. If you don't then I'll have no option but to tell the police you have it and subpoena you to the hearing that I'm in the process of calling. I'm sorry to be so blunt, but people's lives are at stake.'

'Didn't you get the memo?' she asked. 'The way things stand no one is going to give evidence, not to the police and not to your inquiry or hearing or whatever it is. The only way to get to the bottom of this is to smoke them out. I intend to write a story to do just that. Then we'll make a TV documentary. That should do the trick.'

'I have to insist you give me that list.' he told her.

'Insist all you like. You're not getting it. List? What list?'

'You're being criminally irresponsible.'

'I'm doing what I have to do,' she told him, 'to bring these bastards to book.'

'Is that really so? Or are you doing what you have to do to make sure you're the one who gets all the fame and the glory?'

'How dare you! And look who's talking. You just want to be popular and... I don't know...all-powerful or something. You politicians are all the same. All you care about are the opinion polls and your own personal standing. You just want everybody to love you and vote for you and fall down and worship you; you're just a bunch of hypocritical wind-bags and everyone hates you.'

'That's enough of that.' he said, managing to sound like an indignant father. 'You're skating on very thin ice, young lady. I could have you arrested for withholding evidence. If you won't give me the names then you should at least give them to the police.'

'I already have done,' she said. 'That's what I was about to tell you. I've handed everything over to a very high-ranking policeman. Come to think of it he could have been MI5. You see my daddy is quite high up at the Home Office. He arranged it for me.'

Carter looked away from her and gave himself a moment to think. Mainwaring. He immediately realised who her father was: an influential, high ranking, Whitehall Mandarin, not someone of whom one would wish to make an enemy. Still, he'd already made himself a whole campaign bus full of powerful enemies so he didn't suppose one more would make that much difference.

'Very well,' he said, 'you leave me no option. I shall instigate proceedings to have you subpoenaed before the committee. You will be forced to testify under oath, and if you continue with your lies you'll be charged with perjury and sent to prison.'

'Oh, don't be so fucking melodramatic,' she said. 'All

right, I'll let you have the list, just… not right now… it's important that I keep it for just a little while longer in order to trap them properly. I'm sure you're perfectly well meaning and I'm sorry I said that about you just doing this out of self-interest although you did say the same about me – but this is really complicated Much more complicated than you can possibly imagine. There are some very powerful people involved. Look, can you just give me a few more days?'

He closed his eyes for a moment and sighed, could still see her in his mind's eye. So young, so inexperienced, and here he was, the dyed in the wool politico unable to get her to do his bidding. He opened his eyes again and looked at her. They were both in the same leaky lifeboat. Putting their driven selves at risk. Convincing themselves they were doing great deeds. Perhaps they were. Perhaps some part of each of them *was* acting purely in the interest of truth and of justice.

'How about we put our heads together.' he said. 'And sort this out… as a team.'

She gave him a little nod and a smile of assent. 'But I need time,' she said. 'Give me a couple of days. I'll be back in touch, I promise.'

She stood up and he watched her as she strolled over to the main doorway, pulled the heavy door open and walked out. She didn't bother to close it behind her and a wintry blast of freezing cold air blew past her and into the room, as she disappeared off through the slush.

THIRTY FOUR

She got out of the taxi at a large Victorian pub on the edge of Clapham Common and hurried inside. The warm air hit her as she entered and her fingers stung a little as they started to thaw out. Small groups of wannabe hipsters sipped chardonnay and hot mulled cider and used vulgar language in Received Pronunciation.

Emma had got there before her and was slouched at a corner table pressing buttons on her phone. Lucy got a bottle of wine and some glasses. 'How are you?' She asked.

'Me?' Emma said, 'How am I? Bit better now. Since they let me out of Nick. How've you been getting on then, Milady?'

'I'm alright,' Lucy said. 'I'm sorry you –'

'They got you out of my place sharpish. Didn't they? That day.' 'You got special treatment you did. How was that then?'

'I got myself out. I just walked.'

'And nobody tried to stop you. You got special treatment you did. Same as lover boy. He got special treatment. He got a bullet in the back of his head. Funny though, I never saw nothing about that on the news. Did you? Mind you the riots was on and all that so maybe they didn't have time to report any other stories like, know what I mean? Then them two pig twats went mental trying to find that laptop. Threatened to shoot people and stuff. We all kept quiet though and they rummaged around for a bit and then just gave up.'

Lucy poured the wine. 'What happened? To you and your friends?' She looked, around to make sure no one was listening. No one was.

'You couldn't care less what happened to us,' Emma said. 'What do you think happened? They dragged us all out and shoved us into the back of a Pig Wagon. We was in Battersea nick for two days. They never charged us nor questioned us nor nothing. Four to a cell. The nicks was all full, see. I heard Wandsworth was in total lock down while the riots was on so I suppose all the other nicks was as well. I suppose if the riots had spread into the prisons then they'd have had to call the troops out but there's no chance of rioting when you're banged up for twenty-four hours a day, not even allowed out for a shit. A few days later, they dragged us all out one at a time and gave us charge sheets to sign. Receiving stolen goods. You plead guilty you get six months, you plead not guilty you get two years. Then they took us up to Wandsworth Court and the bastards gave us all six months. One after the other. Six months – take her down. Six months – take him down. Bang bang bang.'

'Why didn't you plead not guilty?' Lucy asked, just for the sake of making conversation. 'You didn't want stolen goods in your flat, did you?'

Emma looked at Lucy as if she'd suggested joining the Chipping Norton Set. 'I just fucking told you why. If you pleaded not guilty you got two years.'

Lucy very much doubted that the British judicial system would operate in such a manner but decided not to press the point.

'I had a visit when I was in there,' Emma said, lowering her voice and moderating her tone. 'Them two coppers come to see me.'

'Oh?'

'Yeah. They want that laptop. They'd been to the Block first and tried to force my mates to give it to them. My mates wasn't having that so then they tried to buy it. That didn't work neither, mainly because I'm the only one who knows where it is. They must have sussed that and I got a visit from them, them two fucking weirdos, asking me to tell the boys where it was so's they could get hold of it and hand it over. I told them to fuck off.'

She took a gulp of wine and pulled a sour face. Lucy did her best to not pull any face at all.

'Then, next thing, Big come in to see me and told me that they'd come for Marcus. He'd been staying with a mate of mine. They told her he was being taken into care. She was really upset but there was nothing she could do. She had to admit that she wasn't the mother and that I was, and that I was in Holloway. Then they come back and asked me again where the laptop was. They didn't need to mention that they had Marcus, we all knew they had him. I was fucking distraught but I still told them that I didn't know where it was. I reckoned if I told them I'd have nothing left to bargain with. I told them I'd get it for them if they let me out. And they did. They let me out. But I've got to wear one of these.' She hitched up her jeans to show Lucy the plastic band around her ankle. 'Peckham Rolex.'

'So, now you… could make the exchange?'

'I wouldn't trust them any further than I could kick the bastards. I want you to sort it. I want you to organise it, and I want you to get that newspaper of yours involved. That way they won't dare to hurt him, will they?'

Lucy thought about it, drank some wine and said, 'Yes. That's a good plan. We just need to work out the details. How soon can you get the laptop?'

Emma paused and leaned back in her chair. 'Whenever you want. What's on there though? I had a shufty and I couldn't find nothing that you might call incriminating, know what I mean? Is there really anything on there?'

'Yes. There is. You just need to know where to look for it. At least that's what Terry DeHavilland wrote – in his journal. He's the reporter who first broke this. There are scans on there, of signed witness statements. Lots of them.' After a pause she went on: 'it might not be a simple matter. If he's been taken into care, then there must have been a court order so –'

'There's not been no fucking court order! They've just took him away and banged him up.' This time she was unable to muffle her emotion and her voice wobbled.

'You should help me anyhow. Never mind your fucking laptop.'

'That's not fair. Look, the contents of that laptop

will help to put a lot of very wicked people behind bars. Paedophiles. Like you say, they won't dare hurt Marcus once we let certain people in the media know what's going on. But we can't afford to put ourselves in the wrong, we –'

'It wasn't normal social workers what took him. I just told you, didn't I? It was them two plainclothes coppers. The ones what come in with you that day, the ones what come to me in Holloway and tried to get me to give them that fucking laptop. They took him and no one's seen him since. I been asking everyone since I come out. Coppers. Social workers. Kids' homes. No one knows where he is. Or if they do they ain't telling. He's disappeared.'

Lucy wondered briefly what Norcross and Barrowclough might want with an eight-year old child but the possibilities weren't fit for contemplation. 'Oh.' she dissembled, 'if it was those two who took him, then that makes it easier. But in that case, I really will need that laptop.'

'You're lying,' Emma said. 'You just want your fucking laptop.'

'Yes. I do want it.' Lucy said. 'But I also need it to help Marcus. I can use it as a negotiating tool.'

'You'd better not fuck me over.' Emma leaned forwards and firmly but discreetly took a hold of Lucy's shirtfront. 'Or I will fix you so fucking good you…'

'There's no need to talk like that.' Lucy pulled herself free. 'When can you get me the laptop?'

'Now listen to me and listen good you stuck up cow, I couldn't give a shit about your fucking career any more than you could give a shit about my boy. Sort Marcus out first. When you've done that then call me and I'll give you the laptop. Don't try to fuck me over, neither. Big and his mates know all about this and they're helping me. Not for money neither. Though I reckon that cunting thing is likely worth a few bob, right?'

'That's good of them,' Lucy said.

'Yeah, right. Big rules.'

'Yes, that's pretty clear. Big rules. You're lucky to have such a powerful friend.'

'Don't take the piss, love. Let's face it, he's going to spend most of his life in Wandsworth. But he cares about Marcus. If you'd have taken any interest at all you'd have sussed it. Big is Marcus's dad.'

THIRTY FIVE

They met in the pint-sized lobby of a little-known boutique hotel near Sloane Square. There were hunting scenes on the wall and a smokeless blaze in a phony fireplace.

The place was empty apart from the Honourable Barry Carter M.P. and Lucy. Carter was seated in a flowery patterned armchair that was just about big enough to contain him. He had a pot of tea in front of him, and an empty, crumb-strewn plate that had once supported biscuits.

'What a weird little place.' She said. 'I must have walked past it a hundred times and never even noticed it.'

'Yes,' he replied, 'but that's London for you, isn't it? So much going on right under our noses that we never see.'

She shrugged and gave him a 'get on with it' look.

'Compromise.' he said, startling her a little by the sudden change of subject, 'is at the very heart of politics.'

'Of course it is,' she responded. 'Somewhere in there next to lies and self-interest and nasty old corruption.'

'You are very harsh,' he said, with a trace of fatherly amusement in his voice. 'I was too when I was your age.

As you get older you will learn that nothing, but nothing my dear, can be achieved without compromise. Let me give you an example… when I was a junior minister I was in charge of the nation's sewage system. Not the most glamorous of positions I'm sure you'll agree, but I had to make a success of it or there would have been no advancement. In order to make a success of it I had to be high profile and raising my profile in that particular position could only result in a certain level of ridicule from my peers and the general public. I had to be seen down in the sewers wading through the filth with the rats and the… sewer worker people… despite suffering from claustrophobia and a weak stomach. I had to do it. I did it. Sometimes we have to do things we detest the very thought of doing. Sometimes we have to wade through shit to reach the bright, sunlit uplands of success and recognition.'

'So, what are you saying?' she asked him, with a disgusted stare. 'That I'm going to have to wade through shit to get my story out?'

'Well… yes… you might just have to tiptoe though the odd shallow pool of liquid excrement.

She leaned forwards so he could hear the hoarse whisper with which she addressed him. 'Look. I'm sure you're acting with only the very best intentions, but I am very close to exposing at least two and possibly many more of these… paedophiles. I want you to lay off for just a few days. Then I'll give you everything I have. I promise.'

'Would you like a cup of tea?' He asked her.

She could hear the remains of a Brummy accent, and

that he'd tried his best to lose it. She ignored his offer of tea. He poured her out a cup anyway.

'Everyone knows Lord Warrington is involved.' he said.

'Yes, but no one has been able to prove it. Have they? Have you approached him?'

'No.' he said. 'But I'm going to.' He raised the teacup to his lips in a decorous manner with his pinky on show.

'Don't. I'm setting a trap for him. Wait just a few days and then I can give you enough evidence to convict.'

'I'm not a judge. I can't convict anyone of anything. What I can do is to subpoena and cross-examine certain witnesses and then produce a report based on those cross-examinations, which may or may not be of interest to the Crown Prosecution Service. What I want from you is the list of names and the witness statements that incriminate the individuals on that list. I can understand that you don't want to give me everything you've got all at once, but at least give me something. Something to be going on with.'

'Give me some more time, please? We're on the same side.'

'I would have thought you'd have been happy to co-operate. This way you'll get the chance to write your story at the appropriate time. I'm sure you appreciate that anything that comes out in the press could prejudice the case for the prosecution?'

'Prosecution? What prosecution? What if there isn't one? I'd just be waiting and waiting until –'

'That's a risk we'll have to take. I think there's a good chance we will prosecute. Look, Lucy, you have to let me have what you've got. Don't put yourself on the wrong side of this.'

'No. Fuck you. Have you any idea how much has gone into this... the sacrifices that have been made? Anyway... I don't actually have all the data. Not yet. It's been... encrypted... but I'm getting the password later.'

'When?'

'Later today.'

'All right.' He said. 'I can give you a few hours but don't push it. I have all the authority of the State behind me and I'm not afraid to use it.'

She nodded her agreement. She'd bought a little time. She could still sell the information and she didn't have to tell anyone it was all *sub judice*. She stood up and walked away and left 'Smelly Baz' to what was left of his tea and biscuits.

THIRTY SIX

Adam was at home with his best friend, Seb. The bedroom door was ajar and Lucy could see them clearly. They were both fast asleep on Adam's queen sized bed, completely naked, with their hands on each other's dicks.

She shook the snow from her coat, gave her hair a rub with a towel from the bathroom and then sat down on the Davenport in the sitting room. There was an empty bottle of Chivas Regal and two drained glasses on the coffee table in front of her.

She sat and waited and a minute or so later Adam came out of the bedroom wearing a purple silk dressing gown.

'I'm sorry,' he said. 'I really didn't want you to find out this way.'

She walked over to his well-stocked drinks cabinet, found the bottle of twenty-year-old single malt whiskey that he'd specifically asked her not to open and broke the seal. After pouring herself half a tumbler full she took a hefty swig. She didn't like whisky at all but she managed to hold it down.

'So you're gay? Bi? What?'

'I'm not entirely sure, Lucy,' Adam told her.

'Why did you ask me to move in with you? I always thought you were gay. Why couldn't you be honest? In this day and age.'

'Well… I've always been a bit confused… and you are very lovely… Maybe I just wanted one last shot at being a 'real man.'' He drew speech marks in the air to make it clear that he didn't really think that straight men were any more 'real' than gay ones.

'You're a lying bastard.' She said. 'What's really going on?'

'Come on. There's no need to be like that. We can still be friends. I…'

'Everyone knows you're gay. You've always been gay and you've always known it. You never ever tried to fuck me. Any straight man would have tried to. Any bi men would have.'

'That's something of a moot point now though, isn't it?'

'So, why did you ask me to move in?'

'Because you needed help. You'd got yourself into a right old pickle, hadn't you? Couldn't even trust your own father. And you were traumatised, darling. You'd witnessed a killing for Christ's sake. But leaving all that aside, why did you agree to come if you knew I was gay? You've never pretended to be in love with me. So why? Career move?'

She brought the glass of whisky back up to her lips but the smell caused her to gag so she held the glass away from her but then, on an impulse, she slammed it down on the highly polished coffee table. Some of the liquid jumped up and out of the glass. 'Yes. That's right. I'm just a self-serving little bitch. That's what you think, isn't it? But that's not why. Maybe it was because I admired you – on a cerebral level. Maybe I found your intellect arousing. Maybe I was impressed at how you'd arrived at such an exalted position at such a young age.'

She stopped talking for a second and looked him up and down. He stood up, was about to walk away but then stopped and turned towards her when she spoke again.

'Maybe I *was* worried. Maybe I was worried that something might happen to me. So, when you invited me to move in, maybe I thought, 'why not?' What better sanctuary could I possibly find than the home of the editor of the country's most prominent liberal newspaper. Oh, and Adam, you were so terribly accommodating. Said I didn't have to work, put me on sick leave. No questions asked.'

'You *don't* have to work.' he told her. 'Unless you want to. Maybe you still don't realize how badly you've been affected by –'

'Oh I do. I do realise. I was scared, Adam, but that wasn't why I moved in here. I wanted certain people to know that I was being a good girl and not digging around where I shouldn't be. Moving in with you achieved that if nothing else.'

She picked up the whisky glass again, put it to her lips but then replaced it on the table without drinking. Their eyes met and an unspoken torrent of accusations and denials flowed between them like giant waves passing voicelessly between desert islands.

'But now I'm not scared anymore. In fact… do you know what? I think my old ambition might have returned.'

'That's great news. I'll have to find you a nice juicy story to work on.'

'Oh… I have been working on something, Adam, it's a really massive story but I've got a feeling *The Defender* might not be interested. I'm talking to some telly people though. They're interested in doing a documentary. And I'm writing a book.'

'How wonderful. What's the angle?'

'Knoxley Hall,' she said with a spurt of enthusiasm, 'Terry DeHavilland… Jack Todd… Lord Warrington… Lord Hunter of Hellifield… Bishop Frobisher…'

'That's over. Finished. We can't go near it. No one can. You know that. It's not going to happen. And you know it. Time to move on.'

'Oh but Adam,' she said, with mock solemnity, 'what about those poor children who were molested and –'

'Oh come on, Lucy. You couldn't care less about them. You're a clever girl. Find another story to build your career around. What about this celebrity phone hacking business? That's still got legs. I could give you some leads –'

'No.' She said. 'I'm too far into this to give up now. I'm not a quitter, Adam. Not like you. You just dropped it, didn't you? You got warned off and you just dropped it. Isn't that right? But this story is huge. We both know that. And the fact that people like you won't tell it makes it… even more fucking huge. I'm going to find out what's going on and then I'm going to go on TV and I'm going to write a book. It's all coming out, Adam, every last detail.'

He went over to the drinks cabinet, poured himself a single malt and then returned to sit across from her, regarding her with a cold and hostile manner that she'd never seen him use before. 'Did that laptop ever turn up?' he asked.

Lucy stood up. 'Maybe it did... 'In fact, yes it has turned up. I can get it. Do you want it?'

He nodded slowly.

'Oh, you do want it? Even though you can't use what's on it?'

He looked at her without speaking. She stood up and started to move away from him, towards her room. 'So you can get the laptop?' he asked her.

She stopped and turned to face him, their eyes met and she nodded slowly. His expression was an empty page but then a thought appeared. In headlines. 'Have you discussed this with your father?' he asked her.

She stopped and turned to face him. 'No. Why? Should I?'

'I would if I were you.'

She went into her room and packed all her things. There wasn't much to pack. She carried her cases out into the hall and phoned a cab.

Adam came out of his room and said: 'You don't have to move out right away. You can stay for a few more days, if you like.'

She didn't bother to reply.

THIRTY SEVEN

She got to Dolphin Square about an hour later after a slow and tortuous taxi ride through the worsening weather. It hadn't stopped snowing all day and the British capital, with a characteristic lack of preparedness, was grinding to a halt. Lucy was happy to get somewhere familiar and safe.

Her father wasn't at home so she let herself in. Once inside she peeled off her wet clothes, put on a pair of pajamas and had a little weep before falling asleep on her bed.

Some time later she heard him come in and pour himself a drink. She got up and went through to where he was sitting.

'Hello daddy.'

'Hello darling.'

'Is it still snowing?'

'Yes. And it doesn't look like stopping any time soon. Forecast says it could last a week.'

'Aren't you surprised to see me?'

'No. I'm not. In fact… I was expecting you.'

'Oh? How come?'

'They're not going to let you carry on like this.' he

said. There was anguish in his voice. She didn't suppose there was much point in asking who 'they' were.

'They're not going to be able to bloody well stop me.' She curled her feet up beneath herself on the settee. 'And what has this to do with you?'

'Darling, I have to tell you something. Please listen.'

Lucy shrugged and listened.

'It concerns your mother.'

'What about my mother?'

'I told you she died in a car crash.'

'Yes. Along with my sister, Isabel. I've got photos of them. You were on holiday in the south of France. In the hills above Cannes. They went for a drive. *We* went for a drive. I was a baby. Mummy and Isabel both died. I didn't. I miraculously survived. You stayed in the hotel.' She paused and looked at him. A wave of nausea welled up inside her for no apparent reason. 'Isn't that what happened?'

'They say I was driving.' His eyes were fixed firmly on the carpet beneath his feet. No one seemed to be able to look her in the eyes today.

'What do you mean *they say*? You must know.'

He looked at his drink. 'I was drunk,' he said.

'Oh my God.'

'I don't remember any of it. I'd been drinking for days. I don't remember anything. I came to in the hotel and the local police told me about the accident. There was a lot of press coverage. Local press and then the UK nationals got hold of it because of the baby's miraculous survival – your miraculous survival. I suppose that made it more newsworthy. But they shielded me from the press. The foreign office did, through the consulate, in Nice.'

'Then they came and showed me pictures. It was me driving, it was me behind the wheel. It was all doctored somehow. Falsified. But it looked like it was me.'

He raised his eyes and looked at her with something approaching defiance. 'There was no way she would have got in the car with me when I was in that state.'

'But you don't know for sure? You still don't remember?'

'No. I remember drinking with some expat fellow and then waking up in the hotel room. There was vomit everywhere. They showed me the pics but then they said they'd made everything all right. The autopsy returned a verdict of accidental death. I was in the room. They had witnesses to say I was in the room. Those pictures of me behind the wheel, in the wreck, they never saw the light of day. I *was* in the room. I'm sure I was. I don't remember being in the car.'

'Why would anyone do that?' She went over to where he was sitting and took his face in her hands, made him look at her. 'Why would anyone do such a thing, Daddy? And why are you telling me this now?'

He looked straight at her and said, 'A man came to see me. When they were after that Todd fellow. They had the pictures. They showed me. That was why I told you to turn him in. They want me to get you to drop this, Lucy.'

'Or they'll release the photos of you and tell the press that you were driving, drunk. And that it was all covered up?'

227

'Yes.' he said.

'So they've saved this up for twenty years?'

He looked at her and shook his head. 'There have been other… demands.'

'So I have to stop trying to sell my story.'

'Yes. And there's another thing.'

'What?' she snapped. She'd had enough revelations. She took her hands from his face and turned a shoulder against him.

'There is a certain laptop computer. They say that you know where it is.'

'Daddy, no! I'm not going along with this. They can't prove anything. It was twenty years ago! You were in the hotel room. There's no way that my mother would have taken a young girl and a baby into that car with a drunk behind the wheel. That's just not credible. No. We're not going to let them do this.' She paused and then turned back towards him.

'So you've been doing stuff for them all this time? They've been blackmailing you for all these years?'

He nodded.

'Right. Well it's going to stop right now.' She stood over him and placed her hands on her hips. 'This is dynamite, Daddy,' she said, 'and we're going to use it to jolly well… blow them right out of the water.'

He put his hands on his head. Pressed his palms into his temples. 'So you won't give them the laptop or stop investigating?'

'No. I won't. And not only that we're going to have them prosecuted for blackmail. Oh poor daddy. You poor thing, living under this terrible shadow for all these years. Right. Let's get the ball rolling.' She took her reporter's notebook out of her bag, flipped it open and said: 'Righto daddyo. Let's have some names.'

Daddyo said, 'Stop, there's more.'

'Go on.'

'Selina wasn't your mother.'

'What?'

'Isabel was your mother.'

'She was... fourteen.' Lucy said. ' What do you mean she was my mother? She was my sister. She was fourteen years old.'

Her father said: 'I had no idea she was so young. She could have been... you know... much older. Selina was smart and she cared and she really tried to do the right thing. They were Catholics and there was no question of an abortion, so it was arranged for me to marry Selina. We kept Isabel out of sight, made it look like Selina was pregnant. Padding and so forth. And when you were born they... we... made out that you were Selina's child and that Isabel was your sister. I mean, half-sister.'

'What? What are you saying? That 'they' set you up with an under aged girl?'

'No.' He sounded irritated and impatient now, 'they' didn't set me up but 'they' found out about it later on and then 'they' must have dug up some evidence... birth certificates, that sort of thing.'

He made a move towards her, like he needed a hug. She stood and turned away. Her eyes avoiding his as a flame avoids the water.

'Look,' he said. 'Don't you think I've hated myself, beaten myself up, every day, every single blasted day, for all that time, all those years…'

She broke in on his self-pity: 'So what exactly do they want? The laptop? My silence?'

'Both of those things.'

'Who? Who precisely are we dealing with?'

'Lord Warrington.' he said. It could have been Lucifer, the way he said it.

'Alright.' Lucy said. 'Set up a meeting and tell him I'm prepared to talk.'

He nodded briefly and then looked at her with both fear and hope in his eyes; mostly fear though.

She thought quickly and decided to play along. It would put her in contact with the man who seemed to be behind the whole filthy business. She would agree to give him the laptop but would copy its contents first.

She said, 'Alright, I'll give him the laptop but I insist on meeting him, personally. No minions. Oh and there's one more tiny detail, there's a young boy called Marcus who has to be returned to his parents.'

'What? I don't know anything about that. These aren't the kind of people you can dictate to…'

She walked across the room to the window and stood there with her back to him.Watched the snow come down. Covering things up.

THIRTY EIGHT

A meeting was arranged for the very next day. Down by the river, across the water from the House.

Lord Warrington awaited her in a long, grey overcoat and an expensive looking scarf. The snow lay thick upon the ground. The river was a dirty brown colour and the sky was like a badly cracked ipad that wouldn't turn off.

'I am honoured,' she said. 'I thought you'd have sent a flunkey.' She was pleased that he'd agreed to her first demand.

'Such a delicate negotiation,' he replied, 'requires my personal attention.' He set off at a leisurely pace along the embankment. She made him wait for a few seconds by looking at her phone, but then stepped up beside him.

'Have you brought the item?' He asked her.

'I don't have it with me. But don't worry it's in a safe place. Once the boy has been returned to his mother the laptop will be handed over.'

'I can quite easily arrange for it to be taken by force,' he said, with just the requisite amount of quiet menace, 'but I do prefer to do things in a peaceful and civilised manner, if at all possible. However, please don't try to overplay your hand. And for god's sake don't insult my intelligence.'

'If it was possible for you to just take it, you'd have done so already,' Lucy said whilst gazing out across the Thames. Her voice expressed indifference. She wanted to make him think that she didn't really care.

'Emma hasn't got it. Her boyfriend and his friends have. They're black gangsters. Pretty hard to find. One of them is the boy's father so there's no shortage of motivation on their side to get this deal done. And I want it done too, I promised them that I'd get the boy back to his family home. I'm just the go-between here.'

Lord Warrington snorted. 'People like you break promises like five-year olds break Easter eggs.'

'What do you mean, people like me? You know nothing about me. I don't let scum like you into my life. The only reason I'm here is to help rescue an innocent child from… filth like you. If I can. If not then I'm just going to have to pass this whole business over to someone who *can* deal with it.'

'Oh, don't make my heart bleed,' Lord Warrington said. 'You don't care about the plebs. But you do care about what happens to your father. That's why you're here.'

'There's really nothing to be gained by discussing my motives. Produce the boy and leave Daddy alone and you get your *item*. I'll copy and keep everything that's on there and if anything comes out about Daddy then… I'll tell the world what you and your friends have been up to. You keep your side of the bargain and nothing will ever come out. In which case, everybody wins, right?'

'Oh, I always win.' He said.

She turned her face away from the biting cold wind and showed His Lordship her back for a spell. Then, presently, she turned and faced him.

'Why?' she asked.

'Why do I always win? A certain level of preparedness. Higher levels of education and intelligence than the majority of those who oppose me…'

'No. Not why do you always win. You know what I mean. Why?'

This one word question, spoken gently and without inflection, left her mouth, travelled the short distance between them and seemed to encircle his neck. He coughed and made a mirthless grin. His facial muscles stretched so tightly back across his face that Lucy could see the outline of his skull.

'Enough. I can quite easily discover the boy's whereabouts. He's more likely than not in one of the institutions that I control.'

You know exactly where he is. 'So, hand him over then.'

'I don't see any reason why not.' He said. 'I'll arrange a meeting, a handover.'

They walked along the embankment in silence for a few paces. Then he stopped and looked back across the river at the Palace of Westminster.

'Your father is over there now, playing flunkey to a junior minister. Don't you think that's amusing? A man with a disgraceful past and no visible future kowtowing to a young chap with his whole career ahead of him but with no skeletons, as yet, in his walk-in wardrobe. Although it's only a matter of time.'

'I couldn't care less what happens to my father.'

A flicker of doubt crossed Lord Warrington's face but certainty soon returned. 'Of course you care or you wouldn't be here. Do you really expect me to believe that you care about some godforsaken guttersnipe?'

She said nothing, hoping he would warm to this theme. She wasn't disappointed.

'Do you really think that what happens to the kind of vermin that you seem to be associating with, or their offspring, is of any importance? These people are where they are because they choose to be where they are. They allow themselves to sink to the lowest levels imaginable and then expect the state to support them as they wallow in their own filth.'

Lucy smiled, put her head on one side and maintained her silence.

'Some of us,' he said, 'by providential design, are born into families who have held great power in this land for many, many generations. That power, and the secrets and stratagems of how to use it, have been carefully passed down and now reside with us. We have been trained, from as early as we can remember, to wield that power. Our educations are devised specifically to achieve that goal. We are taught the merits and the benefits of self-sacrifice. We are taught how to be part of a team, how to put the team before ourselves. We are taught how to rule. This involves certain responsibilities and sacrifices but there are also certain compensations. Wealth, luxury, privilege.

'Unfortunately, there are certain maverick individuals, and it has always been thus, who have forgotten the tenets of their education and who abuse those privileges, indeed, use them for the purposes of self-gratification. Allow themselves to become entrapped in the vilest of vices. They are degenerate and dissolute. They invite disgrace upon themselves and by doing so, they invite disgrace upon the whole system that has produced them, educated them and allowed them those great privileges. There are those of us who have been charged with the responsibility of making sure none of the nefarious activities of those individuals is ever brought to light. Because, if that should happen, then the whole system, the whole structure of our society would be imperiled.'

'Oh, I see. Now that makes everything quite all right. If only someone had explained things to me earlier…'

'Only a generation ago… ' Lord Warrington went on, without seeming to notice her interruption, and gazing, almost manically across the river at the Palace of Westminster. '… no one would have dared to interfere.'

Then he stopped and looked at Lucy as if he'd forgotten she was there. 'Those days will come again.' He told her.

And with that he stopped, turned, and strode back towards Westminster Bridge.

THIRTY NINE

'So?' Emma asked Lucy.

'Good news.' Lucy said. 'It's all been sorted out.'

'All sorted out… as in… I get my Marcus back?'

'Yes… and soon. But there are… some formalities that need seeing to. They're worried that once you get Marcus back that you'll refuse to hand the laptop over. They've suggested I should hold onto it as a sort of go-between.'

Emma shook her head. 'I don't believe you. Where is he? Tell me where he is.'

'Lord Warrington told me he's in a place that he "controls." I know that sounds bad but there's a positive side to that. His lordship is only on the board of one of those type of places. I checked. He's on the board of a kids' home in Croydon.'

Emma smiled and looked off into the distance. Lucy didn't need to be a mind reader to guess what she was thinking. 'Look,' she said, 'if you're considering just going down and grabbing him then forget about it. That would ruin everything.'

'Why would it? He's not there officially. I say we get

him out but then still give them the laptop, but we copy everything that's on it and then if they try to take him back, well… they won't, will they? Knowing what we got on the bastards.'

'No.' Lucy said. 'That's just too dangerous. They'll have security. You'll never pull it off. Then they'll move him to somewhere else, somewhere we'll never find him. We have to do it their way. He will get him out of there and give him back to you. Once he's got the laptop, I mean, why wouldn't he?' There was a pause and then Lucy asked: 'Did you bring the laptop?'

'Course not!' Emma snapped. 'You're not fucking getting it. Not until I get Marcus back. You couldn't give a flying fuck about me and Marcus.' The words cascaded from her mouth like punches from a cage fighter. 'This is the way we're going to play it. First we get Marcus out and then you can go and tell your paper, and the pigs, the whole story. Get the bastards locked up.'

Lucy raised her voice, ' I don't have to do this, you know! There are other stories I could be working on. I've got a good mind to just let you handle this yourself. I'm doing my best for you, Emma, and all I'm getting back is abuse and threats.'

She started to rise from her chair but Emma stopped her.

'Alright.' she said, 'so we read it together. Back at my place, and then I keep it until the exchange. There's no internet on it so you can't send nothing to no one and that slot where you plug stuff in is knackered so you can't copy nothing that way neither.'

Lucy nodded. That meant she couldn't get the scans. She had an idea. She could photograph them with her phone. She would go along with it, get what she needed and then just take it from there.

FORTY

They were back in the same little council flat, the one where Todd had died. It was clean and tidy and the nasty smell had almost gone. But the nasty memories lingered on.

'So they kept your flat for you,' Lucy asked Emma,' whilst you were inside?'

'Don't be soft,' Emma replied. 'They sent the bailiffs round, threw all my stuff on to the landing and then boarded up the door and windows. Then Big and his mates took the boards down and put my stuff back in.'

'So you could be thrown out any moment?' Lucy asked. The last thing she needed was a visit from the local council.

Just then the door opened and Big walked through it. He turned his colossal back to Lucy and spoke to Emma in their South London patois: part West Indies, part Wandsworth Shopping Centre.

From what Lucy could make out, it sounded like Big had the laptop but was reluctant to hand it over.

He turned to Lucy and said, 'You any idea how much money I lost because of you?'

'Because of me?'

'Yeah, you and your boyfriend. All that stuff we had in there was mine, bitch, and now it all gone. That was worth a lot. You gonna give me compensation.'

'None of that was my fault. And that stuff wasn't yours, it was stolen. Anyhow, that's all in the past. I'm here to help bring Marcus home and that's not going to happen unless I get that laptop.'

Big turned to Emma. 'She'll promise anything to get her ting back.' Then he turned to Lucy. 'Don't you feel bad about coming back here? This where your lover man got shot in the back of the head.'

'I don't want to talk about that. I don't even want to think about it.'

'She don't care about nothing 'ceptin' hersel',' Big said. 'You can't trust that bitch.'

'This my only chance to get Marcus!' Emma shouted at Big. 'You gotta play along, Big, you said you was going to.'

Big gave Lucy a big ugly stare and put a hand in his bag. It re-appeared with the laptop. It was the one. She would have recognised it anywhere. It had a dent in the lid and one of the hinges was broken.

'You want this?' Big asked her.

She nodded.

'We want something in return. We better get that or you and your people going to get some bad things happen to you. You got that?'

'Yes. Of course.' Lucy muttered. She looked at Emma for support.

Emma said, 'She ain't getting it now. She just needs to go on it. To make sure what she needs is there.'

'Then she won't need it no more. Then she won't need us no more.'

Emma said, 'No. She will still need the ting. Its only fair we let her look on it. Big, she's the only one that can help us. Please Big, do it my way? Please?'

Big grunted and passed the laptop to Emma. 'Ok.' he said, 'I'm going out for one hour. That's all you get.'

With that he left. Emma put the laptop down on the coffee table and Lucy lifted the lid. It fell to one side because of the broken hinge and she had to prop it up with her handbag. She turned it on and tried to get online. *You are not connected to the internet.* It told her.

'Right, then,' Lucy said. 'Do you want to read it with me?'

Emma shook her head. 'What's on there?' She asked. 'Descriptions and stuff? Descriptions of what they did to them kids? Like what they might be doing to Marcus. Now. Right now. Just read it. That's all. That's all you get.'

Emma put her head in her hands and closed her eyes.

Lucy started to scan the contents of the laptop systematically. Every folder. Every document. She glanced through the journal entries that she'd already read in the hotel room, with Todd. There was nothing there. There had to be something else. Scans of signed witnessed statements – or at least a list of names. Todd had found names – or were the only names he had the ones he'd tortured out of Mo? The least she was expecting to find was a list. Left there by Terry DeHavilland. Even that wouldn't be proof of anything; even with that she wouldn't be able to publish, or broadcast. But just knowing who the bastards were would surely give her the requisite information to take to the documentary production company and to the newspapers. Get her name on it. Non-disclosure agreement. And money. Not the *Defender* though. Todd had been right. *They're in on it.* An incredible notion. *But they must be.* But there was nothing on there. Nothing at all.

'There's nothing on here.' she told Emma.

Emma said, 'I don't care. I don't fucking care. You've got to keep your side of the bargain anyhow.'

'How can I?' Lucy said. 'There's nothing here to bargain with.'

'Well you ain't going nowhere.' Emma said. 'You said if I gave you the laptop you'd get Marcus back to me. Big was right. You're fucking dodgy. I'm going to go get Big and he ain't going to be so gentle. He can be a right nasty bastard when he wants.'

Lucy measured the distance between her and the door. Emma read her mind and said: 'Don't even think about it. I'm going to lock you in and then I'm going to get Big.'

She got up and walked out. Lucy heard a key turn in the lock. And then another. Double locked.

All alone in that stinking flat. Could things get any worse? But then she thought of something. She picked the laptop up and had another look. Maybe. Just maybe.

After a few minutes she heard the lock turn. Big and Emma came in. Big seemed a bit concerned.

'We need to get online.' Lucy said. She'd only glanced at Big and now she kept her eyes on the laptop.

'Why?' Emma asked her. 'What fucking difference does that make?'

'He keeps saying it's on here but it's not. He must have emailed it to himself.'

'Then you could pick it up from anywhere.'

'Only if you knew the password and only he knew the password.'

'And he's dead so now no one knows it. So it's all lost. So you better think of something else.'

'I have. I have thought of something. He set up an email account. On this computer. And he saved the password. On this computer. So all we need is to find the email account and that's probably in his browsing history and then we open that account, and it will just open up because the password will be saved. That's why he says it's on here. It's only possible to get into those emails from this computer. That's it. That must be it. We need to take it somewhere where we can get it fixed so we can get online.'

'You ain't taking it nowhere.' Big said.

'Then how in God's name can we get into his emails?' Lucy yelled at him.

Big didn't seem to like being yelled at but he took it anyhow.

Emma though had grasped Lucy's theory and had an idea of her own. 'There's a guy on the next landing,' she said. 'He knows all about computers. He reboots them or whatever it's called. Nicked ones. He makes them like new so we can sell them to the punters.'

'Get him,' Lucy said. 'Please. Go and get him. He might be able to get us online.'

Emma went out and returned almost immediately with a small black kid of about fifteen or so. He wore large white spectacles that were almost as big as his head and were more suited to someone his mother's age. His name was Wizz.

Once the situation had been explained to him he took a mobile phone out of his pocket and said, 'We got 4G here so I can maybe get online using my phone.'

Then he took out a cable, plugged one end into his smartphone and then cut the other end with a pocket knife and stuck the pared off wires into the laptop's broken network applet. A web page opened. They were online.

'I need his email,' Lucy said, and Wizz pressed a few keys.

He shook his head. 'His default email ain't been used. He got other email addresses, like hotmail or yahoo?' he asked Lucy.

'I don't know,' she said. 'But wouldn't it be in his browsing history?'

'Browsing history been wiped,' Wizz told her. 'What's his name?'

Lucy told him and watched with more hope than expectation as he tried every possible email address that might belong to Terry. He typed them into his phone and what he typed came up on the screen; dot TD @ wotsit dot com then t_d at thingdot co.uk – and so on and so forth – every possible configuration. They all bounced back. Every one.

He looked up at them and shrugged his shoulders. 'That's all I can do,' he said.

Lucy almost screamed with frustration. Then she had a thought.

'Try his sister's name,' she said, 'Jo or Joanne DeHavilland. He said something about her – said she was the only one he trusted.'

Wizz went back to work, tried every possible configuration of those two names. They all bounced back. But then one didn't. Then it opened up.

He'd sent it from her hotmail account to an anonymous yahoo one. There was one pdf attachment, about twenty pages long.

'Is that what you was seeking?' Wizz asked her.

Lucy nodded, grabbed the laptop and quickly forwarded the document to herself.

Emma saw what she was doing and now she grabbed the laptop. 'You fucking bitch.'

Big, who'd been bored by the proceedings and gone into the other room, must have heard Emma's angry yell because he came back in just then.

'She got it,' Emma told Big. 'She sent it to herself.'

Big made himself even bigger and it looked as if things were turning nasty.

Lucy said, 'You're going to have to trust me.'

'Open your email.' Big said.

She stood up and faced him. 'No,' she said. 'What are you going to do? Beat me up?'

Big looked like he thought that wasn't such a bad idea but Emma intervened. 'No,' she said. 'Let's give her a chance. She got what she needs now so she can use it to get Marcus back. But we stay with her until we got him.'

Then she turned to Lucy and said, 'I'm coming with you, girl. I ain't letting you out of my sight.'

FORTY ONE

This time they met on the other side of the river in Victoria Tower Gardens, by *The Burghers of Calais*, who didn't seem to mind. The Palace of Westminster stood iconically in the background, waiting for the next tourist selfie. The wind was blowing in from the west now, along the river from Battersea Bridge and beyond; most of the snow had gone but it was bitterly cold and the occasional flurry of freezing sleet blinded eyes and stung faces.

Lucy had suggested this particular meeting place – she had wanted to be around people – in case of any wrongdoing, but she hadn't realised it would be quite this cold. She moved her body from one foot to the other, stamping and doing her best not to shiver; she didn't want them to think she was afraid.

Lord Warrington appeared from the direction of Parliament Square and strutted over towards her like a modern major general, his furled brolly, which he was using as a walking stick, rose, pointed straight at her accusingly and then fell back towards the earth with every springy step he took. He seemed impervious to the inclement conditions.

'The two of them are over there waiting.' Lucy told

him, as he reached her: 'They have it with them. Where's the child?'

'On the other side of this grotesquery.' Lord Warrington told her, pointing his brolly upwards at Rodin's depressing group of malnourished French dignitaries.

Lucy walked briskly around to the other side of the statue. Norcross and Barrowclough were there, smoking and sneering and Marcus was in between them, looking cold and puzzled and shaking like a sapling in a hurricane.

'Look who it is, it's Juicy Lucy.' Barrowclough said. 'What's up, Luce?'

She was about to respond with a quip of her own when Lord Warrington grabbed her arm from behind her and pulled her back to his side of the statue. She pulled herself away from him.

'Keep your filthy hands to yourself!' she told him.

That didn't faze him much. 'Phone her now,' he said, 'and tell her the boy is here. Then she can come hither, with the item, and the exchange can take place.'

'I don't know if I can trust you.' Lucy said.

'Oh for god's sake! Do you think I'd risk the spectacle of a screaming teenage mother making some dreadful scene within shouting distance of the House?'

Lucy got her phone out and pressed the Emma key.

'Where is he?' Emma asked. Her voice was steady and cold.

'He's round the other side of the statue,' Lucy said. 'I've seen him. They won't let you see him, or him see you, until they've got what they want.' She looked at Lord

Warrington as she said this. He held her gaze, easily. As if this type of transaction were an everyday occurrence.

'Alright.' Emma said, after a pause. 'You've definitely seen him though?'

'Yes and he's fine,' Lucy told her. 'Come to the statue.'

'We'll come now.' Emma said.

'You and I will go and watch the boats.' Lord Warrington said. 'My people will take it from here.'

He sauntered off and Lucy followed him. They strolled over to the embankment and once there she turned and saw that the exchange had already taken place. Norcross was carrying the laptop and Emma was hugging Marcus. Big was hulking around close by; he looked nervous and out of place, like a heavyweight boxer at a christening.

'You've done a good thing,' Lucy told Lord Warrington. 'First time for everything.'

'Shut up and listen to me,' he said. 'I'm not naïve enough to think that you wouldn't have copied every single word of what's on that computer. I will continue to hedge my bets. I will continue to hold an insurance policy against anything that is, or has been, on that laptop emerging from the darkness. You will neither divulge any of the names that are mentioned in those... memoirs... nor attempt to contact any of the individuals involved. In fact you will now cease to take any interest whatsoever in this... matter. You will drop it and forget about it.'

They had been strolling back towards Parliament Square as he'd said this and now he stopped, abruptly, and turned to face her: 'Do you understand?' He asked, with the same level of venomous intensity that Hamlet had used against his poor old widowed mother.

'Oh of course not, your lordship,' Lucy said, not even bothering to hide her indifference. He had nothing on her now. The lever had been broken. 'I'll see to it,' she said. 'You have my word.'

'I'm not asking for assurances,' he said. 'I'm issuing instructions.' And with that he pointed, with his brolly, across the gardens to the road.

A police van was parked at the kerb with its back doors open. Two officers were helping Big into the back. He had already been handcuffed. Emma was screaming and Marcus was crying. A siren blared and drowned out the sounds of woe. The police van set off along Victoria Street and then Emma and her boy-child were pushed, swiftly and efficiently, into the back of an anonymous looking silver hatchback.

'You bastard.' Lucy said, quietly. 'You rotten bastard. You didn't have to do that, we gave you what you wanted, you –'

'I told you not to insult my intelligence,' Lord Warrington said. 'Do you really think I would allow drug-addled members of the underclass to run around unfettered and unrestrained, knowing what they know? Unless I possessed the means to keep them silent? The child will not be released. He will continue to be my insurance policy. His mother knows too much and I need to be able to ensure her continued silence.'

'She doesn't know anything,' Lucy said.

'Of course she does,' Lord Warrington said. 'Don't

take me for a fool. She was in possession of the laptop for months.'

'Give the boy back,' Lucy said. 'What the hell does it matter to you?'

'And what does it matter to you? I'm not entirely sure that you care enough about your father to keep quiet. And I'm not entirely sure that you care enough about the boy for you to remain quiet. But there have been no media revelations as yet so perhaps one of those things is ensuring your silence. It could be both or either of them. So I'll hold both those cards for now. Another possibility is that you've already tried to sell the information and there have been no buyers – in which case you are no threat at all, even less of a threat than your friends are. No one would take their word against mine but I'd rather not have them running around and wagging their tongues at anyone who's prepared to listen.'

'You bastard.' Lucy said. 'You disgusting… filthy… revolting… soul-dead old sicko! You suck the blood out of decent people… and their children… to keep your own worthless life going… that's it isn't it?'

He didn't bother to deny it.

She hurled herself at him, tried to rake her nails down his face but then realised she was wearing gloves and was causing herself more pain than she was inflicting on him.

He pushed her away: 'I wouldn't do that if I were you. This is all being filmed. We are gathering evidence, you see, about how certain venerable old fogies such as myself are being victimised, hounded by the gutter press and by certain opportunistic politicians and police officers. At least one unfortunate old man has already killed himself. And now, phone camera evidence will emerge of a second distinguished old gentleman, ie myself, being harassed verbally and physically by some dreadful careerist female hack who is young enough to be his granddaughter…'

He smiled. He smiled a horror show; his smooth and dissolute botox filled features glowing like some death's head mask that covered a real death's head.

FORTY TWO

'Why don't you just do the decent thing and hand yourself in?' she suggested to her father. 'They might be more lenient with you if you did that. And it's all so long ago and you are getting on. I'm sure it won't be too bad. You know, open prison with a good library. You'll be able to look after the vegetable garden or something like that. You could even write a book. That will give you a nice pension for when you come out. Because I suppose you might lose your civil service one. I'm not sure how that works.'

He was facing the mantelpiece with his hands behind his back. His whole torso was ramrod straight, as tense as a flagpole. Still, no change there, she couldn't remember ever having seen him look relaxed.

'I'm sorry Daddy.' she said, 'I've made my decision and I'm going to go ahead and sell the story. We've got witnesses now. The perpetrators have been named; we have signed witness statements naming them. Unfortunately, one or two of the bastards have already topped themselves, but there are others.'

'Don't be a bloody little fool!' her father snapped at her, his sudden burst of defiance catching her by surprise.

'This will never see the light of day. Haven't you got it yet? The power these people have? Your newspaper friends will be told that if they want to continue hatching their meaningless little stories in their prestigious little nests then they'd better just forget this… affair.'

'No one's going to forget anything. In a few days time there's going to be a media shit storm the like of which this country has never seen. The Home Affairs Select Committee are putting a case together and I'm co-operating. Once the evidence is heard it will be open season. The net is tightening. Daddy. Look, why don't I arrange a meeting with the chair of the committee. You might be offered the chance to plea bargain or whatever. You never know.'

'Plea bargain?' he scoffed. 'This isn't America. You'd be sending your own father to prison. Have you no gratitude for everything I've done for you? Brought you up, paid for your exorbitantly expensive education. Got you a job. Oh yes, I got you that job. Do you think a major broadsheet would have taken you on with your mediocre qualifications? Go and tell your tale, if you must. It will never see the light of day. We know all about this Barry Carter fellow and his committee. That's all just a toothless sop to those journalists and politicians who think they can write what they want when they want to. Go ahead, Lucy, but don't expect any more help from me.'

'Times have changed.' she responded quietly. ' New generation, new methods, new media. We'll drip feed the story from an anonymous social network account and then make the documentary. That's just a few interviews and the release of more names, a bit of door stepping for dramatic effect. By then the police will be involved. There will be a media feeding frenzy and the 'something must be done' brigade will come out in force. And something *will* be done.'

'Come on Lucy, you don't really care if anything is done or not. All you care about is that it will be your story and that you will be forever remembered as the courageous young woman who did her best to bring all this nocturnal beastliness into the cold light of day.'

'Right! You bastard! You've fucking well asked for it now.'

'Go on, do it then!' He put this head in his hands and said, 'I'm tired of it, Lucy. So bloody tired of it all.'

She looked at him, felt no pity; could only despise him now. 'So, you'll do the right thing and go to the police – or Carter?'

He looked up at her and nodded.

She went to the door and opened it but then stopped and turned back. 'I'm not going to let you ruin my life. I'm going to be successful. I'm going to have a brilliant career in journalism and broadcasting. Then I'll marry a TV producer or a newspaper editor and we'll go and live in a great big house on Primrose Hill and have kids. Lots of kids. But you'll never see them. You sick bastard.'

She went into her room, packed a bag and silently left.

FORTY THREE

From the lobby she phoned Henrietta at the TV production company and said: 'I've got what you told me to get. Independent, signed witness statements. My God, Henry, the individuals involved… and there's more to it than just child abuse. It was ritualistic. The kids were sacrificed to some… I don't know… god or something. It's quite a story.'

Henrietta didn't seem all that excited at her news. Her voice was calm and assured, bored even.

'Did you hear from an MP called Barry Carter?' she asked.

'Yes.' Lucy said. 'I did a deal with him. He's holding back until we've made the film.

'All the research is there now; you can do a prelim and name names. Then I'll put the story in the *Defender* or one of the other broadsheets and you can do a follow up piece when you've had time to interview all the victims, they'll name names too, now it's out. Then we can approach the perps.'

'They're out to get him,' Henrietta said. 'Carter, I mean. Even members of his own party are briefing against him. The media are calling it a witch hunt.'

'I can prove it's all for real.'

'Alright,' Henrietta said, after a pause. 'Come in and see me. It sounds like you'd better be careful.'

'Yes. Look, my father is involved and I have to move out. Do you have somewhere I could stay for a few nights? Just until I sort something out?'

'Your father? Your own father?'

'Yes. Crazy isn't it? Well, have you got somewhere for me to stay?'

'Yes. Of course. Come to the office. You can stay at mine.'

The snow had turned to pelting sleet. She tried to e-hail a cab on her smartphone but there were none in range of her so she had no other option than to stand under her brolly until a black cab came along. But none did.

Then, after a few minutes, a white van pulled up just in front of her and the back doors opened.

Emma was sitting inside. She motioned for Lucy to get in. Lucy did so and sat down. She tried to wipe the rain off her face with her hands. The van moved away abruptly and she fell sideways. Emma put a hand out to stop her fall. Then held on to her arm with a firm but not too friendly grip.

'Right,' she said, 'I'm going to get Marcus back and you're going to help me do it.'

Lucy continued to wipe the rain off her. 'How did you get out?' She asked.

'We got bail. It was all a bit weird. Someone vouched for us. Someone we don't even know. At any rate we're out.'

'Look,' Lucy said. 'There's nothing I can do about

Marcus. I'm sorry but there just isn't. In any case I'm going to expose those… bastards and when I have done… well they're bound to let Marcus go. They'll see he's part of this, that Warrington used him to buy our silence. Don't you see? The only way to get Marcus out is to expose this ring of… pedo fuckers… once and for all.'

'I've got the names too. I could expose them if I wanted to.'

'You couldn't. You don't have the right contacts and you don't know who's in on this and who isn't. You could quite easily approach the wrong people.'

'And I could quite easily approach the right people. Anyway, you're in luck. That's not the way we're going to play it. We're going to withhold the gen until we get Marcus out and then when they come after us we'll tell them that we'll keep quiet as long as they leave us alone. Oh and that means you as well.'

'But then I won't be able to expose them.'

'Tough shit.'

'But I must be able to expose them. Think of all those innocent children. They deserve justice. And think of the ones who will suffer or even be killed if we don't stop these evil –'

'Oh change the record, love. You don't give a shit about any of that.'

'What? Don't you dare say that! I know you're upset and worried but don't accuse me of that. That's just not true!'

But was it true? Did she care more about her own career than she did about the victims?

'So what's going on with you?' Emma asked her. 'Where you off to? Why the suitcase?'

Tears started pouring down Lucy's cheeks. 'I just can't bear to stay with him any longer.' she sobbed.

'Why not?' Emma asked her. 'Go on. Let's hear it. Better out than in.'

So Lucy told her the story. About how her father had got a thirteen year old pregnant and how her mother and grandmother, who had been masquerading as her mother and her sister, had both died in a car crash in the south of France when she'd been a baby. When she finished she looked up at Emma expecting sympathetic words or an arm around her shoulder. She got neither. Emma's face was as hard as flint.

'So you're going to shop him?'

Lucy nodded. Her lips whitened. The back of the van seemed even smaller, even more constrictive than when she'd first got in.

'No you're not, love,' Emma told her. 'None of this is coming out until I get my Marcus back.'

She banged on the partition behind the front seats and the van pulled over. Then Emma stood up and got out. Lucy heard the doors lock. There were voices but she couldn't make out what was being said.

After a few minutes the doors opened again and Emma said: 'You're going back there and you're going to tell your old man that he has to help get Marcus out. Or we'll shop him. Sorry love, but I don't give a shit about him any more than you do about my Marcus.'

'He can't do anything.' Lucy told her. 'He's completely

in their power. All he does is sit around and wait for the next set of instructions. There's really no point –'

'We're going there… now.' Emma said.

And they did. The next time the van's back doors opened they were back in Dolphin Square.

They walked in to the building and past the porter's desk. He was sitting behind it, for once, reading *The Planet*. They got in the lift and rode silently upwards for a few seconds. Then they got out and walked over to the apartment door. Lucy took out her keys and opened it. That was when the vile smell hit her. It was the smell of shit.

Her father's body was hanging from a flex in the dining room. That was where the smell was coming from.

He'd had one final crap before he died.

Emma turned and ran.

FORTY FOUR

Once the autopsy had taken place, and the verdict of suicide had been reached, Lucy got a call from a representative of the government department where her father had worked. He told her that her father's erstwhile employers had offered to take care of all the funeral arrangements. She accepted the offer, hoping to get the whole grim business over and done with, as soon as possible.

The government, she was informed, had retained the services of an excellent firm of funeral directors who would take care of all the practical details: there was to be a service at St Margaret's in Westminster after which her father's mortal remains were to be disposed of at a small crematorium in Belgravia, not all that far from Dolphin Square.

But then the arrangements hit a snag; the parish priest of St. Margaret's withdrew his invitation. Suicide, it seemed, was an abomination, and the lives of those unnatural monsters who had chosen to defile themselves in this manner were not to be celebrated within the walls of that particular house of God; despite the fact that discrimination against those poor souls who had

261

died by their own hand had not been enforced for some decades.

Alternate arrangements were made and Lucy was comforted to learn that one of her father's colleagues had arranged for the service to take place at a private chapel to which he had access. Lucy, without any other options to consider, agreed to this arrangement.

The chapel was in a subterranean vault full of arches and pillars. It was airless and dimly lit and Lucy could see or hear nothing of the proceedings from her seat at the back of the room where she had been placed, between the man from the ministry and the funeral director.

Lucy knew no one. Her father had had no living relatives but he did have a number of acquaintances that she had expected to attend but who were conspicuous by their absence.

She had assumed that as the chief mourner she should be seated at the very front, not at the very back, but she had no energy to complain about the seating arrangements. She could barely hear the words of the minister but could make out just enough to realise that were being uttered in some foreign language, with which she was not familiar.

After the service, the coffin was carried back out to the hearse in which it had arrived. Everyone got back in their cars and followed on behind Lucy's dead parent, presumably to the crematorium where he would be consigned to the flames.

But Lucy wasn't taken to the crematorium. She was taken back to the Dolphin Square apartment. She protested loudly but the man from the ministry just shrugged and told her that he was only following instructions and that, in any case, there would be no point in their going to the crematorium now because the proceedings would already have been concluded.

Then he made his excuses and found his own way out, leaving Lucy to grieve alone.

When she looked back on this period of her life she found it astonishing that she had been so lacking in assertiveness with regards to the arrangements around her father's funeral. The horror of finding her father and the grief that followed had transformed her, temporarily at least, into a weak, pale shadow of her normal self.

She wanted to move out of the apartment that she had grown to detest, but that wouldn't have been practical – there were still some months left on the lease and the rent had been paid right up to the expiry date. She still felt drained and depressed and was incapable of working. Her mobile phone stayed off and when the house phone rang she ignored it. When she was hungry or needed wine to drown her sorrows, she ordered in.

One morning, after several days of this semi-drunken self-pity, she awoke feeling restless and angry. She had to have something to do; she had become used to the adrenalin-fuelled intensity that the whole Knoxley Hall affair had afforded her.

She just couldn't let it lie. She turned the whole affair over in her mind once more; how it had transformed from involving the exposure of evil strangers to being all about her father and herself and her employer.

What was it that Lord Warrington had said? *'I'm not*

entirely sure that you care enough about your father to keep
quiet. And I'm not entirely sure that you care enough about
the boy for you to remain quiet. But there have been no
media revelations as yet so one of those things is ensuring
your silence. I'm not sure which one it is. So I'll hold both
those cards for now.'

The truth of the matter was that neither of those 'cards'
would have prevented her from selling the story to the
highest bidder. Lord Warrington had misjudged her. But
now her father was dead he would, presumably, assume
that his hold over her was slipping. He still held the boy
Marcus but had expressed his doubt that any anxiety over
Marcus's wellbeing would prevent her from revealing all.
He would be a worried man. Her life could be in danger.

Then there was a development. According to one of
the 'heavies' (not *the Defender*) an anonymous witness
to the Knoxley Hall atrocities had come forward and was
naming names. Now it was revealed that there had been
a police investigation into the 'Westminster paedophile
ring' allegations and that the 'anonymous witness' (who
was constantly on the TV news channels in silhouette
only with his voice disguised) had named names. But one
of the names he had named belonged to a dead man: Lord
Hunter of Hellifield.

So the Knoxley Hall story had become prominent
once more but now the focus was on how certain ancient
public servants had been hounded by the police and the
media and accused of terrible crimes against children
when there wasn't a shred of evidence against them.
Questions started to be asked about the identity of this

anonymous whistle blower and Smelly Baz was brought back under the spotlight and forced to publicly admit that he had jumped the gun and that the allegations that he had levelled at certain individuals under the cloak of parliamentary privilege had been baseless.

She called Henrietta and told her that she had more, much more than the shady man, who was being referred to as 'Nick,' was revealing and that she had the signed witness statements that would utterly refute the claims that there was a lack of evidence.

'Very well,' Henrietta said, after expressing her condolences. 'Let's continue where we left off.'

'Alright,' Lucy said. 'But I have to get out of here. Does your offer of temporary accommodation still stand?'

'Yes, of course.' Henry told her, and Lucy felt a surge of relief. But just before she put the phone down she thought she heard a click on the line.

She put that down to paranoia, pulled out a suitcase and started to pack. Then something made her look out of the window. It was raining heavily but through the murkiness she could just make out a silver hatchback parked directly across the road from her window. It looked just like the one that Norcross and Barrowclough had used to take her down to South London on the day that Todd had died and had taken Marcus from Parliament Square on the day of the 'handover.' She strained her eyes to see into the vehicle. There were two men sitting in the front seats. She couldn't be sure it was *them* but she had a pretty strong feeling that it was. She finished packing quickly and went down to the lobby where she was relieved to see that the porter was in his place behind his desk.

'There are some people out front I'd prefer to avoid,' she told him. 'Is there a back way out?'

'Yes Miss. Follow me.'

He took her to a back door that led into a secluded mews. She struggled for a moment to get her bearings but soon realised where she was and hurried along through the rain towards the Ebury Bridge Road. By the time she got there the rain was coming down harder than ever; it was like a tropical storm. A car pulled up behind her. She quickened her pace and it ambled along beside her. She looked around. It wasn't the silver hatchback, it was a longer, sleeker affair – almost as long as a limo. She stopped and waited.

The driver spoke to her. 'Get in, Lucy.' He said.

The voice was familiar. She looked at him, couldn't make out his features, got in anyhow and wiped the rain from her eyes. Then she saw the driver's face in the rear view mirror.

It twitched and then grinned at her.

Todd! You bastard!

FORTY FIVE

Six months earlier

The sirens wailed. Police and rioters chased each other around inner-city London like the black and white pieces on some giant, metropolitan checkerboard. Fire crews moved in to douse the flames, risking their lives whilst the masses watched on TV and facebook and read all about it on twitter and hipster blogs.

Nothing to do with you! Except it's happening in your street right now. Stay at home and pray to the Lord that no one comes to break down your door or smash your windows or force their way in and take all your sentimental valuables.

Google Earth down to the Doddington, that nasty sprawling estate on the Battersea Park Road, to Harold Macmillan House, Number 305. Full of contraband and coppers.

D.S. Barrowclough came back into the bedroom. He was empty-handed and he shook his head. D.I. Norcross pushed his revolver into D.S. Todd's blood stained face, pulled back the hammer and said, 'Right then Todd. No more pissing around. Where is it?'

Todd's face creased and then twitched and then settled itself down into something between a grin and a grimace.

'I've handed it over to someone I can trust,' he said, 'and instructed them, should anything happen to me, to send whatever's on there to every newspaper and twenty-four-hour news channel in the whole wide world. It will go viral boys and then you're fucked. If you kill me, it all comes out.'

Norcross sneered and gave Todd's bloody visage a little prod with his firearm. 'Where is it, Sherlock?' He stage whispered.

'Fuck off, moon face,' Todd replied.

Norcross smiled at the insult and adopted a more conciliatory tone. 'They want it all tied up nice and neat,' he said. 'That means you killed DeHavilland and Frobisher and now you're dead. No trial required.'

'Tell me something I haven't already figured out for myself,' Todd spat back at him. 'So I'm supposed to hand over the laptop or tell you where it is and then you shoot me and then file a report saying I got real nasty and tried to escape and you had to shoot me in self-defence?'

Norcross nodded.

'That's not what's going to happen.' Todd said. 'You might be stupid enough to play it that way but your bosses aren't.'

Norcoss nodded and made a sly smile. 'You've got some bottle, Jack, I'll give you that much. So here it is. You die. Except not really die. See what I mean?'

'Go on.' Todd said.

'The riot cops are coming in and then an ambulance

crew. The paramedics have had their palms greased. See the level of resources we can rely on? I'll let one bullet rip.' He raised the pistol. 'But I'll aim to miss. That's going to be the hardest part. I don't know if I can bear to do it. Anyhow, they'll make you a wound and they'll give you an injection. Put you in a coma for a bit. We'll put you on a stretcher and take you out to an ambulance. Anyone sees you, you're dead.'

'That doesn't work,' Todd said. 'Like I said, if my death is announced it automatically all comes out.'

'You'll have plenty of time to make sure that doesn't happen. That's what the big boys think. Right or not?'

Todd thought for a spell and then nodded. 'So this has already been arranged?' He asked.

Norcross nodded. 'Them upstairs got brains. Mighty clever them big chiefs. Man on a phone said to fake you croaking. You're a lucky boy. I reckon it's because you're such a big, sad, lonely bastard and nobody will really give a shit where the fuck you've gone.'

Todd looked hard at Norcross. He had to believe him. But there was a little niggle of doubt at the back of his mind, which grew into a great big enormous niggle as Norcross pointed the gun at him and pulled the trigger. He felt a burning flash of pain in his shoulder and he screamed and he fell. Blood poured out of the wound like lies from a politician's mouth.

There was a scurrying outside and then a roaring, crashing sound. Like the Stretford End on steroids. They were letting themselves in.

Then the bitter smell of tear gas.

Norcross let another shot go off, but this one missed. He heard Lucy scream.

'Let me through.' She yelled. 'I'm a newspaper reporter. How dare you obstruct me you…'

But it didn't sound like they were letting her in. Her voice became muffled, still shrill and indignant, but further away now. They were taking her away from him. And he cared. He cared about her. For some reason that surprised him. *She'll be okay. She can take care of herself.*

The pain in his shoulder was unbearable but he managed not to scream. Then hours, or maybe seconds, later an ambulance crew appeared. Paramedics. Faceless men in uniforms. One of them stuck a needle in his arm.

Then nothing.

FORTY SIX

He woke up in a bed that was a foot too short for him in a shabby little room with magnolia coloured walls and a badly stained ceiling. His hands were bandaged. They stung like hell and so did his shoulder, which was also bandaged up. He groaned and managed to sit up. There was a drip pole next to him that held a dirty coloured liquid that was being piped into his arm. He had been restrained in some way. He didn't like that much and made an effort to escape, but whatever it was that was holding him down was doing a pretty fine job of it. He yelled out in pain and frustration.

A young nurse came in. White trousers and top and a headscarf. The badge on her lapel announced her name, which was Farzana.

'Stop that right away,' she scolded. 'We leave you alone for one minute and this is what happens.'

'Why am I tied up?' he snarled at her. 'Get these straps off me and bring me my clothes.'

'Very well,' she said, 'if you so wish. They're only there to stop you turning over in your sleep and opening the wound in your shoulder. It's quite a deep wound and the surgeons had to dig a bullet out of it.'

He said, 'I'm surprised it didn't go right through at that range.'

'I think it was stopped by your collarbone,' she told him. 'It's a miracle you've still got one. I won't ask what on earth it was that you were doing to get yourself shot. That's none of my business.'

She gave him a long, stern 'nursey knows best' look and leaned over and adjusted something at the side of the bed. He felt the straps release.

He pulled himself up and said, 'my clothes please.'

The nurse said 'why don't you wait for the doctor to come around and then you can discuss with him whether or not you're in any shape to be discharged. You have a lot of stitches in you.'

He leaned back, exhausted. She seemed a decent sort. Maybe she was right.

'Are you in any pain?' She asked him.

He nodded grimly.

'I'll increase the morphine dose,' she told him and turned a little valve on the side of his drip. The world became a nicer place.

When the fresh-faced young doctor came in, some time later, to examine his wounds, Todd was still pretty much out of it.

'You're out of danger,' the doctor told him. 'From here on in it's just a question of rest.'

There was nothing else for it. So, for the next few days he just let a procession of nurses tend to his every need. They changed his dressings, fed and washed him, and dosed him with morphine every couple of hours. He couldn't remember anyone ever being quite so kind to him.

On the seventh, or it could have been the eighth, day, Lord Warrington came to see him. There he was, that day, seated at the side of the bed, as Todd came out of a particularly long and pleasant morphine induced slumber.

'I can't tell you how pleased I am that you've come around to our way of thinking,' the great man said in a voice that a weasel might use, if weasels could talk.

'Oh. Have I?' Todd asked him.

'The world thinks you're dead. You don't have any family so there are no complications on that front. So, you need a new identity. We've arranged that. Your name is Tobin, John Tobin. You work for me now.'

'Jawohl mein Fuhrer,' Todd replied wearily. He would have given a Nazi salute if it hadn't been for his bad shoulder.

'Most amusing.' Lord Warrington said. He didn't seem amused. 'Now,' he continued, in a business-like tone: 'You're a military man, aren't you, old boy?'

Todd couldn't be bothered to reply.

'So, presumably you understand the importance of closing ranks. Our side, right or wrong, what? You're one of us now and we look after our own. We know you know things but your presence here means you're not, not ever, going to tell anyone anything. That's right isn't it?'

'Thing is,' Todd said, 'I already have.'

Lord Warrington's face clouded over. 'But that's not what was agreed. Who have you told?'

'Oh, don't worry,' Todd said in a gouchy, chilled out

273

sort of way. He's one of us. A military man, like us. He's in Baghdad, advising the Iraqis. He's top brass. He won't let the side down. So long as nothing bad happens to me.'

'I see,' said Lord Warrington between gritted teeth, 'so that's how it is. Well perhaps you'd like to reveal the identity of this mysterious military gentleman.'

'I'm not that fucking stupid.' Todd told him, somewhat dreamily. His own voice sounded far away and muffled, like the train announcer on Baker Street Station.

Lord Warrington scowled and then scribbled down an email address on a piece of paper and handed it to Todd. 'You have any number of options; you can go off and start a new life anywhere else in the world should you so wish but on the other hand you could stay here in London, such a marvellous city and aren't we lucky to live here? And you can be my personal bodyguard. I've heard you're a bit… handy… we'll be an excellent team.'

'Why not?' Todd yawned back at him. 'I'll need to make a living. Decent wages and time off for good behaviour? Work/life balance so important don't you think?'

The unctuous smile that had been playing around Lord Warrington's lips vanished in an instant and his demeanour changed abruptly from one of geniality to one of outright hostility. 'You'll be watched,' He said. 'One false move and we'll take you down.'

'You take me down,' Todd said, 'and you go down with me. There's still the question of the laptop. It's being held for me. It will be handed over to the media should I fail to check in. And I'm not talking about the British media. I mean the foreign media. 'I don't think you own them yet, do you? I'm talking about scans of signed witness statements. And not all from victims either. Some of them are from the abusers who were told they'd get an easy ride if they turned Queen's Evidence. You wouldn't want them falling into the wrong hands, would you?'

'I see,' said His Lordship. 'Well, we'll have to have a good long think about what to do with you, won't we? In the meantime, you'll have to stay here. You'll be well looked after. When you're well enough to leave we'll find somewhere for you to live and then you can start your new job as my bodyguard. Believe me, Todd, you wouldn't want anything to happen to me. I'm the good guy. I'm just a big softy compared to some of the people who are involved in this and they all know you're alive but that you've become a bit of a toothless tiger.'

With that he left and Todd dozed for a spell. The nurse came in and started to give him his daily dose of morphine.

'No,' he said. 'Enough. No more.'

'I'm only following orders,' she said, 'I've been told –'
Todd's look silenced her and she picked up her little tray and left.

FORTY SEVEN

Less than a month later, Todd was ensconced in a one bedroom flat in a luxury block near Vauxhall Bridge. Spectacular views of the river. He had a new name and a bank account with five grand in it.

The Voice called him on his new phone the day after he'd moved in.

'How did you get this number?' Todd asked him.

The Voice said: 'After all this time and you still ask bloody stupid questions like that.'

'Right. Who the hell am I to ask you anything?'

'Are we to assume that the laptop is lost?'

'Not necessarily,' Todd said.

'We need the scans.' The Voice told him.

'So do the other side.' Todd said. 'And neither of you is getting them. Life insurance.'

'You'll do as you're bloody well told, Todd.' The Voice was angry and quivered a little, like a badly tuned harp. 'Don't forget what you owe me. If it hadn't been for me you'd still be in some stinking glasshouse on the wrong side of Basra. Waiting to be shot.'

'You've played that card,' Todd told him. 'That's all in the past. You're not going to play it again. You want me on the inside, where you've always wanted me. I can be more use to you there. You don't need the scans. You just need to know they exist. You just need the other side to think you have them. You'll never use them as evidence, will you? There'll be no justice, will there? There'll be none of the old 'tried and sentenced by a judge and jury' malarkey. You'll just use them so you can blackmail the poor, sick bastards into giving you whatever it is you want them to give you.'

'It's the best we can do.' The Voice was calm again. 'They've got the media and the police and plenty of politicians doing their bidding, Todd. Play along with us and we'll finish the bastards for good. Do you think we approve of what they've done? Don't you think we want them fixed? Just as much as you do?'

'That's the first time you've told me that.' Todd said, 'Thanks for letting me know.'

'Get the scans, Todd. Then we'll finish the job and you can get the hell out.'

'Yeah, right.' Todd laughed coldly down the phone. 'Send me back to Basra in a Chinook, most likely.'

The Voice hung up on him.

He'd come off opiates a bit too rapidly and started to get cravings and nausea that only a fix would cure. He phoned Nurse Farzana and asked her to come round and fix him up. She said she couldn't possibly do anything like that but that she knew someone who might be able to help.

Later that day the doorbell sounded. He pressed the button that activated the video camera and saw a familiar female face with too much makeup on it. Her head was covered with a scarf and her eyes by a pair of ridiculously large sunglasses, but he recognised her immediately. He buzzed her in.

'Heard you were dead, Todd,' Dolores told him, once she'd peeled off the outer layer of her designer image and draped herself across his rented settee. So imagine my surprise when I got the call. Here's the gear. Or do you want me to fix it up for you. I know the drill. I used to use it myself but it gave me up.'

Todd took the little package and opened it. It looked and tasted all right so he let her cook about half of it up and then shoot it into his arm. The thought that she'd sold him up once, and Terry DeHavilland before him, and that the scag could be arsenic laced, did occur to him. But he needed a fix and had to take the risk; he couldn't have handed it back to her.

Once the first rush had faded and he was thinking straight again he gave her one of his cold hard stares and asked her who had told her he was dead.

'Grapevine, Todd,' she told him. 'Don't ask bloody stupid questions, you should know better than that by now.'

'Right,' he said. 'Who am I to ask questions? I don't even exist.'

She unfurled a ribbon from the back of her head and let her raven locks cascade around her shoulders. 'Except you do. Which makes you a pretty lucky guy the way things were stacked up against you. Just be grateful that they let you live.'

'They let me live, because if they'd killed me it would

have all come out. Now I just have to hope that no one else lets any of it out or they'll no longer have any reason to keep me alive. Will they?'

'There was an inquest and a funeral,' she said, ignoring his question. 'How do you think they faked all that?'

'They can fake anything. Did you go to my funeral?'

'Of course I did, darling. I'm sensational in black.'

'How much do you know?' he asked her.

'I just do as I'm told,' she said. 'Ours is not to question why, ours is but to do or die. I suppose that's 'pretend to die' in your case.'

He said nothing. Nothing really mattered. There was another decent sized hit in the little package she'd given him so that was all right.

The next time he looked at her she'd got an ipad out of her handbag. She came over and sat next to him and showed him a web page. It was the Wikipedia entry for Lord Hunter of Hellifield. There were images and a biography. His long, dreary life had been devoted to selfless public service. He also owned most of North Yorkshire.

'Know him?'

'Know of him,' Todd replied. 'He's on the list.'

'We think he's been got at by the Met and that he's ready to do a deal with them. Like you said, lover boy, you only stay pretend dead if everything stays under wraps. If it doesn't, you could get proper cold.'

'So, what do we do?'

'You do what you do best, what you were trained to do. What you did in Greasy Abdul Land.'

'That's not part of the deal. So far as I remember. Tell them I'm not interested.'

'Look,' she said. 'Someone has to do it. Time for some rough justice, Todd.'

'I ain't arguing with that.' Todd told her. 'But why do I have to do it? Why not Norcross and Barrowclough? They killed DeHavilland didn't they?'

'They're being watched,' she said. 'Did you think the whole sodding Met is in on this? There's some other coppers, spooky bastards – snooping around. Look, Todd, if you don't do it then we're all fucked.'

Todd said nothing, avoided looking at her.

'Besides, she said. 'The bastard deserves it. He'll get away jock free if you don't snuff the old twat. Think of that and think of how it will make his dirty old pals feel. Sitting there in their swanky private clubs drinking dry sherry and reading *The Times*. Give the bastards something to think about, Todd.'

Todd looked hard at her for a good long spell then said, 'How?

'I've set him up,' she told him, with pride in her voice. 'I'm already in there. Been showing him pictures of some pretty young lads. I think he wants to do a bit more sinning to give himself plenty to confess. Or maybe he just can't help himself. In any case he's asked me to take a pretty little boy round there. But I'll take you instead. Big ugly man. Well string the bastard up, Todd, and make it look like suicide. The cleaner will find him next morning and Bob's your Uncle.'

Todd didn't reply.

'What's on your mind? She asked him.

'I'm worried about the cleaner,' he said. 'Might get traumatised.'

FORTY EIGHT

The very next night at a quarter past twelve, Dolores rang the doorbell of Lord Hunter's Kensington town house and then stepped back a couple of paces so she could be seen through the peep hole. Todd was standing to one side where he couldn't be peeped and, when the door opened and Dolores stepped through it, he pushed his way in and slammed the door shut behind him.

'Who the hell are you?' the old man shrieked. He was a feeble looking, white haired old stick with fear and guilt written all over his face like tattoos on an Albanian gangster.

He turned on Dolores. 'What the hell are you playing at? I've paid good money and I bloody well expect –'

'Shut up,' Dolores told him. 'Don't make things any worse than they already are.'

Todd stood tall and smiled an ugly smile. The old man looked at him and shivered.'Do you have even the slightest idea of who I am?' he faltered.

'I told you to shut up.' Dolores said.

'If it's money you're after, there's nothing here.' There was something close to terror in his voice by now. 'But I can get some. How much do you want?'

Todd looked around him. Oil painted foxhunting scenarios in gilded frames and a statue, a classical male nude in an alcove. Not life sized but not far off. At the centre of the room there was a crystal chandelier. Todd wondered how much weight it would bear.

'We don't want your money,' Todd told him

'This is about Knoxley Hall isn't it?'

'Of course it is.'

The old man flopped down on an expensive looking settee. 'Then there must be some kind of misunderstanding,' he said, semi-assertively, 'I've already been contacted by... they wouldn't say who they were, but my guess would be MI5. I've agreed to cooperate. It's all coming out isn't it and quite right too... I mean... yes... I did some things but nothing really bad – I mean not as bad as some of the others – and these... chaps, they said that if I told them everything then there would be some kind of deal on the table. I suggest you go back to... whoever it is who's giving you your orders and I'm sure they'll confirm what I'm saying.'

'You really do think you're above the law, don't you?' Dolores said, 'Have you ever once even considered that there might be even the slightest possibility that you might get caught.'

The shadow of confusion crossed the old man's face. 'Things were different then,' He said. 'Chaps looked after each other. You see, one had to be in. Or rather, they made one think that one had to be in and then once one was ... in... they...'

Dolores slapped him and he put a hand up to his face

and started crying. 'You're a dirty, filthy piece of shit, aren't you?'

'Yes. Yes, I am.'

'Say it!'

'I'm a dirty, filthy piece of shit. Yes. I am.'

It looked like Dolores wanted to slap his face again but it was covered by his hands now so she slapped him around the head a couple of times instead.

'Stop it. That's enough,' Todd told her. 'You're having too much fun.'

He moved over and in front of Lord Hellifield, towering above him 'You!' he thundered, 'move your hands! Be a man. Some kind of a man.'

Lord Hunter took his hands away from his face and looked at Todd. Then at Dolores. Then back at Todd.

'You're a stupid fucker.' Todd told him, 'You confessed to the wrong crowd. They were testing you. Now they know you're prepared to cough it all up –'

'What? What are you going to do?'

A dark and deadly silence came down upon the room.

'What do you want?' Lord Hunter implored. 'I'll do anything, give you anything…'

Dolores sat down next to him and put a hand on his hands, which were on his lap. It was a kind and friendly gesture.

'When I was a little girl,' she said, 'I had a nasty, wicked old uncle who used to put his hand up my skirt. Come to think… ' She looked up at Todd, '…I rather enjoyed it. Anyhow, I knew what he was doing was wrong and he knew what he was doing was wrong and so I told him I'd tell my Dad unless he gave me lots of money and sweeties and toys and stuff. After a bit he stopped doing it and stopped coming around to see us. I think my Mum knew what was going on because she kept me away from him while she was still with Dad. But then when Dad and her split up, he started coming around again and it all started up again. I knew that if I told my Dad he'd kill the bastard so I didn't tell him in case my Dad did kill him and got sent to prison. Cos that would have been my fault wouldn't it? It would, wouldn't it?' And she raised her hands a couple of inches, made them into fists and made a little drum roll with them on the old man's knee. 'It would have been all my fault, wouldn't it?'

Lord Hunter seemed certain that this was a rhetorical question and so said nothing in response. But he couldn't prevent a sorry little choking noise from coming up through his throat and out of his mouth like excess wind from an overfed jackal.

'Yes. That would have been all my fault,' Dolores continued, 'so I couldn't tell anyone and so I had to leave home. At fourteen. I was a runaway. I came to London and got up to all sort of naughty things. Can you imagine that, Milord?' She grabbed his face and pulled it round to face her.' Can you imagine the sort of naughty things I got up to? I'll bet you can.

'A couple of years later and I was on the jolly old smack water. Like he is now, poor bastard.' She raised her eyes towards Todd's monolithic presence. 'But, I was lucky. I got some help. Twelve Steps and all that bollocks and that sorted me out and I came to realise that I was just using the brown stuff to cover up all my horrible, unbearable feelings. See?'

Lord Hunter nodded. There was a flicker of hope in his eyes now.

'You know what I did? I confronted my uncle. That took some bollocks I can tell you. But it was part of my program. I was on a fucking program see? What they call a fucking program. Anyhow, I had to confront and listen to what the old cunt had to say for himself. I was looking for closure, see?

'Course he wouldn't admit to nothing. He wasn't stupid. They could never have proved what he done. But he told me something. Something interesting. Would you like to know what it was?'

He nodded and looked at Todd and then back at her.

'He told me that when he was a little boy he'd been fiddled around with. He'd had a wicked uncle too, poor saddo sod. So, do you see what's going on here? Fucking obvious innit really? The abused becomes the abuser and all that. Got it? Now does this theory apply to you, Michael?'

He could only nod. But he seemed pleasantly surprised that she knew his name.

'Yes,' he said. 'It was when I was at school.'

'Ah. Yes. I thought so.' Dolores raised her hands again and placed them on either side of his white haired head. 'Nasty old British public school system eh? Yes that makes sense. So look – you're not a bad person really are you? You're a sick person, aren't you? I mean you're a real sad sicko. Aren't you? Yes.'

286

He nodded again. Doubt and confusion alternating with the flicker of hope.

'So… really…you need help don't you?'

Now there was real hope in his eyes. He nodded again. 'I'll do whatever you want, anything at all.'

'Yes,' she said. 'Good. And at the same time as helping you we can study you, you know. Like a laboratory rat. And learn all about what makes you do the things you do and then we can use that data to help others like you. Get it?'

He nodded vigorously.

'Then maybe, in time, we can eradicate whatever dirty fucking revolting, putrid, filthy, shitty, crappy, fucking saddo, sicko, fucking sickness it is that you've got.'

'Yes,' He said. 'I can see that that… could be possible.'

'Of course… on the other hand, we could just kill you.'

All hope vanished.

'But that would be inhuman. That would be the sort of thing that the Nazis would have done, wouldn't it? I bet that's what they did to cunts like you. I bet they would have rounded you all up and fucking gassed you. I bet there weren't any fucking nonces in Nazi Germany. Still, we mustn't stoop to the level of that bunch of bastards must we, eh? No. So we're going to take you somewhere nice. Somewhere where you'll be looked after and helped. You need help. Now…' and she shoved his face away from her, 'it's time to go to sleep.'

Todd moved away from them and crossed the room in two long strides; the old man's eyes followed him.

Dolores took out the chloroform-laced handkerchief that she'd prepared earlier and placed it over Lord Hunter's nose and mouth.

It didn't quite knock him out but stopped him struggling long enough for Todd to kill him by breaking his neck.

Then Dolores took out a length of thin, strong rope and Todd made a noose out of one end of it and placed it around the old man's neck. Then he pulled him up and held him in a standing position while Dolores stood on a chair and tied the open end of the length of rope around the centrepiece chandelier. Todd let go and let him dangle there. Like a dead crow's wing.

It had been heavy, stressful work and there was a friendly looking little pub right where their car was parked, so they stepped inside for a drink. Todd had a large Irish and Dolores, of course, had a Bloody Mary.

'You've done that before,' She said. 'Haven't you?'

He shrugged and knocked back his whisky.

They went back to Todd's place. He needed a fix. She went off into the bathroom and left him to stew. He waited as long as he could and then rapped on the door.

'Come out,' he said. 'You know what you have to do.'

She came out with the hypodermic in her hand. 'Is this what you want?' she said.

'Get on with it,' he told her.

'You'll have to catch me first,' She said and she dodged behind the sofa holding the needle aloft, giggling like a schoolgirl.

He wasn't for chasing around after her. He sat down

and waited and a moment later she came around and sat on his knee and ruffled his hair.

'Big boy want his nice reward for being a very good boy then?'

He just held his arm out and leaned back and waited.

Soon it came.

FORTY NINE

She came twice every day after that: mornings and evenings. He could just about make it through on two a day. Anyhow, that was all he was getting. Sometimes he fucked her but more often than not he just didn't bother. They didn't talk much. But one day, out of the blue, he asked her a question.

'What was all that about? All that crap about that uncle of yours? Is any of that even true?'

'Gosh,' she said. 'Are we going to talk about me?'

He gave her his cold, dead-eyed look. She held his gaze for a spell but then stepped away from him with the air of one who doesn't need to prove the power of their will. She looked out at the river for a few seconds and then returned to where she'd been sitting.

'What do you think?' she asked him, moving back into his field of vision. 'Do you think it's true?'

'How the fuck do I know?'

'You just don't know, do you?' she said. 'Maybe it's all just a fantasy. Maybe it's something I just made up. Perhaps we could play it out. Come on Todd, *you* can be my wicked uncle. Would you like that?'

'No.' He said. 'Course I wouldn't. I just asked you a question that's all. If I'd have known you were going to get all weird on me I wouldn't have bothered.'

She threw back her head and laughed. 'Oh Todd. You're fucking priceless.'

Todd wasn't laughing.

'Anyhow,' she said, 'I've got some news for you. Orders from on high. You're coming off the stuff – right now.'

'Like fuck,' he told her. And he stood and took a step towards her. 'Give. Give now or I'll –'

'You'll what?' She spat the words out at him. 'You fucking animal.'

'Just give.' He told her.

She put her face up close to his: 'Why don't you learn some social skills? Why don't you learn to communicate without threatening people? You're just a great big brute. It was fun for a while but, straight up, Todd, the appeal of being with a fucking baboon is starting to wear off now.'

'Fucking give.' He somehow knew she'd have to fix him and sure enough, she did.

'Alright.' he managed to say, when the pain had gone. 'Let's communicate. You're all right. You're an all right girl. Bit weird but nothing I can't live with. I'm sorry that you've tired of me but, you know, we're going to have to stick together. What you think they got in store for us? When we've outlived our usefulness? What's going to happen then? We better make some plans.'

'We can get away, Todd,' she told him. 'We can run. I've got a little money and I can always make more. I know how to get money out of men. And you can look after me. Make sure none of the bastards cuts up rough. I'll take their money, Todd and give them nothing in return and if the bastards get nousy you can drop the twats.'

All council estate girl now.

'I'll think about it,' Todd told her. 'But I thought the pimp was supposed to keep the whore on smack. We got it the other way around.'

She smiled at that and he nodded out for a spell. When he'd come down a bit, but not far enough to need another hit, she gave him some car keys and a scrap of paper with a Mayfair address on it. 'There's a Bentley, downstairs in the garage. You won't be able to miss it. It's the only one there. Pick up your passenger at this address. Be there at twelve and just wait outside.'

'He took one look at the scrap of paper and handed it back. 'I don't need that. I've been there before.'

Brook Street. West End. He double parked and put the hazard lights on and waited. Doing nothing was bad. The craving started. His nose started running and the back of his throat dried up. Then the back door opened and Warrington got in.

'Drive,' he said.

Todd moved forward at a snail's pace and watched Lord Warrington in the rear-view mirror.

'There's something we need to discuss,' Lord Warrington said. 'It's your little friend. The journalist.'

'What about her?'

'Well, as you know, the laptop wasn't found for a very

long time after your… disappearance. She and her council house friends had it. We've now managed to recover it but it seems likely, well, certain in fact, that she's copied the contents. She's trying to make a name for herself. We were pretty certain we had her under control. I don't need to bore you with the details but the hold we had over her has been lost and now she's running around trying to get the best price for the… information and documentary evidence that we both know is on there. We've offered her money but she thinks she can get that anyway from whichever media organisation offers her the best price. And she wants the fame and glory that she seems to think will accrue from being seen as the talented and courageous crusading journalist who has smashed the evil Westminster paedophile ring and told the whole wicked story to a grateful world.'

'Why are you telling me this?'

'Because, if this does come out,' Lord Warrington's eyes narrowed, 'Then we'll have no further reason to keep you alive will we?'

'In that case,' Todd said, into the rear view mirror. 'I suppose I'd better do you, before you do me.'

'Don't be so damned ridiculous!' Lord Warrington sneered. 'The point is, Todd, that you have as much to lose as we do. If you come back to life you're very much in the frame for a couple of murders. None of which you actually committed but, let's face it, you have murdered, so justice will be served in that respect. That's how it works, you know. I was a magistrate for many years and we always found any lowlife scum that were brought before us guilty, in the full knowledge that if they hadn't committed the particular crime of which they stood accused, then they'd have done something else equally despicable and got away with it.'

'You're rattling on a bit. Get to the point.'

'Very well,' Lord Warrington said, between gritted teeth. 'As we used to say in the foreign office, either turn her, which is to say, bring her round to our way of thinking, or burn her, which is to say... well I think you probably know what I mean by that. By the way, her father committed suicide a few days ago so she might be a bit hysterical. Now, drive me back to my club.'

'So why didn't you get darling Dolores to give me this assignment?' Todd asked. 'Like you did the first one.'

'I have no idea what you're talking about. There have been no previous assignments. I chose to give you this assignment myself because only you and I must know of this. As things stand no one else does know. No one else must ever know. I'm relying on your dramatically heightened instinct for survival to understand what needs to be done and to do it.'

Todd swung the Bentley around Grosvenor Square Gardens and back along Brook Street. He stopped in front of the door, got out of the car and opened the rear door for his Lordship.

'I think I'm due for a pay rise,' Todd said.

Lord Warrington hurried inside without promising anything.

FIFTY

It was around this time that the phone hacking scandal came to dominate the news agenda. It was suddenly no longer okay to listen in to other people's voice mail messages and the fourth estate was now divided against itself – roughly along the lines of those who had got caught and those who hadn't, and could therefore moralise against those who had.

Dolores kept Todd informed as to what was going down in the murky world of investigative journalism.

'It's all gone fucking mental,' she told him in the kitchen of his apartment just after she'd administered his daily fix. 'They're all shitting themselves – and serve the bastards right. It didn't seem so bad when it was all celebrity shit but since they hacked that murdered girl's phone it's all gone a bit chaotic. I've heard that the redtops are releasing stuff they've had for years just to deflect the shit storm sideways. You watch! DJs, pop stars, actors, footballers. They got all this from hacking and before that from bribing coppers. It's a warning. They're warning them now. Don't complain about being hacked. Not unless you're as white as the driven snow. And none of them are. What a carry on! Celebrities getting caught for shagging under age girls and the hacks are getting done for hacking their phones and the pigs are getting done for doing fuck all about it. 'Cept taking bungs of course.'

'What's any of that got to do with me?' Todd asked her, dreamily.

'I just thought you might be interested to know what's happening in the world that's all. Not only that. Mo's still doing the rounds. Been back on the telly with his face all blacked out and the voice of an actor speaking his lines. You can tell it's him though.'

'What's he saying now?'

'He's saying it was Lord Hunter. Not giving any other names. The press are calling him a coward and saying Lord Hunter killed himself because people like Mo and that MP bloke have hounded him to death.'

'So it's all coming out then?'

'No. That's just the point. It's not coming out. Or rather, it is coming out but no one is taking the blindest bit of notice because they're all concentrating on the phone hacking story.'

She paused, took a mirror from her bag and started to examine her face in it.

'In any case, nobody gives a shit about it. Especially when it's just some sinister, shadowy little man coughing up the cancer. If there was something else, something more concrete…'

Todd stayed on his back on the settee. His eyes remained closed. His face showed about as much emotion as a concrete pillar.

'Oh. By the way,' she said. 'Interesting development. Remember your little journalist friend?'

'Leave her out of this.'

'It's got to be done.'

'No.'

'It's either you or her. If she spills, you're finished.

Todd said nothing.

'Anyway,' Dolores said, after a spell, 'there's another job to do first. Heard of Sir Donald Sowerby?

Todd groaned, 'Yes, I've heard of him. He's on the list.'

And so it was that that very night on the stroke of midnight Dolores and Todd were sitting in a spacious Hampstead kitchen with Sir Donald himself, yet another feeble, white-haired old man.

'What a lovely kitchen,' Dolores said. 'Do you like to cook?'

'No,' he said. 'Not at all. I have a man who does all that.'

'I'll bet you do.' Dolores said, 'and where is he now, this man of yours?'

'I've given him the night off,' Sir Donald didn't bother to hide his irritation.

'He's gone to visit his cousin in Cleethorpes.'

'Night off eh?' Todd said. He felt like joining in for once. 'Wish I could have a night off.'

'I wasn't expecting this.' Sir Donald said to Dolores. 'I was led to believe –'

'Oh we're just the advance party,' Dolores told him. 'Others are on their way.'

'Others?' Sir Donald, betrayed a whisker of libidinous excitement. 'What others? What manner of other?'

'Let me show you.' Dolores said, and moved over next to him. She took out her trusty tablet and turned it on.

'Would you like it to be him?' She asked, pushing the tablet under his nose. 'Do you recognise that one?'

'Well I… yes I suppose I do but that was ever such a long time back. He'll be far too old by now. Look. I thought this had all been arranged. I was supposed to get the boy who came before. I specifically requested he should be invited back.'

'Oh. Oh I see. So what is it about him that you particularly like?'

'Well… you see… there was a certain… chemistry…'

'Chemistry eh? Hear that, Todd? Him and that other kid had a certain fucking chemistry. What kind of chemistry? I'd love to know.'

'Look. I'd rather not go into that. When will the others arrive? I'm finding all this really rather disappointing and I'm sure you both know that my disappointment will not be tolerated. Not at all. I think you know why. I'm to be kept happy. You should know that. In fact… I'm going to make a call. I'm going to find out just what in God's name is going – '

The old man reached for his phone which was on the table in front of him. Todd reached it first, picked it up and then smashed it on the tiled floor.

The old man looked from Todd to Dolores and then back again at Todd and seemed to get a whiff of what would happen next.

'Please?' He said. 'Please don't.'

'You know what?' Dolores pushed her face right up to his. 'When I was a little girl I had a horrid uncle…'

'Oh, spare me that again.' Todd told her and he broke the old man's neck.

FIFTY ONE

Lucy wiped the rain from her hair and looked straight at the dead man's face in the rear view mirror. His lips curled in the semblance of a smile, mouth only as usual. He'd grown a beard and had his hair cut short but there was no disguising those cold and predatory eyes.

'I thought you were dead,' she said. 'I saw you... I saw your body... there was an inquest and a funeral. I went to your fucking funeral for Christ's sake!'

Todd said, 'I bet you're sensational in black.'

'Fuck you.'

'It was a setup. I only had one option. What was the funeral like? Moving?'

'What do you want? What do you want with me, Todd?'

'I was sent here. We have to talk. They need to keep me alive now so as I don't tell tales out of school. All the facts are with a friend of mine. If I don't check in with him the truth comes out. But if it comes out anyway then... I'm a dead man – and this time for real.'

'Oh. I see. So you want me to not expose this bunch of... powerful... evil... perverted – '

'That's what they sent me here to say to you but, look, I want the bastards taken down just as much as you do. But I'd kind of like to stay alive. Or… come back to life. Anyhow they'll never let you publish the story. They've got the press and the police and the politicians in their pockets.'

'I'm getting sick and tired of people telling me what I'm not going to be allowed to do.'

'If enough people tell you the same thing that usually means it's true.'

'Who sent you? How did you know where to find me?'

His silence told her what she needed to know.

'You're working for… my god you've gone over to them.'

'I'm out for myself and no one else. Just like you.'

He started the engine and they moved off. But they didn't get far. A large white van pulled out from where it had been parked and came around in front of them, blocking their way out.

The passenger door opened and Emma appeared in a pair of scruffy old tennis shoes and a hoodie. She walked through the rain to the driver's side of the car.

'Get in.' Todd said. Emma raised a hand of reassurance in the direction of whoever it was who was sitting in the van and then got into the back of the car and next to Lucy. The van moved off and out of their way.

Todd followed it out of the mews, along Chichester Street and into Lupus.

'Fuck me! I thought you were dead!' Emma said.

'That's what you were supposed to think.' He told her.

Emma looked at Lucy and said, 'Sorry about your dad.'

'I'm not.' Lucy said, without looking up from her phone. 'I hated the bastard all my life. Then I hated him even more when I found out what he'd done. I'm glad he's dead. It makes things easier now I don't have to worry that what I write might put him inside. In fact it gives my testimony an extra layer of credibility. I don't suppose either of you two would understand...'

She paused and waited and no one responded so she tried to get a fix on Todd's black eyes in the mirror. But his eyes moved back to the road so she looked down at her phone instead.

'So what does his lordship intend to do, now that his whole world is falling apart around his shoulders?' she said, to no one in particular.

'Is it?' Todd said. 'He seems to think that he's still in with a chance.'

'I've got all the names,' Lucy said, looking up from her phone, 'and scans of signed witness statements.'

'He thinks I've got them too,' Todd said. 'That's why I'm still alive. He thinks that if anything happens to me then it will all come out.'

Lucy went back to her phone.

'They've got Marcus,' Emma said. 'You met Marcus didn't you?'

Todd nodded. 'Nice kid.' He remembered the talk he'd had with him that day. How hopeful he'd been. How protective of his mother. Brave and fierce. 'Nice kid.' He said again.

'The best way to get Marcus away from them is to get the whole story out,' Lucy said. 'Once this is in the public domain, they wouldn't dare do anything to him and then you can start the legal process of getting him released into your care. If you do anything illegal then you'll only make matters worse.'

'You're not giving those scans to anybody,' Todd said. 'Those scans keep me alive. They're my insurance policy. If you release that information they've got no more reasons not to kill me.'

'Everyone thinks you're dead anyway,' Lucy said. 'Why would they bother killing you?'

Emma said; 'I told them that if anything happens to Marcus that I'd give those names to the papers and the coppers. So same thing applies to me. You're not telling no cunt. You'll be dead if you do.'

Lucy leaned back in her seat and closed her eyes. 'For Christ's sake! You can't be serious! You know this will all have to come out. Once those evil bastards are all inside you can stop worrying about them.'

'I've got a plan,' Todd said. Plan of action. Once I'm done you can publish, go on telly, internet, whatever you want. You'll be famous.'

Lucy watched his eyes in the mirror. 'Go on.'

'I been making out I don't care about what they done… to them kids… that all I cared about was my own skin. Well… I do care about my own skin. I'm staying alive, you can bank on it, but whilst they think I'm their fucking poodle… I can get this sorted. Properly.'

Christ, she thought, *He's going to kill them.*

Then he turned to Emma and said, 'I'll get Marcus away from them. And back to you.'

'When?' Emma asked him.

'Soon as I can. Give me your number.'

They exchanged numbers and Emma said, 'Yeah. I trust you. You do things the right way. Not like her with her constant fucking bullshit.' She tossed her head in the general direction of Lucy and then got out and went back to the van.

Lucy said, 'Look, Todd, I'm in negotiation with a number of major mainstream media organisations. This *is* going to come out. We can do these bastards over but we have to do it in the right way. If you're not prepared to do it my way then I'm afraid we're going to have to part company.'

She grabbed the door handle but Todd was in charge of the central locking and he'd decided that she wasn't going anywhere. Not for the time being.

'Not now,' he said. Wait a few days. There's something going down. We can catch them at it.'

'At what? Hurting kids?' There was frustration in her voice now. 'They need to be stopped now. Before any more kids are damaged by them. I'm sorry about Marcus, but they'll all be cared for properly once that... scum's been skimmed off. Let's face it, he'll be better off in care or with foster parents than he would be on that dreadful estate with a bunch of junkies.'

'You know what? I got to know Marcus a little bit when I was hiding out in that council flat – saw how he was when he was with his mum. He was a happy boy.

Then. Maybe you didn't notice that. Maybe you were too busy trying to get his mother to pin some dodgy sex charge on me. You got that one right, didn't you?'

She looked down at her phone.

'All I'm asking you to do is wait. A few days, that's all.'

'I'm not promising anything,' she said.

He unlocked the door and said, 'Get out then. Go and do what you have to do. If you think they'll let you. You'll just alarm them and they'll close ranks. You'll be stopped.'

'And you? What are you going to do?'

'I'm going to give it to them.' He said. 'I'm going to give them what they really deserve.'

She looked again into his eyes. They were the eyes of a killer. She guessed, as she looked into them, that once you'd started killing you just had to keep on doing it, like smoking crack or eating cream cakes.

'Oh,' she said. 'I see. So you're going to kill them. You can't kill them all, you fucking caveman. There has to be a trial. There have to be convictions. There has to be justice. Think about it. You're going to kill them to get them off your back, not to punish them. Not because they deserve to die.'

'Two birds,' he said. And then, more thoughtfully, 'But justice. Yes. Justice.'

'Let me out.' She said. 'Or are you going to kill me too?'

Quite worryingly he didn't gainsay that.

'You've got to keep quiet.' He told her. 'You've got to put your journalistic ambitions on hold for a spell. You're out of your depth.'

'Are you threatening me? She asked him.

But he wouldn't, surely couldn't, hurt her. She remembered their moment of intimacy. Remembered his vulnerability and just how fucking attractive that had made him. She suddenly wanted to re-live that moment. More than anything. But he was one of them. It just wasn't on. 'Let me out.' She said again.

This time he did.

FIFTY TWO

'How do I know you're not on their side?' Todd asked the Voice. 'It was you set me off like a fucking nodding bunny and I've been nodding ever since.'

'You got yourself into this, Todd. I've given you options that you never would have had. Be grateful.'

'So we're just going to carry on where we left off are we? Just like that.'

'Yes. Of course. Why wouldn't we?'

'They're giving me options. They've set me up a new life. Got a new identity and a nice new pad and a little dolly bird who gives me all what I need. I don't fucking need you no more.'

The Voice said: 'Don't try thinking for yourself, you big stupid bastard. It really doesn't suit you. Remember whose side you're on.'

'I don't know whose side I'm on. I've never known. Who the fuck are you anyhow?How do I know you're not one of them?'

The Voice said: 'How dare you suggest that. I've spent ten years of my life hunting down these bastards and I'm now very close. *We're* now very close. It's not going to end the way I would have liked it to but it *will* end and there will be justice.'

'How's that then?' Todd wanted to know. 'You going to round them all up and put them in the dock? Make sure the judge gives them all life sentences?'

'Not exactly. But there's going to be a judicial inquiry. We'll make sure Her Honour the judge will get all the evidence. Of course there will be depositions and counter depositions and injunctions and subpoenas and extradition proceedings on those who have fled to foreign climes. They'll have it over their heads for evermore. There'll be no end to it.'

'You just said it was nearly over.'

'For you I meant. You deserve a bit of a life now I suppose. New identity and all that.'

'Not bothered about that really. I'd rather just carry on killing them. Can't be caught they say. Happy days.'

The Voice laughed without joy. Didn't seem surprised by that.

'Death's too good for them,' he said. 'We'll torment them for the rest of their lives. We've got the evidence now and they're starting to realise it. We're going to show them the evidence. Bit by bit. Drip drip drip.'

'You're going to blackmail them?'

'Well I suppose there might be a bit of that going down but that's not the primary objective.'

'So what is?'

'Make the bastards suffer and make sure that it never happens again.'

'So you still need me then? I'm good at that. Making people suffer I mean.'

'I'm talking about psychological pain not the physical

kind. Too subtle for you. But there is one final thing that I want you to do.'

Todd said nothing. Didn't ask. Had a feeling that he was going to be told.

'There's going to be a grand hurrah.'

'A what?'

'They think they're in the clear. They think the recent 'suicides' have been a cleansing of the weak. They're having a party. Tonight. There will be children and old men.'

'Where?'

'You'll be told,' The Voice told him.

'The boy? Marcus?'

'Will be there.'

'So what do you want me to do?'

'There will be a raid. It won't be a real one of course but they'll think they're being arrested, think they're being charged. Then they'll be released to a living hell. It will never end for them.'

'So what do you want me to do?'

'Lord Warrington is to get special treatment.'

'Oh?'

'You'll get him out of there.'

'And?'

'Take him to wherever the satnav directs you.'

'What?' Todd pressed the brake pedal. The car stopped abruptly. 'You're letting him go. You're letting the bastard go.'

'That's not what I said.'

'That's it though, isn't it? You're letting him off the hook.'

'That's enough, Todd. Remember your place. This is a strategic move. What I'm commanding you to do is what has to be done. Do it. And then you're free. The children who are still at risk will be unharmed. Freed. Taken to an appropriate place of safety. Do this and you will also be free. And safe.'

'I'll bet you and him went to the same school and all that,' Todd sneered this down the phone at him. 'Old pals stick together don't they? Where you're from. There's no way you'd stitch up an old pal, now is there? How many of these fuckers are your old mates? One or two? All of them? I don't know who you are but I know where you come from. How do I know you're any different from that lot? You sound like them. I'll bet you probably look like them. Bet you belong to the same clubs as them. Brook Street, is it? Were you in there that day when I went in after him. I'll bet you were. I'll bet you were sat there listening. In a leather chair with a glass of vintage port.'

'Don't be ridiculous, Todd' The Voice told him. 'Port is served after dinner, not before lunch.'

'Ha ha what a hoot. It's all a big hoot to you and your lot. Isn't it? All a big game. Christ, you know what? I can't really blame you. Sitting there in your clubs, ruling the fucking world. Issuing instructions. I suppose that's how the Empire was run. But the Empire's gone, hasn't it? And now all your lot has left is this fucking gig. Bit of a fucking come down but better than having to work for a living – '

'That's quite enough. I suppose you needed to say all that but you're wide of the mark. I have nothing in common with that man. He has deluded himself into believing he is some kind of custodian of the dying embers of an older, kinder, more decent world when, in fact, he's a threat to that very thing. *I am* what he has deluded himself into thinking *he is*. I have the responsibility to deliver him to where he belongs. Or rather *we* have that responsibility. You and I together. It just happens to be that it is I who must make the decisions and issue the orders and it is you who must carry them out. That's just the way it is, Todd.'

Todd hung up.

FIFTY THREE

I was a warrior once but now I'm a drug-addled monster who kills old men. I'm a murderer now. And it doesn't matter what they've done. What I did was still murder, still wrong, and the fact that they were old, old men makes it even more wrong. I can forget about it once I've had a dose of the good old Henry Horse but when I'm strung out like a hangman's rope I can't stop thinking about it. Can't get it out of my mind. There they are, grinning their dead men's grins and swinging a little in the cold night air surrounded by their knickknacks and their objets d'art. The fuckers deserved to die so why does it bug me like this? Christ knows I've killed in cold blood before.

So who is Dolores? Whose side is she on? Who sent her to me? Was it Lord Warrington? Or the Voice? She screwed Terry over all right, no doubt whose side she was on back then. But the pendulum's swung back the other way now and I'm assuming she's been turned. The same way I've been turned. From the darkness to the light. But isn't that what they call the devil? The Lord of Light? In any case, where is the bitch? It's time for my medicine! They're coming after me – those old, dead men with their inch long teeth and their claw-like hands.

Come on you bitch. It's feeding time.

The door buzzer sounded. That familiar figure in the entryphone screen. Scarf and sunglasses. She held up a little packet. He recognised the design and pressed the button that opened the door.

She took the hypodermic needle out of her Hermes handbag and placed it, with a spoon and a little plastic lemon full of citrus juice, nice and symmetrically on the nicely polished mahogany coffee table. She sat down across from him and opened the packet. Then she poured some powder on to the spoon, added the lemon juice and sucked the liquid up into the syringe.

He fastened a belt around a bicep to enlarge a vein but she didn't finish the job. Instead she stood up and walked away from him towards his unused open plan kitchen.

'Get on with it!' He growled at her.

'Or else?' She hurled back at him. 'Or else what, Todd? You going to make me? You going to punch me? No. I don't think you're the type who'd punch me. Slap me though. You'd slap me wouldn't you? Make me think a punch was coming. I've had it all before. How many fucking men like you do you think I've had down the years? You're my type, you see. Big brutal bastards like you turn me on. But you know that don't you? Maybe I'm your type too. In some ways. Oh you wouldn't settle down with me. Course not. That's not what I'm for, is it? I'm just someone to stick your great big filthy dick into. Isn't that right? That's what you think of me, isn't it? Isn't that what you think of me?'

'Course it fucking is,' he told her. 'Now give it to me. Come on, Dee, then we can fuck if you want.'

'You won't want to fuck when you've had this and you know you won't, you lying bastard. You'll say anything to get it though, won't you?'

Todd just lay back and looked up at the ceiling. It felt like he was crawling along it like a lizard.

Lizards. That was it. Lizards. She thought they were all lizards. Maybe she thought he was one.

'I need that,' he told her. 'Give it to me, Dee and then we can go and kill some more lizards'

'Men,' she said. 'men fucking men fucking men fucking men…'

On and on like that. Todd wanted to scream but he didn't. He just about managed not to.

He could just about not grab her too. Not squeeze the life out of her. She would squirt the stuff on to the carpet if he did that. That would be bad.

'…men fucking men fucking men fucking men…'

'Shut up!' he said. 'Shut up and think. We are where we are. Neither of us want to be here. But it's where we are. Give. Please. Come on. Give.' It was the closest he would ever come to begging but still she held out.

'The first man who ever fucked me was my uncle. I was twelve years old.'

Oh, change the fucking record!

'He got it for free but after that you've all had to pay. Yes. You, Todd. Not *Them*. *You*, you bastard. You're just like the rest of them. Terry DeHavilland – weak fucker he was. Did what I told him. Sacrificial fucking lamb.

Sacrificed for me, by me, Todd. He died so that I could live. You think you're strong where he was weak? You're weaker than him. At least he had some brains. How many men? I can't fucking count how many. But I can count how many had anything left when I was finished with them. Absolute fucking zero. Absolutely fucking none of the fucking bastards –'

'Alright. Enough. You've made your point. Now give. Come on. Give.'

'Alright,' she said. 'You'll get it. I just needed you to know… all that… and she pulled the belt tight around his bicep and flicked his vein to make it big and then pierced it with the needle and pushed the plunger.

Straight away he knew that something was wrong. He leaned back and closed his eyes. There was some relief but not as much as usual. Not enough. And there was something else. When he opened his eyes the room was bigger, as big as a ballroom. And Dolores was gone.

FIFTY FOUR

'Alright,' said Lucy to Smelly Baz in a pub near Smith Square, 'I'm ready to hand it all over. All of it.' She patted a buff coloured folder that she'd placed on the table in front of her.

'Why now?' he asked her.

'Because it's the right thing to do.'

He let out a short and humourless laugh. 'Spare me the moral crap, love,' he said. 'I'm not in the mood. Haven't you seen the news?'

'Of course I have,' she said. 'You're being challenged. Did you think it was going to be an easy ride?'

'They're calling me a witch hunter,' he said. 'Two suicides are being blamed on me. I can't proceed.'

'There's proof now,' she said, 'and I'm prepared to give you everything. All I ask is that we coordinate things. You subpoena the perpetrators at around the same time as the documentary film is released. Then the media will get hold of it.'

'I see.' he said. 'Yes, I know how that works. And the only paper that gets the inside track is the one that you sell your story to, right? And they'll get the book serialisation rights. There will be a book, won't there?'

'Yes. Yes, there will be a book and why shouldn't there be a book? Look, I've worked bloody hard on this and apart from anything else I've got personal reasons to expose this whole dirty… disgusting –'

'Oh, of course,' he said. 'What an angle! Your own father…'

'Fuck you,' she said. Her voice still soft but very, very hostile. 'How fucking dare you?' She stood up and placed the folder on the table. 'It's all there. You've got everything you need now. And parliamentary privilege to go with it. Do your duty. Try to be brave.'

He laughed again. 'You just don't get it do you? I'm not being got at by that lot.' He pointed at the folder. 'It's coming from my own team – my party. They're not all fucking aristocrats – the pedos I mean. Some of them are on my side of the House. If I exposed them I'd be committing political suicide. I'm sorry but I'm not prepared to do that.'

'You cowardly bastard.'

He looked up and past her and fidgeted, and then scratched his fat arse.

She picked up the folder and was about to leave when something occurred to her.

'How do they know?' she asked him. 'This hasn't even come out yet. How do they know what's going to be exposed?'

All that got her was another weary laugh.

She stood up and walked out. She had nowhere to go, so she just walked. Along the river. After a while she realised she was heading, instinctively, towards Dolphin Square. She stopped and turned and walked in the other direction; took off down a side street.

So what now? Who could she turn to? Adam? The very idea appalled her but perhaps that was the only option. She had to do something. She absolutely had to stay busy, had to have some kind of assignment to throw herself into. Or she would have to face herself. Not ready for that just yet. She despised Adam now but that didn't mean she couldn't deal with him. In any case, was she right to despise him? Perhaps she despised those aspects of him that reminded her of the worst aspects of herself. He was only human. She'd built him up too high, had believed all the crap about him having got to his exalted position at such a young age through hard work allied to integrity and intelligence. Now she realised he'd just wormed his way up through compromise and by prostituting himself intellectually and most likely physically as well. He'd been out for himself all along. She laughed at the thought, at the very notion, that she'd believed him to be genuinely idealistic and that it was his idealism that had propelled him to prominence.

So that was one option, to go crawling back to Adam. She visualised that potential future. Could she face that? First the humiliation and then the mind numbing workaday boredom.

Alternatively, she could hitch her wagon to Mad Jack Todd. Danger. Insecurity. Fantastic sex. No boredom there. Insanity. Adrenalin fuelled uncertainty. Life and death. Derring Do. One wonderful adventure after another with him to protect her. No! She would protect him! She would tame him, all for his own good of course, she would shear off some of his wilder proclivities and then protect him from the subtleties of modern, urban existence. He couldn't go around hurting and killing people. There was no future in that. She would be a crusading reporter and he would watch her back. In any case, he didn't need to hurt people. All he needed to do was look at them and they shut their mouths and backed off.

Then reality came crashing home. It was all a fantasy. That could never be. She wasn't a big enough risk taker to do anything like that. The adrenalin died away. But anyhow, there was one last chance, all was not yet lost. There was always Henry. Perhaps she'd come through, now Lucy had the evidence.

She stopped and looked around her, found herself at the back of the Abbey. There was a group of tourists being escorted around by a shabbily dressed tour guide. She waited for them to move on and then called Henrietta. Voicemail.

'I've got everything you asked me to get.' She messaged.

Then she waited in the shadow of the great Abbey for Henry to call her back.

She'd have spent less time waiting for the next monarch to be anointed.

FIFTY FIVE

The walls of the apartment that had expanded like a concertina immediately after Dolores fixed him up now started to close in on him. The roof was descending, slowly but perceptibly. After a few minutes of this he had to hunch down, right down, onto his hands and knees, at which point he realised that not only was the ceiling descending but that the floor was slowly rising to meet it. He crawled over to the coffee table and looked across its surface where the citizens of a small Chinese city were going about their business. At its very centre was the Temple of the Keys. Car keys to be precise. *Pick us up* they entreated him in unison, *and get us out of here.*

Driving the car was surprisingly easy although he did set off on the wrong side of the road. A large white van that was parked right outside his building waited until he was a few hundred yards away and then moved away from the kerb and followed him.

The satnav took him south across the river at Putney and then right, onto the South Circular, towards Barnes. Soon the terraces he passed were replaced by identical semis and then they in their turn were replaced by a succession of large, detached houses. All Todd saw of them were the gates. He had a moment of lucidity, or at least he thought he did. But then the gargoyles on the gates came to life and started talking to him. *Run for your life, Todd,'* they told him. *Run for your fucking life!*

Something told him not to listen and after a mile or so the chattering stopped. His sat nav told him to go left. He went left. And then right.

The building he was circumnavigating was in darkness. Then it loomed. It was large and imposing. It was gloomy and foreboding. There was a derelict old sign that announced its identity in big, black, gothic lettering.

KNOXLEY HALL

The gate at the back of the house was open and had nothing to say. He drove through the gateway and up a short, unlit drive. When he'd run out of tarmac he got out of the car and walked towards what looked like a service entrance.

There were comings and goings. Mainly comings. People were waiting to be admitted. All men. Lots of men. As Todd approached he saw there was someone or something standing at the threshold. It resembled a man; it was a biped and was dressed in an old-fashioned three-piece suit. But it had the head of a lizard: a chameleon or perhaps a gekko.

As each arrival reached the front of the line he took out a smartphone and placed it on a hand-held electronic reading device that the lizard-headed man held firmly in his long-nailed claws.

Todd approached. He had no smartphone. Couldn't remember where he'd put it. Lizardhead held out a claw. Todd looked him in the eyes and shrugged.

'Name?' the lizardman growled.

'Todd.'

The lizardman touched his ear with his claw and listened, head to one side. Then he looked at Todd, gave a little hiss and stood aside.

Todd joined the line of middle-aged men. It moved, slowly, agonisingly slowly, into some kind of anteroom. There, each man was received: a masked and cloaked individual took the coat of each arrival and in return proffered a black cloak and a silver mask, which were duly taken and donned.

Todd got the same treatment and, once the mask and cloak were in place, followed the man in front of him through a door that led into a great ballroom.

The air was thick with incense. An organ was being played. Some kind of fugue. At the centre of the room was a chalk circle and around its edge were a number of naked boys. Todd counted them. There were twelve. Todd somehow knew there would be. They were spaced around the circle like the hours on a clock.

At the centre of the circle was a hooded man, taller by far than all the other men. In one hand, on a length of silken rope, he held a smoking incense burner, which he swung alongside him, filling the room with a sweet, foul stench. In the other hand he held a long, grey staff that was slightly taller than himself and with which he repeatedly smote the ground. At the same time he chanted. An unintelligible repetition of some no doubt ancient blasphemy that offended the ears and froze the blood. After several minutes of this he stepped in front of each of the boys in turn, smote the floor in front of that boy with his staff and when he did so that boy turned and walked away, left the circle and disappeared into the darkness at the back of the room. Soon there was but one boy left. Todd knew that boy; it was Marcus.

Todd stepped forwards, but a large white sheet that was hanging down across the centre of the room impeded his progress. His shadow loomed above him. It was a screen. Now he saw the projector, high above where he had been standing. It had all been a film, some dreadful, sick, pedo movie. There were no boys, real life, flesh and blood boys. Or had there been boys? There were boys on the screen but that didn't mean that there weren't real boys as well.

Then a face appeared: a huge masked head that took up the entire expanse of what Todd now knew was a screen. Only the eyes and mouth were visible but Todd knew those eyes and that mouth – he'd seen them in his rear view mirror – they were Warrington's eyes and that was Warrington's mouth, and it moved now and booming words came over some kind of public address system:

'Do what thou wilt shall be the whole of the law. Love is the law, love under will.'

The great masked face faded into a cloud of black, acrid smoke and nothing was visible for a while. Then the smoke cleared and Todd could see serpents and rats and cockroaches and other vile creatures. There were boys and girls and there was a woman; an ugly old crone and she was naked. She held a piece of rope, which she placed around a young boy's neck. The child opened his mouth to scream but no sound came and then that image faded and the great head returned and then... all the lights in the house came on and uniformed police officers poured in from every direction at once.

FIFTY SIX

'Is Sir Donald Sowerby on your list?' Adam asked Lucy. They were in a coffee shop in the Clerkenwell Road.

She hesitated for a moment, then decided she might as well tell him the truth, might learn something to her advantage if she did so. But it went against the grain to tell him anything at all, so she just nodded.

'He's dead,' he told her.

'Oh,' she said. 'I hadn't heard.'

'They're keeping it quiet. Family privacy and all that.'

She looked out of the window. Outside, the traffic crawled along like a half-stoned serpent. He'd texted her to say he had some information. She should have known that it wouldn't be good news.

'That's that then,' she said.

'What is?'

'He's the last one. I mean, the last one on the list, the last one we've got anything on. I'm sure there are plenty of others still at it.'

'But there's still a story there, isn't there? I mean, you still have all the descriptions about the weird satanic rituals and… stuff like that?'

'Yes, but it's all from this shadowy 'Nick' bloke. Well

actually I know who he is. He's called Mo Miller. His testimony is completely discredited. Smelly Baz has been forced to make a public apology.'

'What about your TV film?'

Lucy shook her head. 'You're right. It's just not being allowed out, is it? I've got scans of witness statements but they're accusations against dead people who can't defend themselves, so that makes them worthless. Even though they're from people who couldn't have known each other all making allegations against the same people. All alleging that they were treated in pretty much the same way. Some kind of sick ritual. Some kids died, you know. Human sacrifice sort of thing. The establishment. The elite. It's fucking unbelievable. So nobody believes it.'

'Do you know it happened? Do you completely believe it happened?'

'Of course I do, but that's not enough is it?'

Adam shook his head and spoke quietly: 'Lord Hunter's family have got the country's foremost QC on the case and a PR firm, a good one. We'd be mad to go against them.'

They both fell silent.

After a spell, Adam said, 'Have you heard about this care home story that's breaking?'

'No,' she said. 'What's been going on there?'

'Neglect and abuse of old people in care homes. You could go under cover. Get a job in one of the homes.' Adam told her.

She brightened up a little. 'Hidden camera, that sort of thing?'

'Yes. Important work, Lucy. You'd be doing something really worthwhile.'

'I'll think about it,' she said. 'I feel a bit washed out at the moment.'

FIFTY SEVEN

On the top deck of a bus Lucy watched a re-run of the news on her phone.

An immaculately coiffured and beautifully spoken female newsreader was annunciating straight at the camera in an appropriately solemn and slightly shocked tone of voice.

'Good afternoon and here is the news at 3 o'clock. Reports are coming in that the anonymous informant known as 'Nick' who has appeared in a recent documentary claiming he was abused as a child at the hands of the so-called Westminster paedophile ring, and who has named two ex-cabinet ministers as his abusers, is now saying that he is not entirely sure that it was either of those two individuals who actually perpetrated the abuse. Our deputy assistant political reporter is in Westminster for us now with the latest developments. What can you tell us?'

An excited looking middle-aged man with enormous spectacles appeared on screen.

'Well, in an absolutely extraordinary development it now seems that the anonymous whistle blower known as Nick is not as confident of who his abusers were as he was previously. This is how he appeared in a preview of a

Channel Nine documentary which is now not going to be screened. This preview, however, was released to the press just over two weeks ago.'

The silhouette of a man appeared on screen with the caption, 'Nick' beneath it. Then a voice was heard from the background. It was Henrietta. That bitch had used the information that Lucy had given her and shot a documentary without her.

'Can you be absolutely sure,' Henry asked 'Nick', 'who your abusers were?'

'Yes. I've been watching them on TV for years.'

'Do you know their names?'

'Yes.'

'And are you prepared to name them?'

'One of them is Lord Hunter of Hellifield and the other one is Sir Donald Sowerbury.

'And there were others?'

'Yes.'

'How many?"

'A lot... I don't know... maybe ten, twenty... I can't remember. Sometimes it was the same ones. Sometimes it was different ones.'

'You don't know the identities of any of the others?'

'No.'

'But you definitely recognise Lord Hunter and Sir Donald Sowerbury? Why? Because they are famous politicians?'

'Yes.'

'Are you absolutely positive?'

'Yes.'

Back to the roaming correspondent who was standing in Parliament Square, presumably in the hope of catching a famous statesman committing an open-air act of gross indecency, right there and then.

'But contrast that with this statement that has come to light only this morning in which he seems to be saying that he can't be entirely sure that the men who abused him were, in fact, the ones he named in that interview.'

'Nick' was there again.

'So now you're saying you're not sure?'

'Yes. No. Look, I just don't know anymore.'

'But only two weeks ago you told me you were absolutely certain.'

'Yes I know but…'

'But now you're saying that you're not sure?'

'Yes. I mean no. I mean… I don't know anymore.'

'Look, I know this must be very painful for you but…'

The silhouette crumpled and sobbed and the clip ended.

'So there we are, nobody can be really sure anymore.'

'But those two men have both been found dead in their homes. What on earth is going on here? Am I right in saying that there's a definite political angle to this story involving the MP, Barry Carter, who is Chair of the Home Affairs Select Committee?'

'That's absolutely right. In another extraordinary development, the relatives of Lord Hunter are kicking up an absolute storm over this. They are insisting that the death of Lord Hunter was as a direct result of the investigations he was forced to endure at the hands of Barry Carter and, indeed at the hands of the metropolitan police.'

'Thank you...'

'Just hang on though. In yet another absolutely extraordinary development we are now hearing that this 'Nick' character, this anonymous informant, is now saying that he also gave Barry Carter some other names too and that these other individuals were also high profile politicians, but that they were members of Carter's own party. Now, If that's true then that would imply that Carter has only made public the accusations against those individuals who were his political opponents but not of those who were members of his own party.'

'I'm going to stop you there because we're just hearing that the Home Office has issued a statement condemning what they are calling unfounded and politically motivated accusations against innocent men who devoted their lives to public service...'

Lucy turned her phone off in disgust, took out her earphones and looked out of the window at the bustling pavements.

She turned it back on again just before she alighted and saw that Smelly Baz had withdrawn all previous allegations and issued a statement saying that he was very, very sorry indeed.

FIFTY EIGHT

J ust then her phone buzzed. It was the Emma buzz. *Ignore her,* thought Lucy. *What's the point in talking to her? We're no longer of any use to each other. I can't help get Marcus back.* But then Emma's picture appeared on the screen and she pressed 'accept'.

'Hello, milady,' Emma said. 'It's been a while. I thought you might have been in touch. Although, now I think of it, why would you? You couldn't give a shit about us, could you?'

'Of course I care!' Lucy snapped. 'I'm not a fucking monster. There's nothing I can do that's all. I can't help. I tried didn't I? Why don't you go to the police or write to your MP? They can't all be bent. You'll get him back if you really want to – if you're really determined.'

'If I really want to? Just what the fuck do you mean by that?'

'Nothing. I didn't mean anything by it. I'm sorry... I...'

'Anyway, I have got him back. We've got him back. He's with us now and we're doing alright. I'm off the gear. Staying off it. Big's making sure of that. He says if I just so much as look at a piece of tin foil he's going to beat the crap out of me and I reckon he means it too. Big's got a proper team together again and there's going to be plenty of money coming in so we can rent a private place somewhere decent up near the river – away from the block.'

'You got him back? Oh, that's wonderful news. Look, I know you hate me but I'm really happy for you. But how? How on earth…?

'We'd been watching them see. Well, we'd been watching you and then he come on your tail too so we started following him. One night he drove down to a place in Barnes, turns out it was that place, Knoxley Hall. And there was something going down, lots of posh twats turning up in cabs. All men in dinner jackets.

'We just sat there and waited and after a couple of hours the pigs turned up mob-handed. About three vans full. All the lights went on and next thing you know all them posh fuckers are all being escorted out with bracelets on.

'We saw Lord Warrington get in the back of the car that he'd arrived in and we was going to point him out to the old Bill when your lover boy walks out and the coppers saw him. They never went near him though. Fuck knows why. It was like they'd all been told to leave him. Anyway, when he got nearer and I just couldn't believe my eyes at first… but right there alongside him was… was my little Marcus…just as right as rain. So we jumps down and your old shagging partner sees us. But he didn't seem at all surprised that we was there, I reckon he must have known we was there all along. He looked like he was well gone on something. I mean, he's a weird looking fucker at the best of times... but he was even more wild-eyed than usual and his hair was all over the place. Christ, you should have seen that look in his eyes. We just grabbed Marcus and legged it back to the van.'

'And Todd? What happened to Todd?'

'He went over to the car and got in it and drove off.'

'And Lord Warrington was still in the back?'

'Yes. He was. He definitely was.'

'But there's been nothing in the news about any raid.'

'Are you calling me a liar?'

'No. No. Of course not.'

'Well... anyhow... I thought I'd let you know. Cos now you can tell the story can't you? Now you can hand the evidence over to the police and have those bastards nicked and banged up. Big and his mates know some right nasty bastards in Wandsworth. Make their lives a fucking living hell. That's what they deserve, right?'

'Right. Yes, that's right. Of course they do,' Lucy said. 'Look, I've got to go. Goodbye Emma, all the best, love.'

She hung up and turned her phone off.

FIFTY NINE

Todd, holding hands with Baby Bear, made his way across the rain-lashed car park towards the big white caravan where Daddy Bear (a great big black Daddy Bear,) and Mummy Bear stood waiting. Baby Bear now let go of Todd's hand and with a growl of joy ran over to Mummy Bear and threw himself into her arms.

Then the three bears morphed back into Big, Emma and Marcus and they all got into the van, which headed off down the driveway at breakneck speed.

Maybe it was wearing off then, whatever it had been, whatever it was that Dolores had spiked into him along with his daily medicine.

Why had she done that? Had she been following instructions or was she just plain evil? Todd came to the unsatisfactory conclusion that either of those explanations was equally plausible.

He got into the car and turned the engine over. The Sat Nav had been programmed and was telling him where to go. It told him to turn right out of the gates so he turned right out of the gates. It told him to continue down that road so he continued down that road.

After a mile or two he looked in the mirror and saw

that Lord Warrington was sitting in the back seat. He hadn't been there earlier, must have been hiding on the floor. Cowering.

'Turn it up.' Lord Warrington said.

Those words held no meaning for Todd so he just said nothing and kept his eyes on the road.

'I said, turn it up!' This time it was a command from a man who was used to issuing them.

Todd realised the radio was on. So he wasn't hearing voices in his head then. That was a relief. The news was on. No mention of the raid. Just a lot of stuff about celebrities' phones being hacked. A lot of the poor celebrities had been left feeling violated and traumatised.

'All right,' Lord Warrington said, 'you can turn it off now.'

'How come you didn't get nicked then?' Todd asked him.

'Oh for goodness sake, haven't you figured it out yet, Todd? No. I don't suppose you would have, you're not exactly blessed with a great deal of intelligence, are you?'

'No.' Todd replied. 'Not brainy at all. More of a brute force kind of person. Extreme violence, that sort of thing.'

'I knew about the raid,' Warrington said, after a pause. 'I was told it was going to happen.'

'That figures.' Todd said. 'Still, all those other bastards who've just been nicked… I'll bet they all get the chance to finger you. Coppers always want the ringleaders, don't they?'

'There will be no charges brought.' Lord Warrington replied. 'There will be no publicity. Did you see any

336

reporters there? Was there anything on the news just then? Big raid like that would have been a big media event, don't you think? No? No. I wouldn't have thought that you'd know much about these things.'

The satnav was taking them east. Back towards Town.

'Kids.' Todd said. 'There were kids in there.'

'Were there? Are you sure?'

Todd thought about it. 'There was at least one,' he said, 'and lots of others on film.Just because it was on film doesn't mean it didn't happen. Some bad shit happened to some kids and now they're damaged. When that sort of thing happens… it's damaging. Changes happen. Bad changes.'

'It sounds like you're speaking from personal experience.' Lord Warrington said, thoughtfully. 'No one will be prosecuted but they will be punished.'

'How's that then? How does that work?'

Lord Warrington laughed out loud. 'How does it work? Magic, dear boy. Pure black magic.'

The Sat Nav took them past the turnoff for Wandsworth Bridge and then down a side road towards the river, towards the Heliport. There was a checkpoint and a barrier across the road. Todd pulled up so Lord Warrington could talk to the man in the box. He showed the man something on his phone and the barrier lifted.

They idled down to the stopping off place for Departures. Todd stopped the car, got out and opened the back door. Lord Warrington got out and stretched. Todd was within neck breaking distance but there were people about. Two of them were called Norcross and

Barrowlough. Norcross took a hand out of his jacket pocket and opened his palm to show Todd a handgun. It was the one that had shot him.

'Get his bags,' Norcross said.

Todd got them.

'Now, get back in, Sherlock, and piss off home.' Norcross said. And he jerked his handgun at the driver's door.

Todd got back behind the wheel and fumed at the sight of Lord Warrington, flanked by Norcross and Barrowclough, heading for the terminal. He didn't like the odds much but he thought he'd have a go. He opened the door and was about to make his move when his phone beeped. It was a text, from The Voice. It just read: *'leave it.'*

'That cunt's around here somewhere,' Todd thought. He stood for a bit and looked around but there was nothing to be seen. So he got back in the car and drove himself home.

Later on the Voice called him. 'You've done well, Todd. It's over now.'

'What about justice? Or don't you give a shit about justice?'

'They will be punished.' The Voice said. 'The men you saw at the party will be punished – every day for the rest of their lives. There will be no prosecutions just now but the threat of prosecution will hang over them… forever.

'That's what Lord Snooty Bollocks said. No trial though, eh? Don't they deserve a fair trial?'

'No is the short answer to that. There will be no trial. But they will be punished.'

'What about the rule of law? I thought that was your big thing.'

'Not in this case, Todd. If I were you I wouldn't worry about it. Like I said, it's over. You can carry on being John Tobin. Wait to be contacted.'

'I suppose it's all about the bigger picture isn't it?' Todd said.

'Now you're getting the idea. All is calm and ordered and Her Majesty's subjects can go about their business. We wouldn't want her to think that those who govern in her name are unfit to do so, now, would we?'

'No. Course we jolly well wouldn't. Let's not rock the boat, eh?'

'Indeed not dear boy, indeed not.'

'Just one more thing, *old boy,*'

'Yes. What is it?'

'Who killed Terry DeHavilland?'

'Oh, what does that matter?'

'It matters.' Todd said.

But the Voice didn't seem to think so because he just hung up.

SIXTY

Lucy continued to live in the Dolphin Square apartment that she had shared intermittently with her father, where she had found his dead body, and from where his embalmed cadaver in its bizarre black casket had been transported to the equally bizarre funeral.

But she didn't like being there anymore. There were just too many unpleasant memories associated with the place; particularly the one of her father hanging from the living room light fitting with liquid shit dripping out of his trouser bottoms.

She had the place completely re-decorated. A small army of tattooed decorators came every day for about a fortnight, shouted instructions to each other in Serbo-Croat, painted the walls and ceilings and tore up the carpets before fitting new ones. She barely exchanged a sentence with any of them for the whole time they were there, but once they were gone an intense feeling of terror descended upon her. The place stunk of paint but even so she was sure she could still sense the aroma of her father's swinging, stinking corpse; she couldn't bear to be alone in the place and spent as much time as she could wandering the streets, sitting in coffee houses, pubs, art galleries, libraries. Anywhere.

But when night fell she had no other options than to return to Dolphin Square. She longed for the oblivion of sleep but it seldom came, and when it did the nightmares came too; her mother/sister, grandmother/mother would appear, they would disapprove of her, they would disown her, they would abandon her; then her father would swing into view on the end of a rope.

She went for days on end without speaking to a soul apart from her doctor, who gave her sedatives and sleeping pills. They only served to make her feel and look like a member of the living dead.

She realised she was giving up on life and decided not to. It took a huge amount of courage and an enormous effort of will but she forced herself to phone Adam and ask him if he had any work for her to do. She would have covered the Chelsea Flower Show if he'd asked her to but he had grander things in mind for her; he told her that if she wanted to she could start work again on the care homes exclusive that they were planning to break. She would go into a care home in Margate where, according to Adam's sources, old people were being wickedly and wantonly abused. She would pose there as an agency worker – all wired up with a hidden camera and microphone; all ready to uncover the heinous acts of cruelty that were being perpetrated.

She agreed to do it. It would be challenging, would take up all her energy and concentration and thus take her mind off all the bad things that had happened.

But on the day she was supposed to start, as one of *The Defender's* IT boffins was wiring her up, the feelings

341

of shame and rage that had been bubbling around inside her suddenly surged up to the surface and exploded like a suicide bomber's vest.

'Get it off me!' she yelled. 'Don't fucking touch me, just leave me alone!'

The inoffensive little man who'd been doing the job removed the equipment and she walked out. Adam tried to phone her but she didn't pick up.

She went back to Dolphin Square, went into her bedroom and screamed into her pillow. That helped a bit.

She couldn't bear to let it go. There was a story that had to be told. *That* story. But there was no point in writing it as a piece of investigative journalism. No one would touch it. The bastards had won in that respect. But then an idea came to her; she would write it as a fictional account. She re-read the non-fiction draft she'd written. It was awful; dry and worthy. Why would anyone want to read that? A series of depressing accounts from semi-educated losers of how, as children, they'd been used as rich men's playthings. She couldn't even bear to read it herself. And now she realised that her own self-interest shone out through the turgid prose like the eyes of a hyena.

Then the idea struck; she would write it up as a piece of fiction. Change all the names and places, muddle up all the time frames so that everyone would know, but no one would be able to prove, that she was writing about real people and real events. Then she would post it on the internet under a false name. She would market it herself. No need to go near any literary agents or publishing houses or documentary film companies or newspapers.

Clicks. That was what they wanted. She'd give them clicks alright.

She started writing: how Adam had sent her to meet Emma who had told her that. Todd had forced her to give him a blowjob in exchange for him not charging her for a drug offence. That had incensed her, enflamed her feminist sensibilities and had, she realised now, made it easy for Adam to trick her into going to Terry DeHavilland's house in Islington to confront Todd. Adam was one of them, he had lied to her, had convinced her, with the help of Emma, who he had bribed, that Todd was an abuser of women, when, really, she had been sent there because they needed a witness to the fact that Todd was in Terry's house (the implication being that he was there to destroy evidence) before anyone was supposed to know that Terry was dead.

Her fingers danced around her computer keyboard like demented ice skaters. The story was writing itself: her undercover assignment at *The Brook Street Club;* how she'd started to doubt Adam and to believe Todd, the meeting with Mo in the pub in Earl's Court, the night they'd spent together in that cheap hotel in Waterloo Road reading Terry's journal.

She wrote solidly for a whole morning and then she read back what she'd written. Todd. It was all about Todd. That big ugly bastard with shoulders like a barn door lintel and a chest like the back of a sideboard. And a nob like Apollo Thirteen.

It was then that she realised that she wanted everything to be as it had been before: running around with him, fighting the bad guys, hunting and being hunted; alongside him. She remembered how good it had felt to be alongside him. No one could take him on. He was a super-hero! Then the riots and his 'death.' She realised now how much that had affected her, how devastated she had been. But how she'd bottled up her feelings like fizzy lemonade.

At that point she stopped writing. What was to come next was just too painful; the discovery that the girl that she'd thought was her sister was really her mother; that she was the product of a union between her father and a thirteen year-old child.

Then the sordid dealings with Lord Warrington around Emma and her son that had culminated in the death of her father. How she had become obsessed with the pursuit of fame and glory and how that obsession had come about by her need to forget it all, to cover it all up.

So she stopped writing and looked inside herself, contemplated the great chasm within her being and realised that it was a Todd sized chasm. She wanted him. She needed him. She would bloody well have him. There was a hole that needed filling and Todd was the man for the job. He would rescue her from her miserable existence. She could move in with him. She would work and pay him rent. She wanted only to work and to be with him. He had been taken away from her once, had died and then come back to life. Now she realised just how much she'd missed him in those weeks when she'd thought he was dead.

It was nothing short of miraculous that he'd been returned to the world and to her. He'd always been damaged but now was even more so. Well, they were both damaged now. Surely it was only right that they should heal together.

She had to see him again. She just had to. The fantasy of him, that phantasm of him, became her escape, her only hope. She would go to him, she wanted him so much and she desperately nurtured the notion that he also wanted her.

She sat and looked at his number for a whole hour before she finally pressed the green button. Then she got voice mail – not his voice, just a default voice mail message. That was typical, he wasn't the type to waste time recording a silly message instructing people to do whatever it was they were going to do any way. Or not. She hung up quickly without leaving a message. She was shaking with excitement. She redialled and this time left a message.

'Please call me.' she said.

Later on he did.

SIXTY ONE

They arranged to meet in the Tate gallery cafeteria.

He was already there when she arrived, looking very out of place, that great hunk of a man in a cheap, grey suit and an open-necked black shirt. He was almost too big for the furniture.

He looked up at her. His appearance had changed. His face was thin and haggard, flesh hung from his cheeks like mouldy wallpaper from a council flat wall. Eyes like shrunken sultanas. He had a laptop in front of him. Not *that* one though.

She sat down opposite him; tight blue jeans and a white chiffon blouse, hardly any make-up. The girl next door.

'So,' she said, 'it's over then.'

He nodded and his eyes held hers. 'Nothing can be done,' he said. 'Nothing at all.'

'No. And now it's hard to do anything else, don't you think?'

He nodded again. 'Yes. I know what you mean.'

'Are you alright?'

He looked at her and smiled. 'What is it, love? Why did you want to see me?'

Was that affection in his voice?

'Why? Oh… it's just that… I'm re-writing it you see. I know we can't do it in a conventional way so I'm going to fictionalise it. You will be the main protagonist. I'll be the other one. The two protagonist model is very fashionable in modern fiction writing. We can use Terry's journal as a documentary account. That's a totally acceptable literary device and so I suppose that makes him a protagonist too but that's all right – the multi protagonist paradigm is actually rather trendy.

'And… we were… some kind of a heroic team weren't we? Sometimes together, sometimes apart… working for the forces of good against the forces of evil… haha… I mean… I know that sounds ridiculous but… well we were, weren't we? And then you… you died… I mean… I lost you. I thought you were dead.

'I thought that could go in around midway. I mean, as a turning point. I know it's a bit of a clichéd turning point device killing one of your protagonists off like that but it actually did happen didn't it? That will give you an almost… messianic aura.'

'I didn't understand any of that,' he told her.

'I'm writing a novel,' she said, much more slowly, 'based on Knoxley Hall, on the murder of Terry DeHavilland and how they tried to pin it on you.'

'Oh.' He said. 'I see.'

He looked thoughtful for a moment. 'So what is it you want me to do?'

'We'll need to spend some time together to talk it all through. Would you like that, Todd?'

He shook his head and looked up. She followed his eyes.

Dolores was sitting at a nearby table, wearing some sort of long hooded cloak that gave her an air of mystery.

It was like a slap across the face with a wet bar towel. 'No! Come on! She's a fucking viper. She'll destroy you, Todd.'

He looked right at her and shook his head. 'She's alright. She just got all caught up in it. Just like we did.'

Lucy said: 'She's not alright. She's fucking poison. She'll take you down. My days! That's what you want, isn't it? No. Please Todd. Don't. Please. Don't.'

Then her voice broke a little when she spoke again. 'Don't you care for me? Just a little?'

'I do care for you but we don't belong together. You're still young and you're in the clear. They don't have nothing on you. Me and her got stuff hanging over us. We got to keep each other close. You can start again, we can't. Just forget me – you've got Adam.'

'He's as bent as fucking arseholes!' She spat out. 'In every fucking way.'

There were hot, bitter tears on her cheeks by now. 'You're with *them*. She spat at him. 'You've gone over to *them*. You drove Lord Warrington away. Where did you take him? You helped him get away.'

'That was the deal,' he said. 'Some of them are dead and the others are all on yellow cards. Two yellows means a red and a red means…' He drew a finger across his throat. 'It's over. It's been stopped.'

'That's not fucking good enough, Todd. They all got away with it. They're all as free as nice old granddads, drinking port in their old men's clubs. Sitting on the boards of orphanages and approved schools. You let *him* get away. And now you're with *her*. For Christ's sake, Todd, why?' She didn't wait for a reply. 'Oh. I know why. You had to save yourself. You own lousy skin. But just look at you. Look at what they've done to you. Let me help you, Todd? Please?'

Let me save you, Todd.

'They're being punished, he told her. 'They're either dead or they're wishing they were dead.'

'I wish I were dead,' she told him.

He ignored that and said, 'It's all been taken care of.'

'What?' The tears were flowing freely now. 'What the fuck does that mean?'

'Come around here.' And he made room for her next to him.

She did it and it felt so good. She could feel his energy, his masculinity. She wanted him. Oh god how she wanted him. She thought he was going to put an arm around her shoulder and comfort her. But he didn't. He opened up the laptop, turned it on and clicked on a link.

It was a desert scene. There were white stone outhouses in the distance and, in the forefront, a man in a mask with only his black eyes showing. At first the camera showed only his face but then it panned out and down along the huge man's black *jilbab*. Behind him was a great black flag with white Arabic lettering, unmistakably the flag of the 'so called' Islamic State.

In the man's right hand was a large, unwieldy, scimitar style knife. The sunlight reflected from its shining steel. Then the camera descended further. Three men came into view. They were wearing orange jumpsuits and they were kneeling in front of the man who was about to become their executioner. Hands tied behind their backs.

Lord Warrington.

And Norcross.

And Barrowclough.

When the knife came down Lucy screamed and turned away. 'Turn it off! 'Turn the damned thing off.'

He turned it off.

'He's still got away with it,' she said.

'And just how the fuck do you work that one out?'

'That's not justice,' she said. 'That's just fucking murder. That's all that is.'

'Why? Because you didn't get to expose them? Because the sodding CPS didn't put them on trial and because you didn't hear a judge tell everyone how fucking evil they are.'

'What about the victims? Now they'll never get justice.'

'We'll make sure they see this.'

'And you think that will satisfy them?'

'That's all we can give them,' he said.

'Who's we?'

He looked up to where Dolores was sitting. Lucy looked that way too. *Fucking femme fatale.* She was sitting and looking at them. Her eyes looked out from beneath the grey hood. It was the same expression that the big bad wolf had on just before he scoffed Granny. It was an expression of the purest joy and satisfaction.

'No!' Lucy said, like an angry parent putting her foot down. 'Todd, no! She's going to destroy you. Look at her. That's all she wants to do. That's all she wants you for.'

Samson and sodding Delilah!

Todd shrugged and his haunted eyes found hers. 'No. You don't know her like I do. She's all right. Bit fucked up but who am I to talk.'

'Todd!' Lucy implored. 'Todd, come home with me. We can be good together. You remember how good it was… that night. Don't you? I can help you. We can help each other. We can have a good life together.'

Todd closed the laptop. 'No. No way. Sure it would be good for a while but then I'd get restless. I'll need to do something soon. I'm a soldier. I'll need to find that sort of work. You wouldn't be able to handle that… that kind of a life.'

He stood. Dolores stood. She started to move towards them.

'Keep her away from me,' Lucy hissed.

Todd raised a hand and Dolores stopped.

'Goodbye Lucy.' Todd said, softly. 'You're going to make something… really good out of your life. I just know you are.'

'I'm not,' she said. 'I'm no good. I'm worse than her. I promise you I am.'

She couldn't stand the look on his face so she closed her eyes tightly. Then she pressed her fingertips against her forehead and said:

'I'm bad. I am. I'm very, very bad.'

Then with her eyes still closed she heard herself whisper:

'Go on then, go. Get the fuck away from me.'

And when she opened up her eyes she was alone.

POSTSCRIPT

(Courtesy of Wikipedia)

Eight-year-old Vishal Mehrotra went missing in July 1981 in Putney, less than a mile from the Elm Guest House in Rocks Lane, Barnes which is alleged to have been used by a Westminster paedophile ring. Seven months later the upper half of his torso was found buried in woodland in West Sussex. The boy's father, Vishambar Mehrotra, a retired magistrate, said that he feared the Metropolitan police covered up links between his son's killing and activities at Elm Guest House. In May 1983 the inquiry into Vishal Mehrotra's death was wound up by the police.

Also In 1983, the Conservative MP, Geoffrey Dickens claimed there was a paedophile network involving 'big, big names – people in positions of power, influence and responsibility' and threatened to name them in the Commons. Dickens met with the then Home Secretary, Leon Brittan, and gave him a dossier containing the child abuse allegations. A second copy of the dossier was reported to have been given to the Director of Public

Prosecutions. Neither copy of the dossier has been seen since.

On 29 November, 1985, Dickens said in a speech to the House of Commons that: 'The noose around my neck grew tighter after I named a former high-flying British diplomat on the floor of the House... as important names came into my possession so the threats began. First, I received threatening telephone calls followed by two burglaries at my London home. Then, more seriously, my name appeared on a multi-killer's hit list.' Dickens's son later confirmed that about the time when the dossier was given to the Home Secretary, the MP's London flat and constituency home were both broken into.

Simon Danczuk MP has alleged that before his appearance at the Home Affairs Select Committee where he was to answer questions on child abuse, he was urged by a Conservative minister not to challenge Leon Brittan over his knowledge of the alleged paedophile ring at Westminster. Danczuk said of the encounter that 'I'd never spoken to him before in my life but he blocked my way and ushered me to one side... He warned me to think very carefully about what I was going to say the next day. The minister told Danczuk, 'I hear you're about to challenge Lord Brittan about when he knew about child sex abuse... It wouldn't be a wise move... It was all put to bed a long time ago.'

On 7 July, 2014, the then Home Secretary, Theresa May, announced that a full review of historic child abuse allegations would be carried out by Peter Wanless, chief executive of the NSPCC, assisted by a senior legal figure.

This would cover how police and prosecutors handled information given to them, and was expected to report by the end of September of that year. She said: 'I want to address two important public concerns: first that in the 1980s the Home Office failed to act on allegations of child sex abuse and second, that public bodies and other important institutions have failed to take seriously their duty of care towards children.'

In addition, a 'Hillsborough-style' inquiry, the Independent Panel Inquiry into Child Sexual Abuse, would be held, led by a panel of legal and child protection experts and that this wide-ranging review would be chaired by Baroness Butler-Schloss. But the Baroness stood down on 14 July after mounting pressure from victims' groups and MPs over her suitability regarding the fact that her brother was the Attorney General at the time of some of the abuses in question.

Also in July 2014 Former cabinet minister Norman Tebbit said that there 'may well have been' a political cover-up of child sex abuse in the 1980s. Tebbit, who served in various ministerial roles under Margaret Thatcher, said that the culture at the time was to protect 'the establishment'. He said that it was seen as 'more important to protect the system than to delve too far into claims'.

In October 2014 Baroness Butler Schloss's replacement, Fiona Woolf, also stood down after concerns were raised over her connections with involved parties, including Lord Brittan.

On 14th November, 2014 The police investigation

known as Operation Fairbank was set up following claims by Labour MP Tom Watson in the House of Commons that the police should look afresh at claims of a 'powerful paedophile network linked to Parliament and No 10'. Watson referred to Peter Righton, a former consultant to the National Children's Bureau, who was convicted of importing and possessing illegal pornographic material in 1992. Watson said that files on Righton contained 'clear intelligence of a widespread paedophile ring… one of its members boasts of a link to a senior aide of a former Prime Minister…'

Also in November 2014 Scotland Yard said that it was setting up a related investigation, Operation Midland, with homicide officers. Operation Midland arose from claims by a man aged in his 40s who was a child at the time of the alleged incidents. The man claimed that he was given to a powerful group of paedophiles by his father and was taken to hotels and apartments, including the Dolphin Square development, where he was physically and sexually abused by 'senior military and political' figures. He claimed to have witnessed three murders by members of the group: one 12-year-old boy was strangled to death by a sitting Conservative MP; another boy was murdered at an orgy at which a Conservative MP was also present; and another abuser struck and killed a 10-year-old boy with his car to intimidate other victims. The officer leading the investigation into the alleged murders, Detective Superintendent Kenny McDonald, said in December 2014 that experienced officers had concluded that the allegations were 'credible and true.'

In an interview with *The Guardian* in November 2014 Tom Watson said: 'There is no doubt in my mind that sexual abuse by powerful figures took place.' Watson said that he was aware of the name of the senior aide of a former Prime Minister who allegedly smuggled indecent images of children from abroad, but that it would be wrong for him to name the individual. Watson said: 'In one particular case of one person, there have been multiple allegations from unrelated people, some more credible than others, about severe cases of abuse. And in my mind I'm pretty certain that the person has broken the law and abused kids.'

On 4 February, 2015 Theresa May announced that the new Chair of the Independent Panel Inquiry into Child Sexual Abuse would be Dame Lowell Goddard QC, a New Zealand High Court judge who had no ties to the UK bodies and persons likely to be investigated. The existing panel was disbanded, and the inquiry was given new powers as a statutory inquiry. The Statutory Inquiry opened on 9 July 2015, with an introductory statement by Justice Goddard. In November 2015, she announced that twelve separate investigations would take place as part of the Inquiry, including investigations into MPs, local councils, and church organisations.

On 20th November 2015 Tom Watson was forced to make a written apology to Lord Brittan's widow, Diana, after a committee of MPs said he had behaved 'inappropriately' by describing the late Conservative home secretary as being 'as close to evil as any human could get' days after he died.

Over the years, starting in 1991, specific allegations of sex abuse of children by the Labour peer, Lord Janner of Braunstone dating from at least 1955 were made to authorities. This did not lead to any official action, beyond Janner being questioned once, between the first allegations and 2015. After it was decided in 2015 that he should have been prosecuted earlier, the accusations were due to be investigated in a 'trial of the facts' in April 2015, because Janner was deemed to be too ill for a criminal trial. But he died before this could happen.

On 4th August, 2016, Home Secretary Amber Rudd announced that Dame Goddard had resigned from the Inquiry; no explanation was given.